Lillian's Story

One woman's journey through the 20th Century

By

Sally Patricia Gardner

Henry May Publications
Copyright © 2006 by Sally Patricia Gardner
All Rights Reserved

Also by Sally Patricia Gardner: *The Sweetest Empire*

Painting by Numbers

Finding Cordelia (due out 2013)

Contents:

Foreword

Dramatis Personae

Prologue

Acknowledgements

Foreword

Lillian's story could only have been written by someone with great experience of life – someone who has survived great sorrow and known great joy.

Everything I read felt like my own life – the sadness and the joy, the love of animals, the comfort of friendship.

This book is so truthful and I love truth in everything.

Dora Bryan, OBE, MA

Lillian's Story – Dramatis Personae.

Part One, The Early Years
Suffolk

Lillian's Family: Father
Thirza, her sister
Mother
Her brothers: Jack, Frank, The Twins and Timmy,
Uncle Jethro
Pastor Reynolds, a clergyman
Martha, Lillian's friend
Mr Nash, farmer and landlord
Mr Knight, a butler.
Mrs Knight, a cook
Josephine, a servant
Mrs Curtis, Mistress of Hadslow Hall
Peter, a stable lad
Jimmy, a stable lad and gardener
Sophia & Isabel, daughters of Mr & Mrs Curtis
Freddy & Raymond, Mr Curtis's sons by his first marriage
Mr Noggs, a sweep

London

Mr & Mrs Willett, Lillian's employers
Marcus, a chauffeur
Collette, a 'French' maid
Miss Ritchie, a governess
Sebastian, the Willetts son
Mr Richard, a butler

Mrs Phelps, a widow
William, Lillian's eldest son
Cynthia, Thirza's eldest daughter
Jack, Lillian's youngest son
Rose & Peggy, sisters and Lillian's friends
Mrs Everton, a pillar of the Church
Tilly, her daughter
Norma, Thirza's second daughter
Margaret, her youngest daughter
Mr & Mrs Grieves, pianists
Maxy, a versatile musician
Elsie, daughter of the pub landlord
Michael, Sebastian's friend

Suffolk

Donald, Lillian's half brother
Ivy, her half sister
Lettie, her sister in law.

Part Two, The War Years.
Suffolk

Mr Naismith, owner of the village shop
Eric, his son

London

Percy & Alan, Jack's friends
Mr & Mrs Smith, Lillian's neighbours
Lucy Fryer, a young mother
Daphne, a neighbour
Eileen, Lillian's friend

Sid, Collette's husband
Moira, her youngest daughter
Gladys, her eldest daughter
Billy, her eldest son
Ronnie, her youngest son
Mr Deeprose, her father
Mr Bryant, landlord of the pub
Stan, a Canadian airman

Part Three, The Austerity Years. London

Dr Marsh
Rosalind, Lillian's eldest granddaughter
Angarhad, Martha's daughter-in-law
Harriet, an actress

Part Four, Better Times Brighton

Barry, a driving instructor
Natalie, Thirza's grandaughter
Mike, her grandson
Teddy, Margaret's boy friend
Neville, Moira's husband
Andrew, Lillian's grandson
Frederick, her grandson
Gerald, an actor
Nerys, Donald's daughter
David, her brother
Edward, Timmy & Letty's son
Lena, Stan's wife
Nicholas, Rosalind's boy friend

James & Sarah, Lillian's twin grandchildren
Ivor, childhood sweetheart of Nerys
Steve, Rosalind's boy friend
Phil, Collette's grandson
Paula, Ivy's friend
Richard, an American
Samantha, Collette's granddaughter

Part Five, The Final Years
Brighton

Pheobe, Lillian's great-granddaughter
Davina, Andrew's girlfriend
Ben, Sara's fiancé
Jillie, a receptionist
Poppy, Andrew's girlfriend
Matthew, Lillian's great-grandson
Lily, her great-granddaughter
Victoria, James's girlfriend
Nigel, a mini cab driver

And a special mention should go to:
The dogs, in order of appearance:

Spot,
Tess,
Berry,
Goldie,
Rufus,
Wilfred

And the cats:

Minnie,
Mickey,
Biggles,
Sophie,
Darcy,
Pete.

Prologue

The young clergyman climbs down from the pulpit to stand between the two coffins. Looking down, he places a hand on each. A silence envelops the packed church, but there is no shuffling of feet, no sense of unease.

"Dearly beloved brethren," he begins. Then he throws back his head and treats his congregation to a wide smile. "How unusually apt that phrase is today. Surrounded as I am by family, theirs and mine. I have such a strong feeling that Lillian is going to be very cross with me if I get this wrong."

He pauses as a ripple of laughter runs round the church.

"So I shall try very hard to get it right. Not only for her, but for all of us here who loved them both. We have shed our tears already. We know how much we shall miss them. But these are lives to be celebrated, and I intend to try.

"Where to start? Was Lillian an extraordinary woman born into ordinary times, or an ordinary woman born in extraordinary times? Both, I suspect. The very first time I met her she tore me off a strip for daring to suggest that working wives were a new phenomenon. I was suitably chastised, but also aware that she had enlarged my understanding of the world she grew up in.

"No, that's wrong. Not the world she grew up in. That was even further back. Lillian was a Victorian. That's a difficult concept for those of us who knew and loved her. Born at the turn of the century. Almost literally. In January, 1900.

"Born into a very different world…"

9

Part One: The Early Years

January, 1912

Tomorrow I shall be twelve years old and my new life will begin. Thursday, 11th January in the year of Our Lord 1912. Father says we must always say that to remind us of Our Father Who Art in Heaven. Like saying grace even when there is not an awful lot of food to go round. Pastor Reynolds says people who don't remember Him all the time and thank Him for everything burn in hell, so I try very hard to remember.

I have to remember for my brothers too as they say they don't believe it and don't care anyway. So Thirza and I pray very hard every night for all of us. Sometimes it's difficult being the only two girls in the family and having five brothers. Thirza is going to miss me. I think I might be too busy to miss her a lot but I shan't tell her that.

Tomorrow, tomorrow!

Thirza's head comes round the door.

"Lillian, Mother wants you downstairs. What are you doing, just sitting there? Come on. She's got your dresses ready. Oh, Lillian, I wish I was going with you."

I stand and give her a quick cuddle.

"You must work very hard at learning your letters, so you'll be able to write to me soon. Then it will be almost as if we are not apart at all."

"They are nearly good enough now, it's just that only I can read them." We both giggle and I take her hand and jump her down the narrow stairs. Mother

10

looks up as we arrive at the bottom in a noisy heap.

"Lillian, I hope you won't be coming down the stairs like that at Hadslow Hall."

But she is smiling as she says it and I know she is not really telling me off. Placing the pincushion that I made her at Christmas on the arm of her chair, she holds up a dress.

"Come along, child. Time to try on."

She slips it over my head and I pull it down and straighten the sleeves. It is beautiful. The material is so soft and the delicate grey colour looks like the wing of a bird.

"Oh, Mother…"

I am speechless with joy. She pushes back my hair gently. I think she would like to say something but words do not come easily to her. But there is a tenderness in her touch and I know, as I always have, that I have the best and most loving mother in the world.

So many new clothes. More than I have had in my whole life. I already have a black dress for going to church on Sundays, which Mother has let out for me, but she has made me two new pinafores as well. And Mother says that I will be given a work dress – just imagine, they are going to give me a dress, and food, *and* they will send Father some money every three months.

Today Mother is going to cut off my flannel bodice. We are all sewn into them at the beginning of October after Mother has rubbed goose grease into our chests and backs to keep us warm. Usually they are not cut off until April but as I won't be walking to school anymore mine is coming off. And, best of all, I am going to have a bath tonight. The boys are already bringing in the buckets from the well in the garden and Father has brought out the big round iron tub, which hangs near the hay cart. When the cooking pot comes off the fire it is going to be put on to heat up just for me.

We are having a special supper tonight in my honour as I won't be here tomorrow. I am travelling right to the other side of Suffolk so we shall have to start really early. Jack is going to drive me in the cart. Father will be too busy as Mr Nash from the big house wants to see him. Father says he'll want to make sure that the horses are fit and well as it won't be long before the ploughing starts. Anyway it will be fun going with Jack.

Jack is my only brother who is older than me. He is very clever. Mr Henderson wanted him to stay at school. He said that if Father would let him be a pupil-teacher and help him, then he would see that Jack sat the examination to go to one of the big schools far away. But Father said we are not rich enough for that sort of nonsense so Jack works on the farm with him. He gets paid a wage now – like I will from tomorrow! Jack still goes to see Mr Henderson a lot and usually brings books home to read. He often shows them to me but I don't think I am as clever as him because most of the time I don't really understand them.

Mother has made a rabbit stew and the special dumplings she knows that I love. We shall all sit round the table together tonight and later I shall have my presents. I know that everyone has made me something because they all keep telling me to "go away" and say that I mustn't look at what they are doing. When I was little we didn't have a table. We all used to sit on the floor round the pot and dip our bread into it. Mother said that was how gypsies lived and no way for respectable people to behave. Father brought home an enormous piece of wood one day and he and Uncle Jethro sawed and chopped and turned it into our lovely table. Martha, who lives in the cottage next door, says that we are really posh because no one else has a table.

Supper time at last. The stew is wonderful. We are all wondering what I shall be having tomorrow when I reach Hadslow Hall. Mr Nash says it is a very grand house so I expect they will have very grand food. Everyone is trying to imagine "grand food". Timmy says "pig stew" and the twins tell him not to be silly, but after all he is only three years old.

Frank says "roast boar" and Jack nearly falls off his chair laughing. Frank got that idea from a book that Jack has been telling us about with knights and things in.

Jack says, "That was a long time ago. I don't think anyone is that grand now."

Timmy says, "Not even the King?"

Jack has to confess he is not sure about that. But he reckons that the food won't be that different from ours, just more of it and not all on your plate together. Mr Nash asks him to help up at the big house sometimes so I expect he knows from that.

It's nearly time for my presents. Father leans back in his chair and tells us to clear the table. When we are all sitting down again he leans forward and clears his throat, which we know means that he has something important to say.

"Lillian," he says, "your mother and I have a special present for you. Not only because it is your birthday, but because you are going away."

And he pulls out from under the table a beautiful wooden chest. It even has a lock on it. I shan't have to put my things in the old hamper. I throw my arms round him and then round Mother. It seems that Father and Jack have been making it for weeks and everyone else has been in on the secret.

I am overcome when I open it. Mother has made me six handkerchiefs with lace round the edges and my name – Lillian – embroidered in the corner of each. I recognise the lace. She has taken it off her next best petticoat. I suddenly want to cry. I look at her and see that she has tears on her cheeks so I give her a hug and start to look at my other presents so no one will notice.

Jack has given me a book full of blank pages. It has a stiff cover and he has written on it in big writing "Lillian's Book". And Frank has given me two pencils to go with it. I am going to write all about my new life in it so when I come home to visit I shall not have forgotten anything. Oh, the twins have whittled me a flute. I manage to play "Three Blind Mice" and we all get the giggles. I am not very good, but I promise to practise on it. My brothers really are so clever and kind I resolve not to get cross or impatient with them ever again. Even Timmy has made me a hair slide with Jack's help. And just when I think there can't possibly be any more presents Thirza gives me two of her hair ribbons. I must be the luckiest girl alive to have such a family.

The tub of water is going on the fire. Father puts the clothes horse round it with the big bed blanket draped over it so I shall be private, and Mother fetches the scissors and cuts off my bodice. It is always such a funny feeling as the grease is all gone but the bodice is a strange green colour and smells very odd. Some of the families soak them to use again the next year but Mother says we are not *that* hard up and burns them. I feel more free, but not so cosy. The water is soon hot enough and the boys put the tub in front of the fire. Everyone leaves me alone behind the screen and I climb in. It feels wonderful. I have never had the bath to myself before and I know that I must be a real grown-up lady now.

I stay in, making it last as long as possible, until I hear Mother say, "Lillian, child, you will be getting goose skin if you stay in there much longer."

I can see that she is right so I reluctantly climb out and prepare for bed.

Thirza and I share our bed with Timmy. We sleep at the top and he has the bottom. The twins and Frank have the other bed. Tonight there is a lot of toe-tickling and laughing and being silly. Eventually Mother comes up and orders us to be quiet and go to sleep. Thirza and the boys have to get up very early at the moment as the lanes are so muddy the walk to school takes even longer than usual.

She bends and touches my hair. "And you, girl, have a long journey tomorrow."

We settle down, though I feel very wide-awake. Mother and Father sleep on the bed downstairs. I think that it must be nice to be so near the fire. Jack goes across the lane to Uncle Jethro's to sleep, as since Aunty Meg died there is more room in his house and Jack helps with the children. We all use the same privy and the door squeaks. I hear the squeak and Jack's voice greeting Uncle Jethro as sleep overcomes me.

15

Tomorrow this will be my old life and I shall be living my new one. Tomorrow.

This is the strangest birthday anyone in the whole world ever had. Mother wakes me up very early. I dress in the dark so as not to wake the others, though Thirza sits up and pulls on my hand as I am going downstairs.

"Happy birthday," she whispers drowsily, then, sitting up, "you will write to me, won't you?"

"Of course I will. As soon as I can," and we hug each other tightly.

None of the boys wake, which I am quite glad about as I think a lot of goodbyes might make me feel a bit sad. Mother has lit the lamp downstairs and I sit by the fire and have a mug of warm milk. Mother tells me that Bert, who is in charge of the cows, has brought a jug round really early for us as his farewell present to me. People are so thoughtful and nice. Jack comes in and we have some bread and dripping, and Mother gives us a parcel of bread to take with us. My new wooden chest is already strapped on the back of the cart and Father harnesses up Nelly. She is my favourite of the farm horses so I am really pleased that Mr Nash said Jack could have her for today.

I don't really want to talk a lot about saying goodbye to Mother and Father because I suddenly know how much I am going to miss them. But I concentrate hard on being a grown-up and promise Father that of course I will be a good girl and work hard…and then…one last hug for Mother…into the cart…and we are off. I twist round so I can watch them disappearing into the darkness. I am thankful that it is still dark so Jack can't see that I am crying just a little bit.

It is the longest journey I have ever been on. When the daylight breaks we stop and have some bread and stretch our legs. Then on we go. Our next stop is at a horse trough for Nelly but there is barely time for me to get down before I am up again. My back is so sore from being bounced around on the hard seat but at least it isn't raining. We have a big rug to pull over our knees and Jack wraps it all round me as he says that he is keeping warm with the driving. He says that we have to go about forty miles but I can't really imagine that. We have to allow an hour and a bit to walk to school and I know that is just over two miles. The cart is a lot faster than us walking, of course, but I still think such a distance will take us all day.

In fact it is still light when we arrive at Hadslow Hall. By this time I am feeling all my old excitement again. Father has arranged for Jack to stay in the stable block overnight so he and Nelly can rest. Jack unstraps the chest from the cart and carries it up the steps for me. Hadslow Hall is not as large as I had imagined it would be, it's hardly bigger than Mr Nash's house really. We pull on the bell rope. I can hear someone coming.

A man in a black suit answers the door. He is very tall. He smiles at me.

"Are you Lillian?" he asks. He has a kind expression but when I say yes my voice comes out all high and squeaky so I nod in case he didn't hear me.

He tells us that we have to go round the back of the house to the servants' entrance and asks if Jack can manage the chest. He says his name is Mr Knight. When we arrive at the servants' entrance someone is already standing there waiting for us. She is wearing a large white apron and I wonder if she is the cook. She takes us into a big kitchen, which is lovely and warm, and we realise how cold we are. Mrs Knight, as she tells us she is, makes us two very large mugs of tea.

There is a girl a bit older than me washing up at the sink and she turns and winks. It makes me feel warmer inside as well as outside, if you know what I mean. Mrs Knight explains that she is indeed the cook and that her husband, Mr Knight, is the butler. Mr Nash hasn't got a butler at the big house so I am not quite sure what a butler does. The girl at the sink is called Josephine and Mrs Knight tells her to look after me for a minute.

"Don't look so scared," laughs Josephine (I think she laughs a lot. She's got that kind of a face. I can see that Jack likes her from the way he is looking at her). "Mr and Mrs Knight are really nice, and you and I are the only live-in servants here. So nobody's going to eat you – not yet anyway! You'll meet the stable lads later, they have their meals with us. A good couple of boys they are, too. Not at all fierce, I promise you. Then there are the two girls from the village who come in the morning but go home before supper. One of them's about your age, I reckon, though the other's a bit older."

Mr and Mrs Knight come back into the kitchen then and he says I must tidy myself up, as the Mistress wants to see me. Mrs Knight combs my hair quickly and brushes the stuff from the rug off my black dress, which I have travelled in. She tells me to bid Jack goodbye, as he must go down to the stable block now, and there will be no time in the morning to see him again. I had not realised this. I throw my arms round him and I think that there has never before been a moment in my life when I have not known that I could call him and he would be there. I must not cry. I am a grown-up now.

Mr Knight takes me along the hall. It feels very large and long. He knocks at a door. A woman's voice says, "Come!" He ushers me in and the door closes behind him. I am standing in a big room with a very high ceiling. There is a large fire in the grate and, sitting in front of it, is a *very* large lady.

"Come forward into the light, child," she says.

I move nearer to her. I am shaking. I tell myself it is because I am cold but I know it is because I am afraid.

"What is your name?" she asks.

I tell her, "Lillian."

She falls silent. Then: "The girl who just left was called Ellen. That will be your name here." She pulls a bell rope near her chair and Mr Knight appears. "She will do," she tells him. "You may take Ellen away now and explain her duties and the standards we expect in this house."

I am stunned. I walk in silence behind Mr Knight. Back in the kitchen Mrs Knight starts to outline my duties but I do not hear her. I am Lillian. I am not Ellen. I will never be Ellen. What is this world I find myself in?

I have never slept in a bed by myself before. First of all I feel very cold and I miss the warmth of Thirza's body next to mine, but I am so tired I fall asleep anyway. Mrs Knight saw that I was in no state to absorb what she was telling me and made Josephine take me up to bed. We share a room in the attic that is much bigger than the room that seven of us share at home. And we have a bed each. Josephine said she would show me where to put my things in the morning. She is so good. She helped me to take off my dress and I almost fell into the bed. But now I am wide-awake. I think that it must still be the middle of the night as it is so quiet. The events of the previous day are galloping in my head. I must say it is pleasant to be able to stretch all my limbs without anyone moaning at me in their sleep. I think I shall get to like this.

But I will not like being called Ellen. Tomorrow I shall ask Josephine always to call me Lillian when we are together, because that is who I really am. I do not like the Mistress but I shall pretend to myself that I do. We used to play "let's pretend" at home so I know I am good at it.

Ooooh, this is such a nice comfortable bed…

I can hear the sound of a match being struck and the room is suddenly full of shadows and shapes. Josephine is out of bed and has lit her candle.

"Lillian," she whispers, but I am already out of bed. "Here, come and wash your face and hands," and she points to a bowl on the chest of drawers. We splash the freezing water about and then dry ourselves quickly on the towel she holds out.

She hands me a black dress like hers, which I have not seen before. It is quite a lot too big for me. She says it was Ellen's. I ask what happened to Ellen. To my surprise she looks away and says she doesn't know, though I am sure that she does. We tuck my dress up and over the belt. I think I probably look a sight. But when I say to her, "Josephine, please will you always call me Lillian when we are alone, not Ellen," and she says, "Bless you, of course I will," and gives me a quick hug, then I don't care what I look like anyway.

20

She takes my hand and we go down the steep stairs by the light of the candle, with me trying hard not to fall over my skirt. We catch sight of our joined-up shadows, bobbing massively on the wall beside us and are consumed with giggles.

We have to clean out the three grates and lay the fires before the Mistress and the rest of the family wake.

"It's a really tiny family," Josephine explains. "Just the two little girls, though there are two much older boys away at school. I've got seven sisters and four brothers, though only one of them is still at home as they are all much older than me. You and your brother seem really close. He's very good looking, isn't he?"

Funny, I've never thought about Jack like that, but I am happy to agree with her and I tell her about Thirza and Frank and Timmy and the twins, and before it is fully daylight I feel as if I have known her for years.

We have to carry the ash through the house. We must be very careful not to drop any. We put it in a big metal bin by the back door. Then we bring back with us a scuttle of coal for each room and enough paper and wood to lay and light the fires. At home ours stayed in all the time, but of course there was only one fire, not three, and Father and the boys chopped wood to keep it going. Now we have to light the fires. Josephine shows me how to hold a big sheet of paper over the grate so the flames whoosh up the chimney, and I am so startled when they do that I drop the paper and nearly set fire to myself. She is such a giggler we are both set off again, though, in truth, I was a bit frightened for a moment.

Next we have to fetch the pots of water that Mrs Knight has been heating on the kitchen stove and quietly take them up to the bedrooms. I knock on the Mistress's door and wait.

"Come…"

I enter and pour the water into the basin. No other word is spoken. I begin to think that perhaps that is all she ever says. We go into the girls' bedroom together and they are awake. They look like two little cherubs lying together in an enormous bed, peeping over the covers. They leap out and Josephine introduces me. I catch my breath, though I understand that she has to say Ellen, but then the girls throw themselves at us for a cuddle and, laughing, I don't really care for it is nearly like being at home.

Mr Knight serves the breakfast for the family. Josephine says that when there are guests we all have to help as the sideboard nearly collapses under all the dishes of food. Most of the time it is just the family breakfast though and that is a simple affair. We sit in the kitchen with Mrs Knight and the stable lads, who are called Peter and Jimmy, and there is toast (as much as you can eat) and hot tea and lots of laughing and teasing and moaning and groaning and I realise with gratitude that they are making sure I do not feel left out.

I am learning names. The family are Mr and Mrs Curtis (though every one calls them the Master and the Mistress), and the girls are Sophia and Isabel. They are only three and four years old and they haven't grown to their names yet, so it's Sophie and Issy unless their parents are cross with them. The absent boys are Freddy and Raymond, who are fifteen and seventeen years old, and Josephine says they are very nice.

Peter makes us laugh with his imitation of Mrs

22

Curtis and even though Mrs Knight says he shouldn't do it we can see she is trying not to laugh herself. I am beginning to see that no one likes the Mistress very much. Josephine says that she is a lot younger than the Master and Freddy and Raymond are his sons by his first wife who died. She seems to spend all day lying on the sofa. We don't see much of her. Good. Mrs Knight says she was very ill after Sophie was born and has been delicate ever since. Delicate seems a strange word for such a big lady. I think she was probably *always* ill-humoured.

Jimmy, the other stable lad, loves the garden and knows all the plants and shrubs just like Uncle Jethro does. He is sixteen and he reminds me a bit of Jack. The two girls from the village are not particularly friendly but we are all so busy during the day there isn't much time to talk anyway.

After breakfast every day our first job is to do the washing-up. Mr Knight brings the dishes through from the main house. Our part of the house is separated from the family by a big green door. Then we have to sweep and dust – we do a different room every day. Josephine shows me how to dust the very fragile things with a little brush so we don't have to pick them up. We have a big mop thing for the walls and ceilings. Then we have to fill up all the oil lamps in the rooms. There are so many of them. Sometimes as many as five in one room.

When we have finished that we go and make the beds and tidy up the bedrooms. Mrs Knight comes up with us when the linen is changed. After that is done we help to set the tables for lunch. The village girls clean the kitchen and peel the vegetables. A lady comes from the village twice a week to collect all the washing and she brings it back the next day and we help to sort it out and make sure it is all put away in the right places.

We usually have bread and dripping for lunch and then spend most of the afternoon helping to prepare dinner, which the family eat at half past four. Josephine helps Mr Knight to serve it and I will be allowed to when I am older. Then, when we have cleared up from the family we have our supper. That is the best time of the day with lots of laughing and lots of food to eat. Sometimes the bell over the door rings and Mr Knight has to leave us to answer it, but that doesn't happen very often. After supper we do the mending while we sit round the table in the kitchen. Josephine and I try to stay awake but we are usually nodding over our work by eight o'clock, and Mrs Knight sends us to bed because we have to get up at 4.30 in the morning.

I am supposed to have a half-day off a week but the Mistress said today that as I have nowhere to go there is not a lot of point. Mr Knight says, "We'll see about that," when I tell him this, so I am waiting to see what happens. I *have* got somewhere to go, anyway, as Josephine lives in the next village and she says I can go with her to meet her family.

Josephine says we are lucky to be in such good employment. "I could tell you some stories," she says mysteriously (she never does, though) and I know she is right, but, well, I do miss Mother and Father and Thirza and Jack and the others much more than I thought I would, though I wouldn't admit it to anyone. And I sometimes think that I would give anything to have half an hour to myself with nothing to do but read one of Jack's books, even if I didn't understand it.

But the most important thing is that all of the other servants call me Lillian, not Ellen. The Mistress might be able to take my half-day away but she can't stop me being me. I tell myself that I have two families now and, as we sit down to supper, I feel a rush of affection for this, my new family.

January, 1917

Wednesday, 10th January, 1917 – no I won't say "In the Year of Our Lord" – I won't I won't I can't. The boys were right all along – it's a nonsense. There is no caring God. Jack is dead. My loving, handsome, clever brother is dead. The letter came this morning and I put it in my apron pocket because I thought it was to wish me a happy day tomorrow but it was to tell me that Jack is dead. Mother says they don't even know where his body is – somewhere in a place called Flanders across the sea. If you are up there, God, then what are you thinking of? Jack, where are you? Don't leave me, Jack – I loved you so much. I am in a cloud of darkness – it is as if no one can penetrate it. I hear their voices, feel their arms round me but nothing is really touching me. Jack...oh Jack...

They are trying so hard to help. Jimmy is to drive me home. Mr Curtis says I must go immediately. There will only be Mr and Mrs Knight left here then. Josephine left last year, she is a VAD now, and we have not heard from Peter for a long time. Jimmy came back before Christmas with part of his arm blown off but he says that as he can still drive the cart and do the gardening he is one of the lucky ones. Freddy and

Raymond are both army captains and Freddy is home on leave. He has given me a note to read but not yet, he says. I think now that I have been so stupid. I really never thought that anything could touch my lovely Jack. I didn't even worry about him a lot. I will never, ever, see him again – I cannot bear it…

We are almost home. It is the first time I have been home for nearly two years. I did not think it would be like this. I must be strong. I am the eldest now. I shall be strong. Father is outside to meet us. I run into his arms and Jimmy follows slowly, not wishing to intrude. Father holds me tightly and for a minute he says nothing, then utters "Mother is inside" as he releases me.

It is dark but Mother has not lit the lamps so at first I can only see shapes in the firelight. Then Thirza throws herself at me with loud sobs. I hug her briefly then put her aside for I have found Mother, hunched in her chair.

"Mother," I say, and she looks up. She stares at me as if I am a ghost and I think that she looks a hundred years older than when I last saw her. I think that she does not know me. "Mother, it is Lillian," and I fall to my knees and bury my head in her lap.

"Lillian, my child," she says and her hand creeps over my hair and in spite of all my resolution not to cry a great sob escapes from me.

My brothers emerge from the shadows and we all hold and touch and entwine in a wordless knot of grief and loss and love. Even in the middle of our pain I know how blessed we are to have each other and I ask the God who I don't really believe in to help us through this awfulness.

I set the twins to lighting the lamps and send Frank to fill the log basket from the store in the shed. Father comes in and brings Jimmy with him. Jimmy brought me the other time I came home. He has an aunt who lives in a nearby village but Father says he is to stay with us tonight. Jimmy takes Timmy to help him bed down the horse and get the cart away. Thirza and I start to prepare the vegetables that Mother had intended for a hotpot. In that other world, before the telegram came. No – I must not, cannot, will not remember that. Concentrate on supper. I am the eldest now.

There is a tap on the door and when Father opens it Mr Nash is standing there. He touches Father's hand for a brief moment, then clears his throat, pushes a basket into Father's arms and is gone back into the night. The basket holds a large basin of piping hot stew. The cook must have prepared it specially and I am touched that Mr Nash has brought it himself.

We cannot persuade Mother to eat anything. I think none of us has much appetite. But I chivvy them along and pretend that the journey has made Jimmy and me hungry and Father understands and plays up to us and then the little ones discover that they really are hungry after all. We eat in silence. Then Timmy says, "Do you remember that day when Jack came home late and ate all of the stew because he thought we'd had ours already, and we were playing in the garden waiting for him to come home and we hadn't eaten anything?" And of course we do remember.

And Henry says "Do you remember…?" and we do and the table is suddenly noisy with laughter and tears and memories.

Then we fall quiet again. And into the silence

Jimmy raises his mug and says, "Here's to Jack. I only met him the once but I felt I knew him well as Lillian spoke of him so often. He always sounded a grand fellow."

And that feels right. We all raise our mugs and say "Jack" and Mother looks across at Jimmy and says, "Thank you." And I know that we will, somehow, survive.

It has been decided that I am not to go back to Hadslow Hall. Father has written to Mr Curtis explaining that my family need me here. I am to become parlour maid at the big house. I shall sleep at home but will work there from 7.30 a.m. to 8.30 p.m. It is an extraordinarily generous offer. I am to have a whole day off every week and Father tells me that Mr Nash is paying a good wage for me, as well as supplying me with a dress and two aprons.

If Jack were here I should be ecstatic, but I feel numb. I am glad I do not have to leave Mother, though. We cannot have a funeral, of course, as we do not have my lovely brother to bury. Pastor Reynolds has been and says that Jack died bravely in the service of our country so God will take him into heaven very quickly. I wanted to ask if that applied to those fighting on the other side as well but I didn't dare. I know his words comforted Mother and Father. I wish I could recapture some of my old certainties.

I am making a shepherd's pie for supper and hope Mother will eat some. She is deathly pale and her hands tremble all the time. I do not know what else to do for her. The little ones are quiet but I know that the two years Jack has been gone from their short lives is an enormous time to them and he was already less than real. I am glad for them but I envy them, too. The pain is like a constant kicking in my stomach. Thirza keeps touching me when we pass as if we shall both draw sustenance from that. Perhaps she is right. The older boys are working with Father. There is not usually so much to do at this time of the year, so I know they are keeping busy because men are not allowed to cry.

Jimmy has gone. He is going back to Hadslow Hall, but probably not for long. His parents live in a place called Epsom, a long way away. His arm still pains him, I think, even though he says it does not, and his family want him near them. He is going to write to me.

I have just remembered Freddy's note. I go upstairs to read it. It makes me cry again but they are not bad tears.

Dear Lillian,

You were never Ellen to Raymond and me. You came to our house as a child and when we first saw you, you had already become part of our household. We loved your optimism and your determination to be true to yourself. Even our stepmother was won over in the end, though I doubt she would ever admit it. You have grown into a woman we should be honoured to call our sister. I am so sorry you have left us in such tragic circumstances. I have no doubt that your love for him lit up your real brother's life and I hope that may eventually be of some comfort to you. Before our mother died, she told Raymond and me that those who are left behind have an obligation to live their life to the full. I believe she was right. Remember that, dear Lillian. I trust that we shall meet again in happier times.

> *Yours affectionately, Freddy.*
> *PS Back to the front tomorrow. Please pray for me.*

Oh, Freddy, I will. I am.

February, 1917

It is my first day working at the big house. This time I will have my own name. I have known Mr and Mrs Nash all my life. They have three daughters who are all quite a lot older than me and married, so we don't see them very often. Only cook is living in now, and Martha from next door comes up every day to do the rough work. I am to do the light housework, set and serve at table and receive visitors. I am relieved that Mr and Mrs Knight trained me so well as nowadays there don't seem to be the same guidelines that once existed. My brother Frank says that people are just pleased to get servants at all and perhaps he is right. Cook is lovely and is to let me help her so that on her day off I can do some of the cooking. I think I shall enjoy that.

Enjoy? How can I already be thinking that I shall enjoy something with Jack lying dead somewhere? And yet that is what Freddy was telling me, I suppose. Jack wouldn't want me never to be happy again. I *shall* learn to be happy again. And Jack will never really die while there are people living who remember him with love.

January, 1920

I am so happy and so excited. It is 11th January, and I am to be married today. I have such a pretty dress to wear. It belonged to one of Mrs Nash's daughters and it fits me like a glove. It is long and silky and creamy and I am so relieved that the weather is frosty and the ground hard or it would have got dreadfully muddy on the way to the church. Thirza and Mother and I sewed sweepers into the hem just in case but the wet would have spoilt the way it hangs. I have never worn anything so lovely. I think every one of our friends will be at the church and Pastor Reynolds says that with all our family *and* all my new relations the church will be bursting at the seams. But I can tell he is as happy as everyone else is for me.

When I am ready Mother and Thirza hold the back of my dress as I go downstairs to where Father and the boys are waiting, all wearing their Sunday clothes. They are so quiet when they see me, for a moment I think I have done something wrong.

Then Timmy says, "Oh, Lillian, you look so pretty," and Father comes and takes my hand and says, "You're looking grand, girl," and Frank gives me a kiss and I feel like a princess as the twins throw open the cottage door for us.

The walk to the church is such an event, with all the villagers coming out of their houses to wish me joy. Mr Noggs, the sweep, comes out of his house grinning broadly and walks up to me so that I can touch him for luck, and several people carry their black cats across our procession and then let them go so they run back across my path. So many good wishes and good omens.

The service goes amazingly quickly. One moment I am walking down the aisle on Father's arm and the next it seems that I am going back up on my husband's. I am now a married woman, how strange that sounds. But wonderful. I think that somewhere deep inside me I have known since I was twelve years old that I was going to marry Jimmy.

Mr Nash has asked all the family up to the big house and cook has prepared us a banquet! Martha is helping her today. Thirza has already taken my place as parlour maid and she is having a fine old time. When I think how strict everything was when I started at Hadslow Hall I can only wonder how different things are now. The war changed so many things and in spite of all the horror and misery, lots of the changes are for the better, I think.

Jimmy and I are going to work in a house in London. It is near the famous Crystal Palace, which Jack told me all about. Jimmy is to be the gardener and handyman. He thinks that is quite funny and makes jokes about being a one-handed handyman. I think that is why I love him so much, because he makes me laugh such a lot. I am to be cook, would you believe! Mother says that I would never have such a position at my age if there were not such a shortage of people going into service, but Mrs Nash says they are jolly lucky to have me. Actually, I think so too, as I know I am a good cook. Anyway they don't know how old I am. We are Mr and Mrs Spencer and you don't ask married ladies their age.

We are leaving tomorrow. We are going on a train. Just imagine.

February, 1920

Oh my goodness, this is such a splendid house. There is a big outhouse attached to the main building, I think it was a stable once, but now it has a car in it and we have two lovely rooms over the top of it all to ourselves. There are two live-in maids who have their room in the attic just as Josephine and I did all those years ago. Mrs Willett also has a French lady's maid, called Collette, who does her hair and looks after her clothes. The three children have a governess, Miss Ritchie, though Sebastian, the youngest and only boy, is due to go off to school soon, poor little mite. He looks very frail. I would never send a child of mine away like that. Jimmy has an under gardener to do the heavy work.

But the funniest thing is our butler. His name is Richard, though we all call him Mr Richard, and it was several days before Jimmy and I discovered that his name is really Richard Richard! I think he is the oldest person I have ever known. His suit, and he has never been seen even without the jacket, is so ancient it is a funny green colour and privately Jimmy and I are agreed that it has a *very* strange smell. He walks incredibly slowly but he is very charming. When we arrived he bowed to me and said, "You must be our new cook. What a delightful young lady, if I may be so impertinent." And then he kissed my hand! Jimmy said he would have been quite cross if Mr Richard had been any younger, but well, even though I was a bit embarrassed, I knew he meant well and so did Jimmy. I was really quite flattered, too.

By the second day we had worked out that I would put the food on a trolley I found at the back of the pantry and then one of the maids would wheel it through to just outside the dining-room door. That way Mr Richard can wait for it to come and not stagger in looking (and feeling, I should think) all breathless and wobbly. I am going to ask Mrs Willett if I may have a chair put in the hall so he can sit and wait between trolley loads.

Mr and Mrs Willett are very nice. Mr Willett is something to do with a bank and usually away in the day but Mrs Willett is a real socialite, always having friends round for cards or just to chat, and she goes out a lot. They go to the theatre quite often and Mrs Willett tells Collette all about the plays they have seen, and then Collette tells us in the evening.

Collette is not really French at all. She actually comes from Stepney. But her grandmother is half-French and Collette is her proper name, so when she heard that Mrs Willett was looking for a French maid she pretended that she was. I think that was very daring of her. I thought at first it was a bit dishonest but Jimmy says that wanting a French maid is a snob thing just so that Mrs Willett can boast to her friends and, as none of them speaks French anyway, everyone is happy and there's no harm done. I hadn't thought of it like that but I suppose he is right. In fact, Miss Ritchie *can* speak some French, but she says that she would not dream of splitting on Collette and that she thinks Mrs Willett probably suspects the truth in any case.

To be honest, being cook here is easy. Jimmy says "a piece of cake," which makes me laugh. I see Mrs Willett every morning and we discuss what the menu for the day will be, and though that sounds very grand I generally have it all worked out and she just says, "That sounds lovely," and though I say it myself, it usually is. Between Mother and Mrs Knight I have been taught well and I really love cooking so it doesn't feel like work at all. When we have a lot of visitors Mrs Willett asks me how much extra help I need so I never feel under too much pressure. She is very pleased because Miss Ritchie and I have thought up some special nursery treats for the children and little Sebastian is eating better and looking stronger.

Jimmy is completely re-organising the kitchen garden for me. He says the whole garden is in a fair old state because during the war there was only one young lad trying to do it all. Apparently dear old Mr Richard gave him his orders and Jimmy says Mr Richard probably knows as much about gardening as he does about driving the car. Marcus, who *does* drive the car for Mr Willett and has his room at the back of the outhouse, says Mr Richard would like to stop buttling but he has no relations and nowhere to go. I think that is so sad.

Mrs Willett has asked me to help Mr Richard do a rota so all the staff get proper time off as it seems to be a bit hit and miss at the moment. I'm making sure that everyone has a whole day off every week. Jimmy and I always have ours together, of course, and today we are going to walk up to the Crystal Palace.

The Crystal Palace is HUGE – it must be the biggest building in the whole world! Oh, how I wish that Jack could have seen it. There are fountains everywhere in the gardens and even though it is winter most of them are working and shooting sparkly water high into the air. They are so beautiful but as Jimmy says, no wonder they are always saying they are short of money. It must cost a fortune to keep them going all the time.

We couldn't go inside today as it wasn't open. Mr Richard says that in the summer they have all sorts of shows in the gardens and a kind of fair. There is even a roller coaster. We are definitely going to have a go on that when it is back up. But the very best thing of all is the dinosaur park. Jack had a book with pictures of them and he told me that they were the very first animals on earth. There are the most enormous stone statues of them here. Some of them are on a little island in the middle of a lake. We are able to take a rowing boat and go near to them. They are actually quite scary till you get really close and can see that they are just statues. Jimmy says that dinosaurs actually were that size so I am glad that they aren't around anymore.

April,1920

I had a letter from Mother today. She says that I sound like a real woman of the world. Just wait till I tell her that we are going to see a play in the West End of London tonight! Jimmy has bought me a beautiful dress to wear for it, the skirt is well above my ankles and I feel very daring. I should be nervous of wearing it out without Jimmy beside me. Mrs Willett has a phonograph, that's a thing that plays all sorts of music. When I went in to see her this morning she played me a piece that she said came from *Chu Chin Chow*, which is the play that we are going to see. Mr Willett gave us the tickets as he said someone had given them to him but he and Mrs Willett have seen it twice already.

I sort of expected the play to be a bit like the flickers that we go to see and I didn't expect the colour and the noise and the joy and jollity of it all. It is amazing. The story is really the fairy tale of Aladdin that I used to tell to Timmy and the little ones but everyone has different names. There's a lot of dancing and singing and so many funny bits that everyone laughs and cheers and it is like being at a great big party. On the way out we all say "Goodnight – wasn't it good?" to people that we have never met before and everyone smiles at everyone else just because it has made us all so happy. We are definitely going to see some more plays. Jimmy says we can go quite cheaply if we go upstairs in the gods. We are going to have a look in the newspaper to see what we fancy next.

Sometimes I almost can't believe how nice our life is.

January, 1926

William's fifth birthday today, 14th January, and it doesn't seem two minutes since he was born. Marcus has popped up to see us and when Jimmy comes in he is going to take us all for a special birthday ride in his car. William is very excited at the idea of going out in the car after dark. He is sitting on Marcus's lap with his chauffeur's hat on. It is miles too big for him, of course, and he looks so funny.

"I'm going to be a driver when I grow up, Mummy," he says.

"You can come and drive for me, William, I'll have a whole fleet of cars by then," grins his Uncle Marcus.

I wouldn't be surprised if that turned out to be true, given the way things are nowadays. Ever since Mr and Mrs Willett told us they had to cut back, because of

37

some crisis with Mr Willett's job, we've been counting our blessings that we are still here. But we know that we can't bank on anything being permanent the way we used to. Even some of the rich people are feeling the pinch now.

Marcus reads all the newspapers and saw it coming. He already had a plan worked out. He suggested to Mr Willett that he would buy the car from him, and still drive Mr Willett around, but he could start up his own private chauffeuring business as well. They talked about it for ages and then had a proper contract drawn up and now Marcus has the car and still lives here and drives the Willetts for a set amount each week, but is ever so busy driving other people as well. He calls them his toffs. Jimmy says it was really clever of Marcus because it worked both ways – Mr Willett still has a chauffeur but doesn't have to pay him, and Marcus is already making quite a lot of money, and not paying any rent.

They had to get rid of all the other servants, though. There's only Jimmy and me left now. I still do all the cooking, but my goodness, we do cut the corners sometimes. Mind you, though I say it myself, I've got good at making some really cheap cuts of meat go down well. The secret is to cook the meat for a very long time and then dress it up in a simple sauce or suchlike. That way you can conceal the shortcomings and it looks fine when it reaches the table. I *am* quite proud of my cooking. I like to experiment a bit, too. But I don't talk much about it in case it looks like boasting.

We have a woman who comes in to do the cleaning every day. There's not much entertaining anymore. I hear from Collette quite often. She is married now and has three children. I don't know how she manages with them all so close together. Jimmy still has a lad who comes to help him with the garden. They grow a lot of vegetables and the fruit trees are all producing well, so I think that it pays for itself. We are so lucky to have such good jobs still. There is a lot of talk of workers striking in the country. Jimmy says that what the miners and lots of others are paid is disgraceful, but I don't see what people like us can do about it.

I can hear Jimmy coming up the stairs. William charges across the room and throws himself at him and Jimmy twirls him round then pretends to drop him.

"Who's my birthday boy then?"

"Me, me, me!" sings William, Marcus's cap now completely covering his face.

"Put him down before he gets too excited," I order his dad, but we are all laughing.

"Honestly," I say to Marcus, "it's like having two daft kids together sometimes!"

I wrap William up really warmly and get my coat on and then we go straight out as it is nearly dark. I do love going in the car at night. I am almost as excited as William as we zip along the street. Some of these houses have electricity, you can tell because the light is brighter than you get with gas mantles. If they have not drawn their curtains you can catch glimpses inside their houses. Jimmy says it is being nosy to stare but I can't resist. It is like stepping into someone else's life for a moment.

Back home, and I have done us a steak and kidney pudding for our tea, William's favourite. Marcus says that I make the best steak and kidney pudding in the world and can he have one for *his* birthday? He is so cheeky, but of course I say he can. We all sing happy birthday to William and then I put him to bed. He has had such an exciting day. His Auntie Thirza gave him a teddy bear that she had made herself from a pattern in the paper and he was so thrilled with it, and Jimmy and I gave him a big box of paints and both our families sent him little presents. I often think what a pity it is that William hardly ever sees my brothers, but our life is here in London now. I think we are much better off than my brothers, who are all still in Suffolk.

He does know his Auntie Thirza well, of course. She works in a big draper's shop in Lewisham now, and we see her nearly every week as she comes over on the tram most Sundays. At first I was worried about her coming up to live here on her own and not being married or knowing anyone except us, but I must say I think she was right to make such a big move. She was not cut out for being in service and it's worked out well for her. She is certainly looking very smart and pretty and she seems to be having a really good time.

After Mother's death she held everything together at home, but once Father married Martha it all changed. Thirza says it was a blessing in disguise for her, as it set her free. Martha is expecting a baby so we shall have a half-sister or brother soon. I must say that it still all seems a bit strange. Martha is younger than me and she is my stepmother. Lots of girls are marrying older men, though, as since the war there are not enough young men to go round. As long as she and Father are happy, and they seem to be, I think Mother would not have minded. She never seemed to feel strongly about anything after Jack's death. It was as if the spark that made her herself had died too.

March, 1926

Sunday today. We are going to the park this afternoon as it is such a beautiful day. Thirza is here quite early as the trams don't run after midday on Sundays, but Marcus will take her home later. I think he is carrying a bit of a torch for her but I am keeping quiet in case I am wrong. With only Mr and Mrs Willett at home it doesn't take long to serve their dinner, so we are soon all sitting down to ours.

"Money for old rope, this cooking business," says Marcus. So I tell him if he wants his dinner he'd better show some respect for a good cook. "Good?" he says. "Best in the world, you mean."

He is such a flatterer but so much fun with it. After dinner everyone helps with the washing-up and then it is coats on and off we go. William loves climbing on the dinosaurs and Jimmy and Marcus are nearly as bad, so after watching them for a bit Thirza and I walk round by the Crystal Palace to keep warm. I never get used to how lovely it is.

Thirza is unusually quiet. "Is everything all right?" I ask her.

"Mm," she replies. "I was just thinking," and she turns and stands looking back at the three climbers, now astride one of the monsters and making fierce noises at each other. "Do you like Marcus, Lillian?"

"Ah," I say, "so you *are* keen on him!"

Her blush makes her even prettier than usual and I give her a big hug. And tell her that I like him very much indeed. She grins at me and says that perhaps the time has come to let him know, very subtly, of course, that his attentions might be welcome. We have a giggle at how we always have to pretend that the men are making the first move. Then we link arms and march back to where the three of them are now pretending to be cavemen.

I remind them that we have promised to drop in and see dear old Mr Richard before we go home. He has two rooms in the basement of a house in Penge. He is not so lonely as we all feared he would be, as his landlady is a widow with a little terrier, Spot, which seems to spend most of its time down with him. The three of them have become good friends and Mrs Phelps often asks him up to play cards or listen to the gramophone. William loves going to see him, though I think Spot may be the big attraction.

We take a last brisk turn through the gardens together and then pile back into the car. It is getting *very* cold. Marcus drops us at Mr Richard's, then he and Thirza go back home to wait for us. Wicked Thirza gives me a big wink behind Marcus's back.

Mr Richard is in high old spirits today. He makes us a cup of tea and then shows us his newspaper, *The Daily Graphic*, which is full of stories of an impending strike by the miners. He and Jimmy both think that the government should be doing more to help them but I know from what Marcus says that his toffs don't feel that way at all. He says it will take a revolution, not a strike, to really even things out in this country.

I must say Marcus has made me realise that a lot of things are unfair. I didn't think much about it before I knew him, but now it seems really silly to me that I shall have to wait another four years at least before I can vote. Just because I am a woman. Still, Mother died without ever being able to, so I guess waiting till I am thirty isn't too bad when you look at it like that. It just isn't right that Jimmy can vote at twenty-one and I can't until I am thirty. At least Jimmy thinks it is daft too, not like some of the men who still feel that women can't understand politics whatever their age. You don't have to be very bright to know what is right and what is wrong and women are just as good as men at seeing that.

William is rolling all over poor Mr Richard's floor with Spot and they are both getting noisier and noisier, so I tell him we'll take Spot out for a run. We leave Jimmy and Mr Richard putting the world to rights and when we get back Mrs Phelps has joined them. She is talking about "that nice Mr Lloyd George." Hmm. Let's hope she's right.

It is getting late and we have to say goodbye and hurry back up the hill. Mr and Mrs Willett have high tea on Sundays. I have already made the soup, and I am going to do my special Welsh rarebit to follow, with an egg custard to finish up. Life is so much simpler than it used to be.

Thirza and Marcus are down in Marcus's rooms, we can see them through the window. Obviously *very* deep in conversation. When they come up to join us they are both laughing and sort of sparkling so I know straightaway that something has changed between them. After supper, when William has gone to bed, we get out the cards and play whist. Marcus keeps trying to see Thirza's cards and she uses them like a fan to eye him over the top, like Theda Bara in that Rudolph Valentino picture, and we all get the giggles. When it is time for Marcus to take her home, Thirza slips her arm through his. I've never seen her do that before. I'm dying to know what she has said to him but of course I will have to wait till I see her alone. She gives me a big hug and whispers: "Tally ho!" She is *so* modern. She makes me feel quite old sometimes.

May, 1926

It's Sunday, 9th May, definitely a date to remember. Marcus and Thirza are engaged. We are all so thrilled and I am doing a special tea with a cake that I have piped their names on inside a big wedding ring. Marcus has bought Thirza such a pretty ring, it's two diamonds sort of offset so they catch the light. She's flashing it about all over the place, bless her. No point in having it if you're not going to enjoy it, I tell her.

It's nice to have something to talk about apart from this strike. It hasn't really affected us much because a lot of people have turned out to do the strikers' jobs. Marcus says he's been taking some of his toffs to the bus depots so that they can drive a bus all day and then he picks them up to bring them home when they've finished. He says it would be funny if it wasn't so sad. He says it's the well-off banding together to make sure that the poor stay poor and I have to say that I think he's right.

There are families round here whose kiddies go to school with cardboard in their shoes and Mr Baldwin either doesn't know or doesn't care about stuff like that. He's calling on people all the time on the wireless and in the papers to help break the strike. Mr Willett has got himself sworn in as a special constable. Jimmy says he's a good man who just doesn't understand. I'm sure he's right. Mrs Willett is talking about volunteering, which has given us all a bit of a laugh. When I told Collette she said that she could just see her sorting the mail or being a clippie wearing her favourite tea gown.

I'm not going to think about it any more this afternoon. Mr Willett has just brought us up a bottle of sherry to toast the happy couple, as he put it. Jimmy says, "Told you he is a nice man really," as soon as the door closes and we all dissolve into laughter.

August, 1926

Rudolph Valentino is dead. I heard it on the wireless just now and I feel sort of sad. He was so handsome, so alive, so, well, sort of special. He somehow made shivers go up and down your spine, and when he looked into Pola's or Vilma's eyes it was like he was looking into yours. When he came to London last year Thirza and Collette and I went up to see him, even though Jimmy said we were quite mad (but only in a nice Jimmy sort of way, he didn't mind really). We were right in the middle of the crowd and we had to try and lift each other to see him and we did catch a glimpse. Nothing more, but it was exciting and fun and it sort of made us feel that we almost knew him. We went to see the film together the next day too, and it was lovely. *The Eagle*. One of his best. I don't believe there will ever be another film star quite like him. Not for me, anyway.

October, 1926

Marcus was given some tickets for *Lady be Good* at

Drury Lane, and he and Thirza have already seen it, so they passed them to us. They are babysitting too. Jimmy and I don't often get out in the evenings nowadays, so this is a big treat. We've heard so much about the Astaire brother and sister and I must say that Fred is a wonderful dancer. Jimmy says he must be made of rubber. And the music is astonishing. There's a number called "Fascinating Rhythm", which makes you want to leap up and dance in the aisles. Thirza says they call the music syncopation, whatever that means. But it does sound different – like it's got a sort of echo inside it.

I do love going to the theatre. Tonight our seats are in the circle in among the toffs. Jimmy borrowed what Marcus calls his monkey suit and he looks so handsome. And Thirza lent me her grey satin coat, which I am wearing over my yellow dress with the fringe round the hem. Marcus says we look a right couple of toffs ourselves. Jimmy says he could get used to this. I know what he means.

January, 1931

I am thirty-one years old today. I have the nicest birthday present of all, even if it has come at a bad time. I am going to have another baby. After William was born we hoped for another but it just didn't happen. Until now. I am quite sure that I am in the family way because today I felt it kick. I am so excited. I haven't dared let myself be till now. I have never been regular enough just to know and anyway Thirza said a girl she worked with missed for four months and then came on again and was not pregnant at all, so I hardly dared to

46

hope. I can tell Jimmy he can uncross his fingers as soon as he comes in.

Jimmy is assistant head gardener at Crystal Palace now. There have been so many changes. Mr Willett just dropped down dead one day at work. They said it was all the worry and strain of his job and his heart just gave out. It was so awful, poor Mrs Willett was distraught. The children were wonderful, really held their mother up, thank heavens both the girls married so well. She has gone to live with Fanny, the eldest, in Wiltshire. We saw Sebastian at Christmas. He is in his first year at Oxford but when he is in London he always comes to see us. He is such a big strong lad now it is hard to believe he was such a little shrimp.

Mr Willett dying like that was such a shock to everyone, but Mrs Willett made sure we had time to find something else once she had decided what she would do. We are not nearly so well off now as we have to pay rent, of course, but we found a nice little house in Penge right near Mr Richard. He is so frail nowadays and unfortunately Mrs Phelps is getting quite feeble as well, so it is a good thing that I can pop in and keep an eye on them. Luckily Spot is still very sparky and I think he keeps them both on their toes.

Marcus and Thirza and little Cynthia live over in Norwood, so we are all near to each other. Marcus is doing so well. He has four cars now and employs men to drive them. He has taught Thirza to drive and she comes over quite often. She says she is going to have her own car soon and then she can come as much as she likes. I am so pleased that this baby will grow up knowing one of her cousins. Funny, I don't know why I think it will be a girl but I do think of her as a her.

Though I must admit I was quite sure that William was going to be a girl, so…

Marcus and Thirza have asked us over for Sunday dinner today. A special birthday one, Thirza says. Even more special than she knows. I am looking forward to telling them about the baby. Thirza has been crossing her fingers for me too. She will be so thrilled.

Jimmy gave me such a lovely birthday present this morning. Ages ago, when he came back from the war, Mr Curtis gave him an old pocket watch of his, but Jimmy has never used it much. I think I've used it more, what with rushing around doing all these cleaning jobs. But today he gave me my own wristwatch. It is the most beautiful thing I have ever owned. The gold has a sort of delicate pink shine to it and it is octagonal instead of being just round. When I ask him how he managed to afford it, he tells me that he sold his pocket watch. He blusters a bit about me always running late but he knows that isn't true.

Then he puts his arms round me and says, "Just wanted to show the best wife in the world how much I love her." I don't have the words to say how I feel so we have a great big hug and then he puts it on my wrist. I am *so* lucky.

Everyone is delighted about the baby. Thirza asked Mr Richard and Mrs Phelps for dinner as well so we have to wait for them to come home from the service at St John's, but Marcus picks us all up on the dot of twelve. I am surprised that Cynthia hasn't come with her dad, but then, when we get to Norwood, in the sitting room is a big banner with "Happy Birthday Auntie Lillian" written on it and Cynthia pops out from where she is hiding behind the door and throws herself at me with big Cynthia chuckles. That starts us all off, of course. She's such a little moppet. She looks a lot like Shirley Temple, though Thirza says that is because she spends ages putting her hair in rags at night to make the ringlets.

They have all brought presents for me. Marcus and Thirza give me a simply stunning hat. I joke that I won't have the nerve to wear it but I know that I will. It is red and fits close to my head with a beige flower on one side. And Mr Richard and Mrs Phelps are obviously in on the secret as they give me a red scarf to wear with it. William gives me a big box of chocolates. He tells me that he bought them himself, from the money Mr Hill pays him for delivering groceries after school. What a perfect birthday.

It's the day after my birthday and we are going to the pictures tonight. I am going to wear my new hat and scarf. Jimmy and William say this is my extra birthday present from them. Jimmy says that even if we are a bit broke we can still afford to go in the gods at the Penge Empire. They only used to do Music Hall but now they have plays and talking pictures as well and this evening they are showing Greta Garbo in *Anna Christie*. My two men know how much I want to see it. It is supposed to be very good and she always takes a really good part. I like her a lot and it will be interesting to hear what her voice sounds like. I must say I do like the talkies, they are more natural. William keeps saying that because she is foreign she might sound funny. I don't care if she does.

July, 1931

49

Little Jack is nearly two months old. How the time goes. He's such a good baby. He hardly ever cries and I only have to get up once now for a night feed. I took him over to Thirza's for the first time today and we went on one of the new trolley buses. They do feel a bit strange, not quite as solid as the trams but everyone says they are the buses of the future and the overhead electric lines are going up all over the place.

We were nearly there when the trolley bus stopped quite suddenly. We were all wondering what was happening when the driver came round the bus with a long stick and hooked the poles on the roof of the trolley back up onto the lines. I let William get off to watch. Everyone had a good laugh about it, but sometimes you can't help wondering if this new-fangled stuff is as efficient as the old things were. The conductor says these are cheaper to maintain. It's always about money in the long run, I suppose. Marcus brought us back in one of his cars. It was a lot quicker but William and I did want to see what these trolleys were like, so I'm glad we went over there on one.

There are so many new things happening. Thirza says Marcus is thinking of having a telephone put in so his toffs can telephone him for a car rather than sending a boy round. A telephone. I can't begin to imagine having one of those. I sometimes wonder what Jack would have made of all these things. But he was so clever he'd have understood how they all work much better than me. I do miss him still. I wish he could see the boys. He'd probably have kids of his own by now. Sometimes I find it quite hard to remember what he looked like. Perhaps little Jack will grow up to be like him. Wouldn't that be something?

January, 1935

It's the day after my birthday and we are having a meeting of all the people in the streets round here. Just about everyone comes and we decide that we are going to organise a big party for the King's Silver Jubilee in May. I am really quite excited about it. Heaven knows there is so much doom and gloom about at the minute it is nice to have something cheerful to think about.

I am going to be in charge of organising the food with Rose and Peggy from Maple Road and Mrs Everton from the Church is going to see to all the decorations and things like that. The Jubilee is on 6th May and that is little Jack's fourth birthday so that makes it even more special for us. I don't suppose the King and Queen will mind sharing their celebrations with him.

The money is really getting quite difficult. Jimmy has had to take a big cut in his wages even though he has hardly anyone working with him now. He seems to work all the hours that God sends. We know that we are lucky he still has a job at all with so many out of work, but ever since that last bitterly cold winter he has had a nasty little cough that he can't seem to shake off. We really can't afford for him to see a doctor. Mrs Phelps makes him some of the linctus that she used to give to Mr Richard. It does help but the cough still won't go away. He's always had a bit of a tickle, of course, ever since the war. But not like this.

I have got several cleaning jobs, some that I go to twice a week, but I can't fit in anymore because of having to take Jack with me. All my ladies are very nice and sometimes Mrs Everton asks me to cook for her when they are having a big do. The trouble is that she doesn't pay very much. I think she feels that as it is the Church I should be doing it for nothing. Jimmy says that it is typical of her kind but I know that she just doesn't understand.

However short the money is we are determined that we will let both our boys stay at school for as long as they want to be there. We are not going to let history repeat itself. They will not have to leave school like my brother Jack did. Things may be bad but they are still better than they were then.

William is going to try for a bursary this year as he would like to be a teacher. You would never think it, watching him cycle around with a big grin on his face delivering the groceries. He is a real charmer (and he knows it) and a lot of the ladies tip him. It is hard to imagine him being a teacher. I think Tilly Everton is quite keen on him, she's always hanging around. Mrs Everton would have a fit if she knew. But I don't think William notices girls yet. He is a good lad, always ready to help his dad and me. He still makes time to go and take Spot for a walk every day, though Spot doesn't want to go far anymore. Mrs Phelps' legs are so swollen she can't get him out herself. I think she misses Mr Richard. We all do.

Thirza is coming over today with her girls. Cynthia is so bossy with Norma, quite the little mother really. Fortunately Margaret isn't old enough to know what is going on yet so let's hope she is going to be a strong personality too. Mind you, she certainly has a good pair of lungs on her. Thirza copes wonderfully with them all and she still looks so young and pretty. Not like Martha. She and Father came up to see us last year. Martha has got so fat I would never have known her, which is a pity because it does make her look much older than she really is. Father looks very thin and elderly but I suppose he must be getting on a bit by now. He still has to work on the farm, and of course having two fairly young children must be a bit of a strain. I can't help wondering how Martha will manage if Father dies before the children are grown up. Jimmy says I mustn't be morbid but I think I am just being practical.

April, 1935

Rose and Peggy and I have finished working out all the food for the Jubilee party, and all the business of who is getting what and who is going to pay for what. And then, just when I was feeling quite pleased with myself, I have a bit of a shock. Mrs Evans says she can't afford to have me anymore. Mr Evans has lost his job. He was on the staff at the Penge Empire. I suppose fewer and fewer people can afford to go there now. I know we haven't been for ages. I feel really sorry for her, but I will have to find something else quickly. She is my Tuesday-morning and Thursday-afternoon lady.

Thirza is here when I get back in and she has got the kettle on. Over our cup of tea Thirza says why don't I look for a job at the laundry up the road? I say that I can't because of Jack but when he starts school I think I will. She says that people will always want their washing done and she is probably right. But I still can't do that for nearly a year. She's going to put a card in the shop near them offering to do mending or washing.

There is more money in Norwood so more folks likely not to want to do it themselves. She says if anyone answers she can help me collect it now she has her car. I don't know what I would do without her.

May, 1935

We are having such a wonderful day. The papers have been full of the Jubilee for days and this morning Marcus packed as many of the kids as he could into his big car and took them to Trafalgar Square to see the King and Queen go to St Paul's for the thanksgiving. He said the crowds were enormous so in the end he marched them all through to Nelson's Column and they climbed up high enough to watch the procession. Jack had pride of place on account of it being his birthday, he's quite convinced all the cheering was for him, and Marcus says he waved very regally to everyone from his perch. Next year is going to be a bit of a let down.

Marcus says the Queen was all in white with big feathers in her hat and looked lovely, but the thing the children were full of was a little dog that got under the royal carriage and wouldn't move. The soldiers tried to get him out, and then the police, but the poor thing was obviously frightened. In the end he did run off but he had held up the procession for ages. Everyone is calling him the Jubilee Dog.

We spent ages last night getting everything ready for today. We decorated Maple Road with lots of Union Jacks and put a big banner across the road saying 1910–1935, and Thirza did a big crown in the middle of it. We've put the trestle tables from the school down the middle of the road and Mr and Mrs Grieves have got their big piano out onto the pavement and their boy Maxy has come out with his accordion and we are all dancing to the music. William is helping to organise the kids with Tilly Everton and young Elsie from the pub. They are having a lovely time playing Musical Chairs and In and Out the Dusty Windows. Such a lot of giggling and pushing and shoving going on, it's an entertainment just watching them.

Then, when we are finally all glad of a sit down, even the youngsters, we have tea. Bloater paste sandwiches, and egg and cress ones and some ham ones. And, of course, jam ones for the tiny kids. Lots of sticky fingers but no one cares. Then we finish up with red and green jelly and trifle. All the children are starting to get tired so we stay sitting round the tables and sing all the old songs. Everyone tries not to giggle when Maxy plays "Nellie Dean" because we all know that's what his dad sings when he comes home sloshed from the pub.

About eight o'clock, when the light is starting to go, I fetch the Jubilee cake that I made and bring it in with a big flourish. I've put twenty-five candles on it and the kids all group round and blow them out. We cut very tiny pieces so that everyone has a taste and then we finally pack the children off to bed. It is midnight before we finish clearing up but what a day it has been, none of us will ever forget it.

August, 1935

I've been taken on part-time at the laundry. What a relief. I am going to do shifts, and if Jimmy is a bit late Peggy is going to keep an eye on Jack for me. It should make the money a bit easier.

Thirza is trying to make me go with her to these keep-fit classes that are all the rage at the moment. Bless her, I told her I haven't got time not to be fit.

The wireless is on and someone is talking about that speech that Mr Churchill made last year about Germany re-arming and saying we should be spending more on defence. It makes my blood run cold. As if we haven't got enough problems without spending money on guns and such. Didn't they have enough last time? I don't believe there will ever be another war – people just couldn't be that daft.

January, 1937

Sometimes things just don't seem to make any sense at all. Yesterday they said on the wireless that anyone going off to Spain to fight in their civil war might go to prison for two years when they get back. All those young men believing they've got a cause, whatever would be the point of sending them to prison? I wouldn't really have taken much notice of any of it but our Sebastian, bless him, went rushing off a couple of weeks ago with one his friends, Michael.

"But, Lillian," he said, when he came down to tell us, "we have to fight for justice."

Justice, indeed. It'll finish off his mother, poor dear, if he gets sent to prison. I can't make head or tail of the rights and wrongs of it and neither can Jimmy.

Thank heavens William is safely at teacher-training college, the lads there seem to have their feet more firmly on the ground than these university types. I sometimes think those boys have more money than sense. Jimmy says you can only afford to fight for justice when you don't have to worry about earning a living. Sebastian and Michael both work in the same bank. I reckon that they would certainly be more careful about risking their jobs if they had ever had to worry about where the next meal was coming from. Collette came over to see us and she says it's always one law for the rich and another for the poor, and they'll come back and fall on their feet straightaway. I expect she's right, she usually is. I do hope Sebastian is being careful, though.

Jimmy is coughing really badly again. He is going to work at Kelsey Park in Beckenham at Easter and I shall be so relieved. The smoke from that dreadful fire when the Crystal Palace burnt down is still hanging around up there and I am sure it is getting on his chest.

I can't bear to go up there and see the ruins of that lovely building. People came flocking from miles around to watch it burn. The fire engines that might have saved it couldn't get through the traffic. Ghouls. And the noise! There were some enormous explosions but Jimmy says no one seems to know what caused them. Down here in Penge the air was thick with the smoke, you couldn't see across the road. Jimmy says the fire is still smouldering and they reckon it will be for some time. The worst bit of all, he says, is the dead birds. They let them out of the aviary, thousands of them, hoping they would escape, but they couldn't fly in the smoke and they dropped into the fire. Those beautiful birds. He says you find bits of them all the time.

Everyone feels that we need cheering up with so much misery around. Peggy suggested that we organise another street party for the Coronation. We had such fun with the Silver Jubilee party it seems like a good idea and it will take our minds off the gloomy stuff. This one will be in May, of course, just a few days after Jack's birthday. He'll be sure it's for him, like he was before. Cynthia made him a crown to wear last time, I wonder if she'll remember and do it again. I think that nice Duke of York, with his pretty wife and those two lovely little girls, will make a much better king than the other one. Jimmy says they are probably the only people in the country who are not worried about losing their jobs, but he doesn't mean it.

We are managing quite nicely now what with me working at the laundry and him going to be chief park keeper. That'll be easier for him than gardening. I think his arm hurts him sometimes when it is very cold though he would never say.

We are going to see Max Miller at the Empire tonight, *and* we are sitting in the best seats. It's my birthday treat from Marcus and Thirza. I am really looking forward to it. We saw him once before and he is *so* naughty but ever so funny. I am going to get all dressed up and wear my good hat that they gave me a couple of years ago.

Thirza is finally cutting my hair off today. She's been on at me for ages to let her do it, she is really good at hairdressing. She says if Marcus ever goes broke she'll do it for money but till then she does all her friends and family just because she likes doing it. It feels very strange as the weight of it falls away but I am already thinking I should have done it years ago. I love the feel of it being so short.

When Jimmy comes in he pretends he doesn't know

me and says to Jack, "My goodness, I didn't know Jessie Matthews was coming to visit," and Jack goes, "No, Daddy, it's Mummy, it's Mummy," and Jimmy says, "So it is. Yes, now I look closely, I can see she's even prettier than Jessie," and gives me a smacking great kiss.

We're all giggling like mad of course, but I know she's his favourite film star so I have to be a bit flattered even if I do think it's wishful thinking on his part. But I know it does look nice.

I wish my hands weren't so red and puffy. Washerwoman's hands, I say to little Jack. He looks up at me through that blond fringe of his (he definitely *should* have been a girl with those looks) and says, "But Mummy, you are a washerwoman, aren't you?" Out of the mouths of babes.

October, 1937

William has just come in and his coat is ripped and his nose is bleeding. He goes straight into the kitchen but not before I've seen the state he's in.

"William," I say, "whatever has happened? Who have you been fighting?"

I am really shocked and shaking because William never fights, he is not that sort of boy. When he's finished getting the blood off his face, I hand him a clean towel and sit him down and wait for an explanation.

"There was a march," he tells me, "those Brownshirts, Mum. Mosley's lot. Singing the National Anthem and giving that clenched-fist salute. I was trying to get past when someone threw a bottle at them, and then there were police everywhere, and I got caught up in it. Everyone was bashing everyone else. This policeman grabbed me and I thought I was going to get arrested but he let me go. And all I was doing was trying to get home."

I can see that he is on the verge of tears, poor lad, so I give him a cuddle and tell him that his jacket is easily mended and that I know it's not his fault. Then I make him a nice cup of tea.

But underneath I feel frightened and angry. The government won't do anything to stop these thugs. I don't understand it at all. There has been a lot of trouble with them over Collette's way. Her dad was knocked down in the street by one of them and the police didn't want to know. We've just had all the song and dance over the coronation, all the pageantry and the parties, and that made most of us feel very patriotic and proud to be British, but this makes me ashamed. Jimmy is going to be furious when I tell him what happened. He gets so angry at this stuff. So do I. But I wish I didn't feel so helpless.

January, 1939

William is eighteen today. He has been accepted as a teacher at St John's and will start in April. I should be really excited, he's done so well in his exams, but all this talk of war is frightening me. Surely they won't really let it happen again? They said that the last war was the war to end all wars and I just can't believe that there will ever be another big one like that.

Of course I know that there are smaller wars going on. God knows I would have a job not to know.

Especially with Sebastian living here with us ever since that business in Spain. Michael's death has altered him so much. He won't talk about it, just sits in front of the fire sometimes with tears rolling down his face. Then if he thinks you have noticed he pretends he's got a cold.

Jimmy talks to him sometimes but when I ask him what they say to each other he says not much, it's just that Sebastian knows that he, Jimmy, had a bad time in the Great War. Not that Jimmy has ever talked about that. Not even to me. In fact that's the most he's ever said. It's like these men feel they mustn't ever admit that they are suffering. At least I can talk to Thirza about how scared I am. If I try to talk about it to Jimmy he sort of manages to make it sound as if I'm being daft. I know he does it to reassure me but it doesn't because we both know that I'm not being daft.

They are saying that Mr Chamberlain is going to introduce conscription soon. I stopped believing in the Church and all that when my brother Jack was killed but I find I am saying prayers all the time that William will never have to go. Please, please, please, God, don't let it happen.

April, 1939

William started teaching today. He bursts into the house full of it all – no need to ask if it went well, it's written all over him.

"Look at these, Mum, aren't they great?"

The attaché case that Marcus and Thirza bought him as a starting-work present is full of the kiddies' exercise books, which he tips onto the table.

"Look at these drawings. I asked them to do

something that would tell me a bit about them or their families, and I can't believe how good some of them are."

He's right. Houses and dogs and cats and parents and grannies (all their grannies seem to be sitting in rocking chairs knitting. I'm a mite doubtful about the accuracy of these) and most of the pictures are lively and funny. But one shows a little boy sitting on a pavement alone.

"Who's that?" I ask.

"Ah," says William, his face clouding, "that's Graham. Parents drink, apparently. Poor kid smells so no one wants to sit near him."

He's got a class of seven-year-olds and he's quite taken aback that some of them don't seem to know their tables properly or their alphabet.

"I think it's because most of the teachers are quite elderly, Mum, and don't realise that teaching has changed and the old-fashioned way of just testing one or two in class and assuming that everyone is at the same standard doesn't really work. I got the children chanting their alphabet and singing their tables, and I made a game of it with them, like they showed us at college."

"You mind you don't tread on anyone's toes," I warn him. "Don't run before you can walk, my lad."

He grins at me and says, "Don't worry, Mum, the soul of tact, that's me."

I hope he will be. I can't imagine some of those teachers being thrilled to be told that their methods are out of date by an eighteen-year-old.

We heard today that they are introducing conscription, but thank heavens, it's only for twenty-year-old lads. Perhaps this whole thing will have blown over by the time William is twenty. I am absolutely not going to think about it.

We have got a new member of the family. Her name is Tess and she is the prettiest dog you have ever seen. She turned up here one day and we couldn't find out where she had come from so she just sort of moved in. She sleeps at the end of Jack's bed and during the day she goes with Jimmy to the park. She is black and white and very loving and makes us all laugh a lot just by being a dog. Even Sebastian cheers up when she is around.

Thirza's girls adore her, of course, especially little Margaret. She brought her doll's pram over the other day and she put an old bonnet on Tess and stuck her in the pram and amazingly Tess let her do it and just sat there with that funny dog grin on her face. We let her wheel her as far the Empire and back again but Margaret had to lift her out or I think she'd be there still. I wonder where she came from. I do hope another little girl isn't breaking her heart somewhere.

Thirza refuses to let the girls have a dog of their own but she has let them have two kittens as a sort of consolation prize. The girls have called them Mickey and Minnie. Marcus says that seeing they bring dead mice in all the time the names are a bit unfortunate but happily the girls don't know what he means.

May, 1939

They've been talking again on the wireless about evacuating women and children to the country. Jack has been doing gasmask drills at school. Jimmy is volunteering for the ARP. They think this Hitler will bomb London if there is a war. I feel sick. I don't know what to do. How could I leave William and Jimmy? But I don't think I could send Jack away on his own.

Oh please, God, no – not again, dear Lord.

August, 1939

I feel as if my life is coming full circle. I am back in Suffolk. Jimmy and William came up with us and stayed for a few days and then went back to Penge. Martha and Father are being wonderful but I never realised how tiny the cottage was. However did we manage all those years ago, with so many of us living here? Jack and I are sleeping downstairs. Jack is getting on well with Martha's children and I must say they are very good with him. Donald is such a big lad but of course he's thirteen now, and little Ivy is eleven. Although they are older than Jack they let him tag along and seem to understand that it's all a bit strange for him.

But we have got Tess with us, and she's having a lovely time with the farm dogs, and tomorrow Thirza is coming down with the girls and Minnie and Mickey. She is going to stay with Uncle Jethro, he says he will be really glad of the company now all the children are gone. All my brothers have been in to see us. Thank God even Timmy is thirty now, that must be too old to be conscripted, mustn't it?

Surely they will be safe – oh, please God, don't take anyone else away, I don't care how selfish that is, surely once in a lifetime is enough – it may not happen – hold on to that. Mr Chamberlain might find a way out. Peace with honour – I don't care about the honour. I just want the peace. Perhaps it won't happen. Please God, don't let it happen. Not again.

Mother would say, "Pull yourself together, Lillian!" – it must be being back home that does it because I can almost hear her voice. She's right, of course. Whatever happens I must be strong for Jack. For them all. All my men. Thank you, Mother.

Part Two: The War Years

Sunday 3rd September, 1939

They've done it. They've really done it. We are at war with Germany. Marcus and Jimmy and William came up last night and Timmy and Lettie are here too. It is half past eleven and Mr Chamberlain has just finished his announcement. We all knew it was coming but somehow we couldn't quite bring ourselves to believe it was actually going to happen.

Martha and Thirza and I get up and go and put the kettle on. No one says anything for a minute and then Father says, "Well, that's that then," and goes outside. Lettie comes up to me and I see that she is trying not to cry. Poor child, she and Timmy have only been married a few months and –

Oh my God, the radio is still on and they are saying there is an air raid on London….. we all stand stock-still and Jimmy has come and put his arm round me and the children pick up the tension and Margaret and Norma start to cry….then Marcus says, "Stop – listen," and…..they are saying it is a false alarm… . Oh, thank you, God. Thank you.

An aircraft was spotted off the coast and all the sirens went off but it was just one of our own aeroplanes.

We make light of it to reassure the children. William helps me to take the tea round as my hands are shaking so much. The papers are saying that the government can conscript anyone between eighteen and forty-one. They don't think the older ones will be called up but my William has been already. He brings the big teapot out and starts refilling everyone's cups and everything seems so normal. He glances over at me and grins. He is still a child. How can they send him to war?

Marcus sees my face and says that this war will not be like the last one because of the air power. "He might be safer in the army than stuck in London, Lillian." I know he means well but as Thirza says it's not much of a comfort when he and Jimmy are just going back there. They want to leave soon so as to be back for the King's broadcast tonight. I wish we were going too. I am not at all sure about being up here, but the men say that knowing we are out of London is important to them. We'll see how it goes, is what we are saying. If it was just me I wouldn't stay here but of course I've got Jack to think of.

They are leaving now. I suddenly wonder if I will ever see any of them again. I smile and say, "You mind how you go now," as if they are off for a picnic. Marcus's big car roars off and we stand with the kids waving them out of sight. Later, when everyone is in bed, I slip into the garden and sit looking up at the sky. It is a beautiful, quiet night. Tess comes and pushes her head onto my lap.

I cry very quietly so that no one will hear me.

December, 1939

Jimmy and Marcus are coming up today to spend Christmas with us. William is somewhere abroad. We don't know where, of course, but I have a card from him with an Eskimo and a penguin on. Jimmy says is he trying to tell us something. But he is only joking. We think he is probably in France but he's not allowed to say. Reading between the lines in the papers, that's where most of our boys are being sent.

It is all so quiet. All the bombing and gassing and stuff that we were expecting hasn't happened, thank God. Jimmy says that the ARP spend all their time practising first aid on dummies, doing drills on how to put out street fires, telling people to draw their blackout blinds, and yelling "Put that light out!" at houses that have even a chink showing. Marcus says that when they do that it starts all the dogs barking and the babies crying and Hitler could probably find them by the noise alone.

A lot of the women and children have gone back home. I would really like to but Jimmy has asked me to wait and make sure it is going to stay quiet so that we don't put Jack at risk, and I said I would. Anyhow, Thirza says she feels safer up here with the girls so it is not as if I am on my own.

Our two men have just arrived. What a lot of noise and cuddling and hugging. Little Margaret has attached herself so firmly round Marcus's legs that he finally has to fall into Father's armchair, convulsed with laughter. Not to be left out, Cynthia and Norma are draped over him so he is nearly invisible. Poor Thirza can't get near him.

"Obviously have to wait my turn," she giggles.

Jack is much more restrained with Jimmy. "Girls!" he says scornfully and then he shakes Jimmy's hand. Jimmy and I are a bit taken aback but we try not to let Jack see. It makes me realise how seriously Jack has taken all Jimmy said to him about being the man of the family while we are up here. He's nine in a couple of weeks and I don't know whether to feel proud or sad. A bit of each, I reckon.

Tess is running round in circles barking madly and trying to join in the fun. Father and Martha come in from the kitchen with a big pot of tea and we try to restore some order to the proceedings. But it's lovely to have us all together and to be so happy. If only William was here it would be a really nice Christmas.

I reckon this war will be over soon.

January, 1940

It's my birthday and I am forty today. I used to think that forty was terribly old but I must say I don't feel a lot different from when I was thirty. The government put us on food rationing this week.

"Funny sort of birthday present," I said to Thirza. We had to pop along to Mr Naismith at the village shop and register. It was really strange, we had to tell him who we were and where we lived and the children's ages. As if he didn't know already. Father, who has never liked Mr Naismith that much, said he was being a pompous old goat and the little bit of power had gone to his head, but Martha said that as he might now *have* a bit of power we must play along and be careful. She's got her head screwed on, that girl.

Butter, sugar, bacon and ham can only be got with coupons now and not much of them then. Uncle Jethro had the sense to get a couple of pigs a few years ago as a little sideline, so we shall be all right there. Martha's family have a cow and a goat, and like almost everyone else here we have hens, so if eggs go on the ration we shan't be affected by that. Mind you, old Clive the cockerel is getting a bit long in the tooth so Father is hunting around for another one just in case. He says they are bound to ration eggs eventually and then you won't be able to get a young cockerel for love nor money.

We've always grown vegetables of course and Jimmy tells me that our little garden in Penge is still producing well in spite of a slice of it being dug up for the Anderson shelter. We haven't got any shelters here. We had a leaflet round telling us that if we get bombed we must take refuge in the well under the stairs. What a hope, there's just about room for Minnie and Mickey there.

February, 1940

Still no bombs anywhere, thank heavens. We are beginning to think that no one will dare to do it because they know they will get bombed back. There are posters all over Ipswich and even in the village shop…"'Ware spies – keep it under your hat"…actually the chap on the poster is wearing a tin hat and reminds me a bit of my Jimmy… . "Be like Dad – keep Mum"…and lots more everywhere.

Who do they think we are going to talk to and what do they think we know anyway? I can't help feeling a German spy would stick out like a sore thumb up here, but, as Thirza says, you never know.

May, 1940

Mr Chamberlain has resigned and Mr Churchill has taken over from him. Uncle Jethro says he is an old warmonger. I hope he's wrong. Mr Churchill made a speech on the wireless. "I have nothing to offer but blood, toil, tears and sweat." The papers are all saying it was wonderful and inspiring but Thirza and I both think we'd rather he'd offered us peace and all our family to be together again.

I had a postcard from William this morning. It just says "Don't worry, Mum, I'm OK." Father says he won't be allowed to say any more. The news from France is really bad and seems to be getting worse. I try not to think about it too much. It's not as if there is anything you can do...

Today is 26th May and on the wireless we heard that our army is stranded on the beach at a place called Dunkirk – they are being shot at and bombed by the Germans and they can't get off. My William is there – I am sure he is – oh God, what is going to happen to him? – William, my William – where are you? – please be all right – please...

Mr Churchill has said that we must all go to church and pray for a miracle or we will lose the war. On the wireless they say that practically everyone in the whole country is going...

I'm here but I can't pray – I'm just saying "Oh, dear God, no, please, no, not again – our boys are out there – sons, husbands, brothers – killed, wounded – not again, dear Lord, please make it stop – if you are up there, God, please make it stop" – over and over again – perhaps that is a prayer. Perhaps that's all most of us know how to do – perhaps just being here counts. Please God, give us a miracle...

Oh God, I will never, ever, doubt you again.

You've given us our miracle. The sea, which has been so rough for days, has gone blessedly calm and hundreds of people round the coast are setting off in their little boats to fetch our boys off that dreadful beach. Timmy has just left with Mr Naismith's son Eric. The Naismiths have a little skiff moored at Harwich and Timmy and Eric are going to take it over. The twins have gone too, they have a boat at Felixstowe. God protect them all. Thank you, God. Thank you.

Please bring my William home. Safe. Please.

June, 1940

William is back in England. Alive and well.

When I saw the telegraph boy's bike coming I thought...but it was from Jimmy with the best news I could have. My William is safe. Picked up by some fishermen from Hastings. God bless them. I want to be with my men. I am wiring Jimmy to say that Jack and I are coming back at the weekend. Thirza is going to stay here but I have had enough.

I am going home.

It is so wonderful to be here with William and Jimmy again. Jack rushed straight up to his room and had his Meccano all over the floor before you could say knife. You'd think he'd never been away. He's already got Percy and Alan from down the road up there and we are told they are constructing a destroyer. As long as it keeps them quiet they can build what they like as far as

I'm concerned.

I really need to have some time with William. He looks very pale and somehow a lot older. Too much older. I can't help being reminded of when Jimmy came home from the front over twenty years ago. I don't want to ask him what it was like because I understand that it was beyond what he would tell me even if he was allowed. I just want him to know that his dad and I are always thinking of him and praying for him. I suppose I really want to tell him how much we love him but he'd be embarrassed by that kind of talk. So we sit side-by-side in the little bit of paved garden outside the kitchen where we keep the mangle, the bit that has always been such a suntrap, and in the end we don't say much at all. We just sit in the sun. But I do hold his hand and he lets me. He's got to go back to his unit in two days' time.

I've brought back a nice breast of mutton and I'm roasting it for dinner. William is peeling the potatoes for me and I'm telling him all about Suffolk and some of the things Thirza's girls got up to, like Cynthia secretly bringing one of the lambs home last month and keeping it in her bedroom all day till Uncle Jethro heard it and made her take it back to its mum. She was very indignant. Said it looked cold and lonely so she thought it needed a good home. She'd actually put it in the bed she shares with the other two but they were sworn to secrecy. It is good to see William laughing like that.

I'm popping a rice pudding in the bottom of the oven so it will cook nicely as the potatoes bake. I've put some raisins in it so I don't have to add sugar – that's getting a bit short in the shops. Both Jimmy and William look as if they need feeding up. Marcus is coming over for supper. I can make soup from the mutton bones and then mince up what's left of the meat and do some stuffed tomatoes. It's funny, a lot of people are moaning about having to cook so economically but one way and another I've been doing it most of my life. I quite enjoy the challenge, really.

William has gone back today. Jack and I walk down to Kelsey Park and feed the ducks. Then we go to the park keeper's hut and Jimmy makes us a cup of tea on his primus stove. When we've had that we walk back home. I am just taking my hat off thinking that by the time I have cooked supper and done the ironing and mending I will be tired enough to get some sleep tonight, when Jack says, "He will be all right, you know, Mum."

I'm obviously not as good at acting as I thought I was.

Sebastian, Collette and I went to see *Gone with the Wind* at the Empire last night. Talk about take your mind off the war, it was absolutely *amazing*. Clark Gable was so debonair and I felt really sorry for him. Why couldn't Scarlett see he was head-over-heels for her? I do like Leslie Howard but let's face it Collette and I both said if you had to choose between him and Clark…well, I ask you!

Oh, but we did enjoy it. It is ever so long but you never got bored, *and* it was in colour. Wish there were a few more pictures like it to take you out of yourself.

Sebastian has got two days' leave from his squadron. He looks so smart in his blue uniform. He's stationed at Biggin Hill. He says the King is going there next week to present some of the pilots with medals. I think he is more excited about it than he is letting on. I know I would be.

Going into the RAF has been such a good thing for him, for the first time since Spain he seems to have found a purpose. He's always been such an intense lad, ever since he was a small boy, but he is much more like his old self again. He says he needs to make reparation for Michael's death. I tell him what Freddy told me all those years ago about those left behind having an obligation to live life to the full. When he goes, he shakes Jimmy's hand, and whirls Jack round, then he comes and gives me a hug.

"Oh, Lillian," he says, "I may yet owe you my life." I have no idea what he is talking about so I give him a kiss and tell him not to be so daft. "Just keep safe and come back to us as soon as you can," I say. When he has left I feel quite emotional though I don't really understand why.

August, 1940

The weather is so beautiful it's hard to take in all we hear about the fighting that the RAF are doing, even though every night on the wireless they tell us how many of our planes shot down how many German ones. Like it's a game. It seems that we are winning, though I thank God my William is not in the Air Force. I worry a lot about Sebastian. I had a card from him the other day and he said he was by far the oldest one in his squadron and got teased a lot by the other lads who call him the Patriarch. The Patriarch! Sebastian is not twenty-five yet.

There was a terrible attack on Croydon the other day, we could see the black smoke from here. On the wireless they said that our boys brought down thirty-two planes without losing a single one themselves.

Mr Churchill made a speech today praising our airmen. Marcus telephoned Sebastian later to make sure he was all right as we haven't heard from him for a couple of weeks. Sebastian told him that when the chaps heard the bit of the speech that went "never…has so much been owed by so many" one of the lads said, "Be careful, chaps, the Prime Minister has seen our mess bill." Sebastian says they fool around all the time. Jimmy reckons that's what keeps them sane.

I've got a letter from William. It was posted somewhere in England so at least I know he is safe. He says he has been doing a lot of swimming, but I know he can't have as the beaches are mined, so he must be trying to let us know that he is somewhere near the coast. It's nearly September but the weather is still lovely and warm. All the talk in the papers is of the invasion. Mr Churchill says we have 2,000,000 armed soldiers ready to resist. Jimmy says that if the Home Guard is anything to go by, they are mostly armed with broom handles.

September, 1940

There is this terrible noise – I really can't make out what it is. Jack is playing at soldiers in the street with his friends and I go out to see what is happening. There is this black cloud coming towards us – only it's not a cloud it's planes – it's German planes – I can hear the sirens – *oh God – JACK! – JACK!* – I grab his arm and we run for the shelter in the garden and Tess is already in there whimpering and *the noise the noise the noise* and we pull the door closed and we can hear the planes and now there are bombs exploding and Jimmy, where are you, where are you? Must stay calm, tell Jack we are going to sing, start to sing, "One man went to mow," but my voice is trembling and all these funny noises are coming out so we huddle together and I cover his head with my body and Tess is trying to push in and the three of us are frozen with fear.

It has stopped. I don't know how long we have been here. We are so stiff we can hardly move. The door is wrenched open – oh, thank you, God, thank you. It's Jimmy. He pulls us to our feet and we stand there for a moment just holding each other, and then he says, "Come on, Lil girl, they are probably coming back, we've got to get some gear into this tin hut!" It is still light outside and – oh God, there is a hole where the Murrells' house used to be and there are firemen there – but Mrs Smith next door calls out that they were all safe in their Anderson – none of them hurt she is saying – and everyone is carrying clothes and food out of their houses into the shelters. Tess won't come out – she's backed against the wall but Jimmy tells Jack to leave her and help.

I go to put the kettle on but there is no gas and no water, and I suddenly realise that there is no glass in the windows and – *Oh my God, the sirens are going again* – we are back in the shelter – Jimmy has fixed up his old storm lantern so at least we have some light – the noise is off again – I know we are all going to die – at least we are together...

The all-clear is going – Oh God, I must have dozed

off – I can't believe I did – *I can't move* – I start to struggle for breath – there's this awful smell – and Jimmy's voice is saying, "Lil, calm down, girl, we're OK," and he pushes against the door of the shelter until it opens enough to let the light in and I realise that I can't move because Jack is asleep across my lap and Tess is on top of him and everyone is breathing and – Oh dear God, we are alive and I start to laugh but it turns into crying and Jimmy pulls Jack off me and puts his arm round me and Tess is licking my face and then Jack wakes up and I breathe very deeply to try to calm myself down so he doesn't see me like this but there is smoke and dust everywhere and I breathe it all in and start to cough and they are both thumping me on the back, which makes it worse, and then Jack pulls a sweet out of his pocket and gives it to me, and even though it looks horrible it helps me to stop coughing.

Jack is already pushing at the shelter door and has opened it enough to get out, and Jimmy goes after him and I pull myself up and follow them. It's difficult to see much because there's all this dust swirling about in the sunshine, and it takes a minute before we realise that everything looks different. I don't understand why I can see all the furniture in Mr and Mrs Turner's house opposite, and then I realise that the outside wall is not there. The Drapers' house next door to them is quite gone and the firemen are there trying to put out a fire further up the street.

Jimmy has already run across with Mr Smith to help, and everyone is running round the back of the Drapers' house to see if they are all right, but some of the house has fallen on the shelter and we are all calling and trying to dig away the rubble with our hands. Mr

Smith says to me, "Take the kids away," and I know from his voice that something bad has happened, so I call the children to come over our house and see if we can find some food, and Mrs Smith comes with me and we take the children into the house, which is still standing, and I find a bottle of lemonade that I made last week standing on the sideboard, quite all right even though the windows have blown out, and I tell them we are going to have a picnic.

And my voice is quite steady.

Only then the house starts to creak and one of the firemen puts his head round the hole where the window was and says we had better come out till they are sure it's safe, so I walk along the road with the children and some of the other mums catch us up and we all go and sit in the rec with my bottle of lemonade, for all the world as if it is a normal day.

Except the sky is so black to the east of us it is nearly blotting out the sun and the smell of burning is terrible, and we are all filthy and even the kids are quiet.

Jimmy comes to get us. Chris from the fire brigade says our house is safe. They are setting up a canteen in the school hall and getting some water to us. He tells me that all of the Drapers died in the shelter. Bryan was only six years old and Mary was the same age as Jack.

The firemen have gone up to the East End where they say the damage is a hundred times worse. I wish I had some way of contacting Collette. Jimmy is going to see if the telephone in the butcher's shop is working so he can phone Marcus to see if he's OK, but I remind him that Marcus will be out with the ARP anyway.

We go up to the hall and I help to set up the trestle

tables. Some ladies arrive in a van with big canisters of water and the hall has electricity and it is still working so we get some tea going, and they've got soup and bread and everyone is coming in. Mrs Everton and I are dishing out the soup, and Jimmy's managed to get the heaters on because it feels so cold everywhere, and little Lucy Fryer, who never looks old enough to have children, has organised her three and all the others into a sing-song at the far end of the hall, and some of the older people have joined them. We suddenly realise how hungry we all are and Jimmy points out that it's eighteen hours since that first raid started.

Mrs Everton, who seems to have shrunk somehow and looks a lot older than when I saw her the day before yesterday, says she can't go back in her shelter. She hates being in small spaces and says if it means she's going to get killed, well so be it. I hated it too. I know how she feels. With what happened to the Drapers I don't think any of us will ever feel safe in the Andersons again anyway. Mr Smith says they are going into Penge East Station if it all starts again. I think he has the right idea, at least it's solid.

Most of us are going to stay here in the hall tonight. I can't believe it is still only three in the afternoon. It seems a lifetime since we got out of the shelter. Mrs Smith and I are going to walk down together and try to find some clean bedding. Jimmy says he will stay with Jack. The kids are looking so tired. Well, I suppose we all do really.

We come back up the hill to the school hall pushing Mrs Smith's pram. Her Gwen is only two so fortunately she still has it and we've loaded it with blankets and stuff. They are a bit dusty but the cupboard doors were still on so they are not too bad. I've found Jack's old teddy bear and hidden it in his pillow – he pretends he doesn't take it to bed anymore but I know better – and I managed to find the old plimsoll of William's that Tess loves as well. All I could find of Jimmy's to bring was his pipe and a bit of tobacco but I know he'll appreciate that.

We've put some cups into the pram as well. It's like we're going to live there and a bit of me feels silly. I expect by tomorrow we'll be all cleared up. I do wish I knew how Collette and her kiddies were. Perhaps I'll be able to get over there on the bus tomorrow. After all, this can't go on for long.

Mr Grieves must have dusted off the piano because as we get near the hall we can hear him thumping away and they are all singing "There'll always be an England." Mrs Smith grins at me. "Amazing what a cup of tea will do, isn't it?" she says.

Isn't it just?

October, 1940

I feel like a cave dweller. Every night we go to the station and as soon as the trains stop we move off the platforms into the tunnel. That first night (which seems like a lifetime ago) Mr James, the station keeper, tried to stop us, said it was against regulations, so we all bought penny halfpenny tickets and then didn't go anywhere, just stayed in the station. After that the government said it was OK for everyone to use them at night. It's not very nice but you do feel safer and you can't hear the noise so much. We sling hammocks across the tunnel for the kids and take flasks of tea and some food. Of course, it's only us women with the kids, apart from a few really elderly chaps, because all the men are out there doing the fire watching or whatever. The worse part is going out in the morning not knowing what you are going to find. We try not to think about it too much.

We knit a lot of the time, and chat. I've unpicked all of Jack's old jumpers so I can make him bigger ones – he does keep growing, war or not. Eileen said the other day that we are spending most of the war holding skeins of wool for each other so we can wind them into balls – she was only joking but there *is* always someone asking you to "hold my wool, please".

A few of the women play cards and, of course, we listen to the wireless a lot. Jack and Percy and Alan take off the people in *ITMA*, they are so funny, and little Joan Smith does a wonderful Mrs Mopp. She's got "Can I do you now, sir?" off to a tee. And Alan does a lovely Wilfred Pickles – when we put the lights down he always calls out "To all in the North – good neet," and we all yell "Good neet" back at him. Everything stops for *Band Wagon*, of course – we sing along with Arthur Askey and the kids love calling out "Hallo, playmates." It even drowns out the noise of the planes and the bombs sometimes. We have all got to know each other so well. Daphne cuts everyone's hair down here. Mind you, the other night she nearly took off Mrs Everton's ear when there was a very loud bang.

During the day things are almost normal. Well, what passes for normal nowadays. Last week they got the water back but we lost it again that night. They mostly keep the standpipe in Maple Road going, though. The government has started up special canteens everywhere. For those who are bombed out mostly, but anyone can use them. "British Restaurants" they call them, and I have been recruited, as Jimmy puts it. Actually, Mrs Everton asked me if I would work in ours in Evelina Road, and of course I said yes. So I'm cooking again and even being paid a bit to do it.

And that I really am enjoying. It's an ill wind. *Music While You Work* on the wireless and everyone queuing up for my food – and saying how good it is – stops you having too much time to think about it all. I don't know where William is and I wonder every morning when I send Jack off to school and Jimmy off to work whether I will ever see them again. We get ourselves into the shelter before six o'clock and wave our husbands off again to do their bit. Jimmy's mostly on the fire watching. Some of the younger ones have got husbands in the forces and you see the strain on their faces when the bombing is extra bad and their kids cry and ask when Daddy is coming home.

But we pretend this is normal. It might be. Perhaps what was will never come back. God knows what will happen if Hitler wins. They say women are being raped on the streets in France and we hear rumours about other stuff that is happening that just can't possibly be true. I'm sure it can't be. But we laugh and joke and make do and mend and tell each other there's a war on as if it is all the most natural thing in the world, and when one of the kids wakes screaming we make out it's because of what they had for supper. When it comes down to it, what else can you do?

November, 1940

We had to laugh today. That Lord Woolton, who's supposed to tell us how to cook with no ingredients, was spouting on about making our Christmas cakes with carrots instead of currants, and then he said that there would be no rationing of turkeys or, wait for it, caviar, over Christmas. As Eileen said, "Well, that'll make all the difference to our Christmas, won't it?" But I ask you – how can we take some of these people seriously when they come out with stuff like that? The sort who are going to miss their caviar aren't going to have carrots in their Christmas cakes, are they?

Thinking of the toffs, Marcus says that one of the funniest sights after dark up West is them all coming home from their nightclubs with their white shirt tails hanging out. It's because of the blackout, of course, so that they can be seen. Funny old world, us in the station, them in the nightclubs.

Lots of the people round here who have been bombed out have moved into Chislehurst Caves. They've just taken all they can lay their hands on from the house and gone. There's a mobile canteen goes up there twice a day and a van comes round and takes their washing, but it's getting more and more crowded. Lucy Fryer went up there but she said you had to go outside every time you needed the toilets, and that it was quite a long walk, and with her brood she no sooner got back with one than she was off again with another. She's gone to stay with her sister in Reading. Our house is still standing, thank God. I know I could go back to Suffolk, but I feel that I am being useful here and Jimmy and I would rather be together. We thought about sending Jack, but he was so upset at the idea of leaving us.

We've all decided to pool our rations for Christmas and have our Christmas dinner in the canteen, so I am busy working out the menu. There will be about 200 of us with the kids, but I am going to try and stretch it a bit in case any of our boys have leave. How I would love to see William, but Jimmy doesn't think there is much hope he'll get home. He says the artillery boys are our front line at the moment and we must concentrate on being very proud of our son.

A bomb fell right behind the Empire a couple of days ago, and when I passed there I saw that on the blackboard where they advertise the shows someone has written:

Old Hitler dropped a bomb on Penge,
Tried to knock it all to bits
But if he saw us carrying on
He'd have... "blue pencil"...fits...

Cheeky lot – good for them!

Collette and the children are coming over here. They have been bombed out and are sleeping on straw on the floor of some church. Little Moira, the one she always calls her afterthought, has had dreadful diarrhoea. They've had such a terrible time over in Stepney. Her husband went out on duty with the ARP and just never came back. It was that dreadful night in October when the Hun started nearly a thousand fires in London and hundreds of people were killed in the bombing. Poor Collette. She says it would be easier if she had her Sid's body because she keeps hoping he will just walk in. And the children keep asking for their dad and she doesn't know what to say to them.

There is such a lot of bad feeling in the East End, because our men are out there doing their bit and yet these able-bodied nobs from up West are still going to the nightclubs and suchlike and we all know they have shelters underneath those places that are better than some of our homes. Talk about one law for the rich. Collette reckons that if it was the West End that was being hit so badly it would be a different story. The King and Queen went to visit some of the bombsites last week and people started to boo them. The Queen going on about "looking the East End in the face" when she's tottering over the rubble in her high heels and pearls. A lot of us would think more of them if they told a few more of their own kind to pull their fingers out.

Collette's Billy has been called up, he goes in February. I am glad she's got him with her till then. I don't know how she's coping. She's really worried about Moira, I think she's been very poorly, poor little kid. Not sure who looks worse, Collette or Moira. Gladys and Ronnie, her other two, are OK, but they've always been a couple of right little cockney toughs.

Jimmy and I think she needs to get right out of London with them all so I wired Martha to see if they could have them up there. Of course she said yes, and Marcus is going to take them to stay with her and Father when he goes back for Christmas. I wonder what Father will make of them?

December, 1940

It's been a good Christmas Day so far. Jimmy is on

duty this afternoon so he won't be able to stay, which is a pity, but we are planning to have a dance in here this evening and he should be back for some of that. We are hoping the Germans will want to celebrate too, so we don't have to dash for the station. After all, they are supposed to be Christians. Makes you think, that does. Mr Everton says that if their Pope had told them all to stop that would have been the end of it all, but Marcus says that is "simplistic." I really don't know where he gets all these words from but Thirza says he's always reading, not only the papers but books about history and politics.

Everyone is saying nice things about the Christmas dinner, and though I say it who shouldn't, it wasn't at all bad. Thirza managed to get Mr Naismith to sell us three turkeys and he sent them down on the train without charging us for that, and we had loads of Brussels sprouts, and cabbage, and carrots, and I roasted the parsnips and potatoes. I made the stuffing ages ago.

We had all the giblets to make the gravy and the children threw dice to see who would pull the wishbones – all three of them! Jack was one of the winners and he closed his eyes very tightly and then grinned at me and said, "Now we shall have a perfect Christmas." I wonder what he wished, bless him.

The puddings were a real triumph. I was a bit worried because what with gathering up everyone's rations and stuff it was really much too late to make them – I've always made mine in August. Mrs Everton (she's so much friendlier nowadays) came down with some brandy in the bottom of a bottle and it was enough to pour over the puddings and set light to them, so we stuck some holly in the top and did just that, and then Mrs Everton, Eileen, Mrs Smith and me rushed in with all four puddings very quickly before the flames died. Such a great cheer went up you wouldn't believe!

They won't let me help clear up so everyone is rushing around doing everything while I just sit here. I must admit I could nod off. Jimmy has just come up to kiss me goodbye before he goes on duty. Everyone takes good care to say goodbye properly nowadays because, well, you never know, do you? He's come up behind me and is being daft – it must be that bit of brandy – and he's put his hands over my eyes and is saying, "Guess who?" – and oh my God, it isn't Jimmy, it's my William – and I turn round and he's standing there in his uniform and he looks so handsome, and Jimmy is grinning away beside him, and Jack says, "I told you, Mum" – and I can't believe – oh, William. William. Thank you, God.

This is turning out to be one of the best Christmas Days ever, who would have believed that we'd have Hitler to thank for that? Jack and his friends are dragging William round the hall to admire the paper chains they've been making for days – as if there was any chance of him missing them.

I notice Tilly Everton is hanging on to his arm and joining in the fun. I must say she is a pretty girl with her Veronica Lake hairdo hanging all over one side of her face, but she's always a bit stand-offish with me. Jimmy says she's just a bit shy, but I don't know. Anyway, they are still not much more than children, loads of time to meet Mr or Mrs Right.

I'm just finishing making the sandwiches for tea,

good old bloater paste, and we've loads of egg and cress. Some of the dads who are off duty have been playing Musical Chairs and games with the kids. Of course, they've all got thoroughly over-excited, especially the dads. We had to make them all sit down to listen to the King's broadcast, and now they are putting out the cups and plates for tea. I do hope the Christmas cakes are edible, such a hotchpotch of ingredients, but Marcus found me a bottle of sherry to pour in so I'm hoping they will taste alright. I had to put the mixture into four tins because I didn't have anything nearly big enough, and they took days to cook on account of the gas going off all the time.

They say it was all lovely, though to be honest I have some reservations about the cakes, but anyway there is not a crumb left and you can't really ask for more than that. We fold the tables away and Mr Grieves is playing his heart out on the piano and a couple of the youngsters are joining in with mouth organs. That certainly adds to the volume if not the quality. We've done Knees up, Mother Brown at least three times and I've danced the Velita with William, the Gay Gordons with Jack, the Hokey Cokey with just about everyone and now Jimmy is back and we are doing a lovely slow waltz. Out of the corner of my eye I can see William is dancing with Tilly again. I noticed during the Paul Jones that they kept ending up together. I have to admit that they do make a lovely-looking couple. I can see Elsie Bryant, who lives over The Queens Arms with her mum and dad, watching them. She was in the same class at school as William and always asks after him. She's such a nice little thing.

We have been so lucky. No raids so far and it's nearly half-past nine. Most of the kids are flat out on their mums' laps and it's time to call it a day. We turn off the heaters and make sure there are no lights showing before we open the outside door. We all agree it's been a smashing day. William says he's taking Tilly home. I open my mouth to point out that her mum and dad are both here and she only lives twenty-five yards from the hall, but then I meet Jimmy's eyes and I shut up quickly.

Jimmy and Jack and I walk home singing Christmas carols – "Peace on earth, goodwill to all men" – tonight it even seems possible.

January, 1941

I had a card from William today saying that he arrived safely. I was so worried because he was travelling the night of those dreadful raids just after Christmas, but he left early in the afternoon and was just ahead of it all.

Marcus has just come over to try and persuade me to go back to Suffolk with Thirza. I know that she would like me to be there with them, but I keep trying to explain when I write to her that I would feel that I was running away. I know that I am doing a good job with the canteen, too. The government are paying us properly to run it now, which is just as well as money has been desperately short. They don't pay that much, but it makes a big difference.

It's my birthday today, and Jack must have told everybody, because in the middle of serving lunch Mr Smith came in and yelled at everyone to be quiet and then they all sang "Happy Birthday to Lillian." I was quite embarrassed but I must admit I was pleased as well. Mind you, Jack didn't *have* to call out at the top of his voice, "Mum's forty-one today" – wait till I get him home! And of course, it's our wedding anniversary. Jimmy and I have been married for twenty-one years. How the world seems to have changed in that time. And not all for the better either.

Jimmy's cough is often very bad. He's had it for so long that I think I don't notice a lot of the time but this fire watching and all the dust around are playing havoc with his chest. Tess goes with him everywhere nowadays, whether he's at the park or on duty, and I am so glad he's got her as he's often on his own.

We seem to have acquired another animal. Jack found a little starving tabby kitten in the ruins of the Drapers' house just after Christmas. I made some scrambled egg for supper that night and we gave the kitten some on a spoon and then a drop of warm milk, and now he's eating everything we give him and you can watch him filling out. I casseroled some liver last night and he went mad when we gave him some of that. Jack has called him Biggles, as when the sirens go he flies down the road with us to the station. When Tess comes in he goes trotting up to her and she washes him all over. Jack says he must be the cleanest kitten in the world.

Funny thing is, both Tess and Biggles often seem to know that there is going to be a raid long before the sirens go. They sit bolt upright and quiver and Biggles actually took off down the road ahead of us the other day. He was half-way there before the sirens went. Jimmy says animals must be able to hear the planes much further off than we can. What fascinates me is that they seem to be able to tell the difference between ours and the Germans', even little Biggles doesn't bother to move if it's one of ours.

February, 1941

The government finally decided to control the price of a lot of food and stuff. To be honest, it's quite a relief. With everything being so short the prices have been going up and up and now they won't be able to do that anymore. We are always being offered things on the black market, of course, but most of us feel we wouldn't do that even if we could afford it. Jimmy earns nearly £4 a week now, and with the twenty-three shillings I get paid for working in the canteen we are not too badly off. Mind you, the rent takes a fair slice of it. Seems odd to be paying all this money for a house that we can't live in most of the time, but there you are. Mrs Hammond, our landlady, lives somewhere up in Scotland, and we just pay the rent man every week. We've never met her and are not likely to.

We've decided not to keep putting the windows back. It's getting more and more difficult to find glass and it just gets blown out again, so we've boarded them all up. It is almost as dark in the house now as it is in the station tunnel, but at least we don't have to worry about the blackout.

Sometimes I think that the worst thing of all is that we are almost getting used to it. Three houses at the top of the road were wiped out last week and one of the families hadn't gone into the station for some reason. All dead. Three kiddies, their mum and dad, and her mum, their grandma. Nice old lady. I didn't even cry. And when I told Jack his friend Percy was gone, he just said, "Oh, poor old Perce, I shall miss him." This is a dreadful time to be bringing children up. If we come through it, whatever will they be like?

I've just had a letter from Mrs Willett. Sebastian is missing, presumed dead. I don't believe he is dead. I won't believe it. Not Sebastian, who has survived so much. I wire her back straightaway saying, "Keep praying, I will." Oh Sebastian, please be all right. He's been almost like a third child to us. I should write and tell William, he would want to know. But I feel in my bones that Sebastian is alive.

I don't go to church very often but I go into St John's on my way home from the canteen and I kneel there watching the dust move across the light from the windows, and I can't think of anything to say but please, God, make him come back. I do not let myself cry because that would mean that I think he is dead, and I don't, I don't.

May, 1941

Jimmy is off duty tonight and we are going to see *The Road to Singapore* with Bob Hope and Bing Crosby – they say it's ever so funny. Let's hope we get to see it all the way through. When we went to see *Rebecca* they had just finished the second feature, which was not bad, and we were watching the news, when the sirens went and we all went down into the cellars. After we came up they had just started *Rebecca* when the sirens went again, and everyone began to boo

93

and the manager came out and asked if we just wanted to stay and watch the film. We said we did and it was lovely - that Laurence Olivier sends shivers down my spine. The all-clear went about half-way through.

We really did enjoy *The Road to Singapore*, it made a real break and Jack is still laughing about some of the daft things that pair got up to. Apparently Bob Hope is British but you'd never know.

It is 6th May tomorrow, Jack's birthday. Ten years old. We are wondering whether we dare try to sleep at home tonight, it is so nice to wake up in your own bed and be a bit private. We've managed to get Jack a pair of roller skates. Daphne's boy has outgrown them so that was a bit of luck for us. He'll be so thrilled. We decide that we will risk staying at home. Tess and Biggles seem quite relaxed. As Jack says – if they start to quiver we'll up sticks and follow.

I am so glad that we had that night at home the other day because tonight everything is going mad. They say the full moon makes it easy for the Hun to pick out his target. The all-clear has finally gone, thank heavens. Mr Moore is just coming into the station, he and Jimmy were on fire-watching duty together tonight.

He is calling my name. I stand up and say, "Over here."

Oh God, he is telling me that they can't find my Jimmy.

Everyone stands back to let me through as I stumble towards the exit, my legs are so stiff with sitting all this time. Tess comes rushing into the tunnel barking and starts to pull at my dress and Jack says, "Mum, she's trying to tell us where Dad is," and I think she is too. We run up the road behind her and she stops at the row of poplars outside the church, and Mr Moore risks putting his torch on quickly, and we can see a hand and I know it's Jimmy – and I hear myself scream – and his voice says, "Don't stand there screaming, Lil girl, get a ladder and get me down!"

Mr Moore and the lads are rushing into the church to get the ladder and oh – thank you, thank you, thank you – Jimmy is struggling down but he is all right and he is grinning at me.

"Bloody great explosion blew me right off the church tower," he says. I hold his hand very tightly, and say, "Now then, no swearing in front of our Jack."

William is still somewhere in this country. I hope the raids aren't as bad where he is as they have been here. Some people say that the troops are having it easier than the civilians in this war. They wouldn't say that if they'd seen the lads when they got back from Dunkirk. If they really are having a breathing space, thank God for that.

William had two days' leave last month and it was wonderful to have him back again. Mind you, I think Tilly Everton saw more of him than we did. Mrs Everton says Tilly's applied to the ATS. I expect she thinks she'll look good in the uniform. Well, she will, of course. I wish I liked her better.

Marcus has just come round. He says he has decided to join up. I am shocked but of course I forget he is so much younger than Jimmy – he is not forty until the end of the year. He says that he and Thirza discussed it and they both felt that he should. He has already completed all the formalities and done the medical and everything, but he says he didn't want to tell us till he knew for sure. He's just heard that he is to join his regiment next week, so he is off to spend his last few days in civvy street with Thirza. After we've kissed him goodbye, and promised to try and keep an eye on everything for him at this end, I feel quite tearful.

We've had the most dreadful raids all week. In the canteen if one of the regulars doesn't appear we know better than to ask where they are. There is dirt and death everywhere and we go on making jokes about Hitler and laughing at the wireless programmes and swapping our coupons with each other so those with a sweet tooth have more sugar and those who love their meat get more of that. As if it is all a great big game.

The smell of burning never clears and some of the kids have constant diarrhoea from being in the stations with no proper toilets. Everyone had really bad head lice, but Eileen managed to get hold of that soap stuff that kills them and we all sat in the tunnel one night with our heads wrapped in towels. It really stinks, that stuff, it very nearly masked the other smells down there. Eileen said if we got invaded that night they'd think we were a load of Arabs.

Mr Churchill says our spirits are high. Huh. He should come down here sometime. Daphne tried to run out of the tunnel the other night in the middle of a raid, she suddenly went berserk and started screaming. We stopped her and held on to her but she hasn't spoken to anyone since. Geoff brings her down in the evening and she just sits looking ahead of her without even blinking. I don't know how much longer any of us can go on like this.

August, 1941

It says in the papers that Mr Churchill has had a meeting with President Roosevelt and that the Americans are going to give us some practical help. We have no idea what that means but lots of them are sending food parcels to us already. We had one the other day and it was like Christmas. There was a tin of ham, and some sultanas, and a tin of pineapple and some stuff called Spam, which tastes quite strange but is very nice. And some things called cookies, which are actually biscuits. But best of all there was chocolate. We gave most of it to Jack but Jimmy and I had enough to remember how delicious it is. There was also a packet of gum, apparently you chew it until the flavour, which is pepperminty, has all gone and then you take it out of your mouth and throw it away. Jimmy and I don't fancy that but Jack says it is quite good.

Wonderful, wonderful news! Sebastian is safe. Through all these months I've gone on feeling sure that he was alive somewhere. He's back in this country, not only alive, but apparently unharmed. The wire says, "Be with you all soon." I wonder what he's been through. I shall go back to St John's after work to say "thank you". I must write to Mrs Willet, she must be over the moon.

November, 1941

Only another month or so and it will be Christmas

again. The raids haven't been anything like so bad the last few weeks. I think it is because Hitler is concentrating more on Russia than us at the moment. I can't pretend that it isn't a relief but then I feel guilty because they are people just like us and nobody at all should have to go through this.

The school was badly damaged last week so Jack and the others are having their lessons in the church. Everything is short, it's a nightmare trying to get together a proper meal each day, so Jack and Jimmy both eat in the canteen most days. You get more for your coupons that way.

Jack is growing so fast that I don't know what I would do for clothes, but Elsie Bryant's brother Ginger from the pub is older than him, and they have been so good about letting us have some of his stuff. We've been giving them some of our veg from the garden all year for a thank you, and sharing some of the food that Father and Uncle Jethro send us.

I must say this war has bought out the best in a lot of people. Not everyone though. The police have put big notices up saying that looters will be shot. The thing is, it's not people like us that loot, it's these "wide boys" who sell it on the black market. Shooting seems a bit much though, so I hope the notices will put a stop to it.

It is so difficult trying to carry on like everything is normal. I let Jack go to Saturday-morning pictures but my heart is in my mouth till he gets back in case the sirens go and they don't get all the kids out in time. But how can I stop him going? The youngsters spend most of their time playing on the bombsites pretending to kill each other. The pictures at least show them there is another world outside this one.

What a surprise – I'm busy clearing up after the dinner-time rush in the canteen when a group of Queen Alexandra nurses come in. I go over to say hallo and tell them that as they are a bit late we'll rustle up what we can, when one of them says, "As I live and breathe – it's Lillian!" I stare at her for a moment and she looks familiar but I can't place her and – "Oh my goodness – Josephine!"

Josephine, who I haven't seen since we were both in service in Suffolk all those years ago. Well, what a lot of hugging and explaining to everyone else how we know each other. I leave Eileen to take over the cooking because Josephine says they are on their way through to Portsmouth and haven't got much time. We have a lot of catching up to do. We work out that it's nearly twenty-five years since we last saw each other! She had heard that Jimmy and I were married, but nothing else. She didn't know about William or Jack or where we lived or anything, though she said she had often wondered how we were. When she came back to England in 1918 she trained to be a nurse and has been working in all sorts of places, not just in this country but abroad.

We hardly draw breath for over two hours and then they have to go because their train is due. We promise to stay in touch. It was lovely to see her. She has had such an exciting life. I feel really rather boring.

It's a day for surprises. There's a letter from Thirza when I get in. She has joined the WVS and is driving one of the mobile canteens. She started yesterday and says at last she feels that she is doing her bit. All her girls are at school now and Martha and Collette are there to keep an eye if she gets held up. I am so pleased for her. It will stop her worrying too much about Marcus. Nothing like work to take your mind off your worries.

William is being sent abroad soon. Next week he's got a few days of embarkation leave.

I am hoping we will get to see Sebastian soon. Apparently he came back to England in a Spanish fishing boat. Jack is dying to hear the whole story so he can tell his mates. I don't care how he got back, I'm just so happy that he did.

December, 1941

The Japanese have bombed America, at a place called Pearl Harbour. The wireless is full of it. Jimmy has just brought in the evening paper and it sounds terrible. A lot of people were killed and some of their ships and aircraft were destroyed. It *is* really dreadful, of course, but there's a tiny bit of me that can't help thinking that now they'll have a bit more understanding of what it is like over here.

William is home for a few days. I can't get used to this grown man that is my son. Sometimes he feels almost like a stranger, but I suppose he has had to grow up very quickly. I understand that this probably doesn't feel like his proper life anymore. If this ever ends we are all going to be very different people to the ones we were before the war. They don't tell them where they are being sent, of course, so we all pretend it's going to be somewhere like you see in the films – all palm trees with that Dorothy Lamour in her sarong.

We do a lot of pretending to each other nowadays one way and another. Too much facing up to stuff can make you like poor Daphne. The doctor says she's suffering from a kind of shellshock and there's nothing much can be done. Her mum has taken her to stay with them somewhere near Cambridge.

William says he's got a big surprise for us but he's not going to tell us what it is until this evening. I'm not sure why we are waiting, because Jimmy is home, but there you are, we'll do it his way, bless him. I think I know what it is. I reckon he's been promoted again and this time it will be to sergeant. He is such a clever boy, my William.

I make tripe and onions for supper as a special treat for William, both he and Jack have always loved it. Then we have rice pudding with some of my plum jam from before the war. He still likes to stir the jam in and watch the rice go pink so perhaps he's not quite as grown up as I think. Jimmy and William light up while Jack and I clear the table. I've just finished and am making us a cup of tea when there is a knock on the door.

I go to answer it but William is there first and I hear Tilly Everton's voice. I call out hello and does she want a cuppa, but William comes into the kitchen and puts his arms round my waist and says, "Leave that, Mum, I've got something to tell you."

So I go into the front room with him and I have guessed, haven't I, and I am pinning a smile onto my face and Tilly is there looking gorgeous in her uniform, even though her hair is pulled back. William says, "Mum, Dad, Jack – Tilly and I wanted to tell you together – we're engaged to be married," and he holds out Tilly's hand to show us she's wearing this pretty little diamond ring with marcasite round it.

And Jimmy jumps up and shakes his hand and gives Tilly a kiss and I give them both a kiss and Jack dances around with Tess, and all the time I am thinking no, William, don't do this, she's not right for you. But perhaps she is. Let's hope so.

William's going back to his regiment today. I hold him very tightly and tell him to be careful. What a daft thing to say.

Tilly is going with him to the station, her leave is up as well. They are hoping to get married on their next leave, and Jimmy has promised to look for a couple of rooms that they can rent. Mrs Everton says she thinks that's a waste of money as neither of them will be around to live in it, and I'm inclined to agree with her. The Evertons have got stacks of room in the vicarage and they are quite happy to have them there. William says he would rather that they have their own place to come home to, though, so we'll see what we can do.

Mrs Everton seems really pleased about it all. I suppose what with William being a teacher he's turned into quite a catch. I don't have to tell Jimmy how I feel, he knows anyway. When they've left and Jack has gone out to play Jimmy turns to me and says, "Come on, Lil, count your blessings. She's a good girl, and at least it's not a shotgun wedding!"

He's right. I know I shouldn't feel like this. But I do.

January, 1942

At least the raids are not quite as non-stop as they were last year. With my birthday being on a Sunday we are having a little party this afternoon. It's Jack's idea – Christmas was a bit flat this year with William going off just before, and the Evertons asked us to spend it with them on account of us going to be related soon. It was quite pleasant but a bit strange. Everyone being on their best behaviour.

We are planning to have my party in the canteen, and praying that we won't have to end it in the station, with the noise drowning out the music. Jimmy's got the whole day off. Most of the park is given over to allotments now and I think he spends most of the time advising everyone on what to grow where and with what. Nice that all his gardening know-how is coming in so useful.

We've got our own plot down there and Jack spends almost all his spare time doing things to it under his dad's instructions. He's digging it over ready for the spring at the moment. Keeps him out of mischief, these lads are too keen on hunting for bits of shrapnel and such on the bombsites. Ghoulish, I call it. But Jimmy says we should be grateful that they are too young to dwell on the deaths and the injuries. Mr Smith is in hospital at the moment and they think he may have lost the sight of an eye. He was coming home from work and got caught in that big raid near St Paul's. Funny the way that goes on standing there in the middle of all the rubble. The papers call it a beacon of hope. The trouble with that is that if it *does* get hit everyone will get even more depressed.

All my regulars in the canteen have turned up and everyone has brought something, even Mrs Smith has come straight from the hospital. Bless her – she's brought me a beetroot and none of the chaps understand why we are laughing. We are all so pale and washed out and you can't even get a Tangee lipstick, so we use beetroot to give us a bit of colour. Eileen whisks it into a jar and says firmly, "That's Lil's – anyone chopping that up is for the chop themselves!"

Eileen is looking pretty tired herself. Her youngest is in the nursery now and her eldest is working in the munitions factory up near Shooter's Hill. She's developed a cough that is almost as bad as Jimmy's. All those girls seem to get coughs, I reckon it must be something to do with the atmosphere there. I know that Eileen is ever so worried about her.

I've managed to get a cake together. No fruit, of course, and dried egg, but at least it's risen. We haven't sugar for icing so I've made a cardboard cover for it and put my own name on it and Jack has found some little candles for the top. We light the candles and everyone sings "Happy Birthday", and I tell Jack to blow the candles out for me. I'm very touched at the way everyone has brought something along and between us all we have got together quite a feast.

We've got a gramophone in the canteen and I put Jack and his friends in charge of keeping it wound up and tell all the kids they can have a turn at choosing a record. Then we sink into the chairs for a quiet smoke and a chat. Mr Everton is putting out the pencils and papers for a beetle drive a bit later.

It's been a nice birthday. Jack and I even won the beetle drive, which pleased him no end. No raid, thank heavens. We walk back home, later than we expected, just listening to the silence. It feels like the best present of all.

April, 1942

I am so worried. There was an enormous raid on Norwich yesterday and I have this awful feeling that somehow Thirza might be caught in it – I know she does relief driving for the ambulances as well as driving the mobile canteen, and though it isn't very likely I can't get the thought out of my mind. I am trying to phone Mr Naismith but I can't get through.

Such a relief – a wire from Thirza: "All OK here stop nowhere near us stop." She must have known that I'd be worried sick. I've got a letter from her as well, which she must have written before the raid.

She says that Marcus is on embarkation leave, he's being sent abroad like William. Oh, poor Thirza. I sort of thought they wouldn't send the older ones. And Collette's Billy is going, too. Collette is working part-time in a garage in Ipswich assembling aircraft parts, so Martha looks after all the kids for a lot of the time. They are in school for a good part of the day, of course. Apparently Martha has turned out to be amazingly good at this make-do-and-mend. According to the others, the clothes she makes out of scraps are so inspired they would have wanted to wear them even if there hadn't been a war on.

War really does make strange bedfellows. I would never have thought of those three, Thirza, Collette and Martha, as even likely to be friends, let alone working so well as a team.

Oh, Thirza says she has written to Tilly offering her

and William their house in Norwood as a base for the time being. That is so generous of her and Marcus. I suppose it does make sense. It's quite a big house and although one of Marcus's drivers rents the basement, the rest is standing empty. I wonder if Tilly has managed to let William know. They are planning to get married on his next leave, though heaven only knows when that will be.

The raids are not nearly so frequent now, thank God, but you can never relax because the minute you do – wham – the sirens are off and it's run-for-the-station again. Our Anderson has finally come in useful, we are using it as a henhouse. The hens are just starting to lay, which is a real luxury. I honestly don't think anyone is ever going to convince me that this dried egg has ever been near a hen. We've piled even more earth over the top of the shelter so we can grow potatoes on it.

Everything is so short and being on the ration is a bit of a laugh because you can't get most of the things anyway. I'm quite lucky, working in the canteen, it does mean we get to eat reasonably well. Mind you, I use every trick I've ever learned about making food go a long way. We had a letter from the Ministry of Labour the other day congratulating us on our high standards! We've put it up on the wall. Eileen says that my cheese and onion pie is becoming famous. They've started these really cheerful wireless programmes at dinner time and we play them in the canteen – *Workers' Playtime* one of them is called, and it goes down a treat. Perks everyone up.

The government has brought out this Utility Standard for all sorts of things. The clothes are really well made and good quality and even the toffs have to conform if they want anything new, as there simply isn't anything else to buy. I am desperate for a new skirt, I wear slacks in the canteen but I wouldn't go out wearing them. But I can't believe how short these Utility skirts are. I know it's to save material but I don't feel comfortable with them up to my knees. Jimmy is no help – "Go on, Lil, you've got a smashing pair of pins!" – it's all right for him, he hasn't got to wear it. I might go and try one on. I'll see.

If we had some decent stockings it might help. Eileen is using cold tea to dye her legs and drawing a crayon line up the back like a seam. She went to a dance at the Empire the other day and said when she got back home she found she'd smudged her seam all over her legs. She thought it was a hoot. Those dances are quite fun, but of course the only men there are very young or very old. I went with her the other night when Jimmy was on duty, and we had to dance with each other all evening. But Eileen is right, it does take your mind off all the other stuff. That's got to be good.

August, 1942

General Montgomery is going to take over the 8th Army in North Africa. William and Marcus are both out there. I know that William always spoke well of him after Dunkirk. They call him Monty, which is quite funny because it makes it sound like they know him. We only seem to be getting bad news nowadays, and God knows what they don't tell us, so let's hope he knows what he is doing. All we want is our lads back home safely.

Sebastian is here for a couple of days. Jack is following him around constantly. Sebastian is definitely his hero since his escape from France. Fancy him ending up in Spain. "There you are, Sebastian," I say to him, "what goes around comes around."

"Lillian," he says, "as always, you are so right. The circle is finally squared."

Sometimes I don't know what he's on about.

He looks so tired but all these RAF boys do. Tilly is stationed at Biggin Hill so he sees quite a lot of her. He says that William is a lucky boy, all the chaps make a play for her but she just flashes her ring at them and laughs. Sebastian's got himself a girlfriend at last. Her name is Linda and he says she looks like Ingrid Bergman – but of course he might be prejudiced! She's a WAAF and he's going to bring her down to meet us when they can get some leave together. She sounds nice. She's in her twenties and her mum knew his mum when they were both girls. It's such a small world. Mrs Willett must be so pleased about it, she'd love to see him settled with someone.

After Sebastian has gone, I got to thinking about what he said about Tilly. I must start saving some of our rations for a wedding cake. And Mrs Everton and I must see what we can do about getting some more stuff for her bottom drawer. War or not, we'll make sure they have a good start.

November, 1942

The canteen is even busier than usual today. A large bomb was dropped just behind the Empire and there's a big crew clearing up round there and they've all knocked off for dinner. By some miracle no one was hurt, though young Alan was blown off his bike a whole road away. He's OK though – just a bit bruised.

Eileen is coming through the door. What's she doing here? It's supposed to be her day off.

"Lillian," she's saying. "This came for you."

She's got a telegram in her hand and I don't want to look – if I pretend I can't see her then it won't be happening. *I don't want it, take it away* – but I do take it and the whole canteen has gone quiet and *Workers' Playtime* is roaring out but no one is laughing and I can't open the envelope because my hands are trembling and then – "Corporal William Spencer, missing. Believed killed in action." And everything is moving away from me and I can't feel my legs and I hear this voice saying "No, no, no" as I sink into the black.

Someone goes to fetch Jimmy from the park and Eileen and Jack take me home and lay me on the bed. My body is jerking around like it has a will of its own but my brain feels numb – as if everything is going on a long way away. I want it to stay that way.

When it stops I shall have to bear the pain.

December, 1942

The wireless keeps playing that new Bing Crosby song, "White Christmas". I shall never be able to think of this Christmas without it running through my head. We are trying to make it as normal as we can for Jack's sake. Normal. What a word. We've forgotten what normal is. We had quite a bad raid last night, first one this month, and I found myself thinking, "Come on, get me, you've got my William, now put an end to me."

Jimmy came into the canteen the other day and I looked up and didn't recognise him. Just saw this old man standing inside the door. And his cough is awful. On the nights he's not fire watching we neither of us get any sleep. I think this war is going to kill us all.

They sounded the church bells for the first time since it started last month because Monty had a big victory in Egypt. Rejoicing. Too late for Jimmy and me. We've forgotten how.

Tilly and her mum and dad are going to spend Christmas Day with us. I'd sooner we had it here so I can keep busy. She looks terrible, poor kid. We've grown quite close. How pleased William would – no, I must think of something else. Go and clean the oven out. Been meaning to do it for ages.

It's Christmas Day. We've finished dinner and it wasn't too bad given all the shortages, but none of us cared that much. We are sitting round waiting for the King's broadcast. You can see from the papers this war is taking its toll on him too. He's a good man. They say he never wanted to be king but I think he's making a better job of it than his brother would have done. No gumption, that one. And we were all sad when his other brother was killed, the Duke of Kent, leaving all those little kiddies. Makes you feel they really are just like us, not stuck in what Marcus would call their ivory towers.

They are announcing the King now and playing the national anthem so we all stand up. We've just sat down again to listen when I hear someone coming in. It must be Eileen, their wireless isn't working properly. I call out, "Come in, Eileen," and the door opens behind me and a voice says, "Actually, the name is William. Hallo, Mum."

Oh my God – oh my William – he's alive – he's alive – he's here – oh thank you, God, thank you, God, thank you, God.

January, 1943

It's William and Tilly's wedding day. I am so thrilled that they have chosen to do it on my birthday. Mrs Everton and I have decorated the hall for the reception. Jimmy has brought in a load of holly and some mistletoe that he found in the park for the church, and Mrs Smith found some snowdrops growing on the bombsite down the road, and we've put those in front of the altar.

William's leg is so much better, he can walk short distances without his sticks now. They say he'll always have a limp but when they told him that he just said, "Well, so did Byron, and it didn't do him any harm." Tilly has had quite a job getting leave but I think Sebastian finally pulled a few strings, bless him.

Mr Everton and Tilly are coming down the aisle. William has turned and is smiling at her. Oh my goodness, they are such a handsome couple. I think I am going to cry. Maxy Grieves is playing the organ, "Here Comes the Bride", of course. It really is the most special day. Thirza and Collette and Martha are here with all the kids and Father is sitting with Jack across the aisle looking as pleased as Punch. Sebastian is William's best man. I was quite surprised as I've never thought of them as being that close, but I suppose he's always been part of William's life. The vicar is starting the service now… . "Dearly beloved, we are gathered here today…"

The speeches are all excellent. Jimmy made a lovely one about love triumphing even in the darkest days and saying how proud we are of them both. Jack whispered to me, "I didn't know Dad was so good at speechifying," and I had to agree. Sebastian made everyone laugh. He's put in all sorts of jokes about that Lord Haw-Haw and Hitler and all that whole awful crew. Since El Alamein it's been easier to laugh at them and mean it because most of us really believe now that we will win this war eventually.

Mr Bryant from The Queens Arms gave us a small barrel of beer, so after the speeches we all toasted the happy couple with that. Mrs Everton and I had managed to get quite a decent buffet together. All the neighbours weighed in with something. The cake is a bit of a laugh – it's two sponges made with that dried egg and Thirza helped me to make a cardboard cover for each tier. We've painted them white with pink roses and decorated them with leaves and they do look pretty good – but, of course, we have to lift them off to get to the sponges. How I would have loved to make them a proper cake. Anyway everyone enjoyed having a giggle at it and the sponge went down well.

The men are pushing back the tables and Maxy is back at the piano. Tilly and William lead out with William making fun of himself because of course he can't really dance – he's got one arm round Tilly and is balancing on his stick. Then Mr and Mrs Everton take the floor followed by Jimmy and me. Now everyone is dancing, even Jack. Elsie Bryant is partnering him and showing him how to do a waltz. She is such a nice lass.

So many of our lads not here. Marcus and Timmy and Collette's Billy still in the desert. None of my other brothers could get leave, but we've grown so far apart it doesn't matter as much as it once would have done. The last time we were all together was when Father married Martha. I know they would all have been here if they could. Timmy's little wife Lettie is here though. I hardly know her but Thirza says she's a smasher, just right for our Timmy. Funny, I sometimes think that the war has made me very close to my neighbours but distanced me from a lot of my family. But perhaps that would have happened anyway.

They are playing that song from *Casablanca* – oh, that is a lovely film – and here comes William to dance with his mum. I know it's wicked of me, but I'd rather have him home and wounded than over there still.

"Coming for a limp, Mum?" he asks.

"Never mind the dancing," I say. "You just come and sit this one out with me." So he does. Such a wonderful day.

March, 1943

My poor Collette, another tragedy for her to cope with and such a totally unexpected one. We are so used to waiting for the next shock, even while assuring ourselves it won't happen to us, but this is beyond everything. There was a big daylight raid on the East End yesterday and Collette's mum and dad were visiting her auntie in Bethnal Green, so they all made for the Underground. It's not quite clear what happened but a lady carrying her baby tripped near the bottom and in the panic to go down no one saw her and hundreds of people surged in and they all fell on top of each other. They don't know how many are dead but Collette's mum and auntie were both gone when they pulled them out and her dad is dangerously ill in hospital.

She's left the kids in Suffolk and is staying with us. She hasn't heard from Billy for ages, either. She is looking so thin and her hair has gone quite grey since her Sid bought it that night. Please, God, don't let anything happen to her Billy.

May, 1943

Jack's birthday being on a Thursday this year we've decided to have his party at the weekend. We've got a new family member – well, sort of. Stan, who is with the Canadian Air Force, has been billeted on us and is sleeping in William's old room. He is such a charming boy. Jack is now sharing his admiration between him and Sebastian. I think Jack must know everything there is to know about the RAF and every plane that ever flew, so to have Stan here talking flying is his idea of paradise.

Stan has told us so much about Canada. He lives in a small town surrounded by mountains with his family. He says that one day we must go and stay with him and get to know his country. We say that would be lovely, which it would, but probably so would a trip to the moon. He calls his parents Mom and Pa, just like in the pictures, and Jack is trying to imitate him. Jimmy thinks it's a hoot being called Pa but I'm quite glad he forgets most of the time as Mom sounds very strange to me. Stan has a girlfriend called Lena who he is planning to marry when he gets back home.

He says he never knew so much of England was so beautiful and he has quite fallen in love with it. He's been stationed all over the country, so in fact he has probably seen more of it than we have. Jack is trying to explain to him at the moment why Scotland is in Great Britain and not England. It's an uphill struggle. Stan says he thought that Britain and England were the same place. Jack says, "Well, they are, but…" and flounders completely. I'm off to the canteen and shall leave them to it.

The birthday party is a great success. Jimmy, Stan and William (who's just starting teaching again at Beckenham) organise Jack and his friends down in Kelsey Park, and they are running all sorts of races – egg and spoon (only, of course, it was potato and spoon), three-legged, sack, and some silly ones they thought up specially.

They finally flop down on the grass and Eileen, Mrs Smith and I open the picnic we've brought down, and after they've cleared every scrap we give them jam jars and some old nets we've found, and they fish for tiddlers in the stream until the light has nearly gone. When we've done the big count-up to see who has caught the most (happily, Jack – well, it is his birthday) we tip them back into the water. Then we sing "Happy Birthday" to Jack one more time.

We are all walking back together with the kids marching ahead to "Colonel Bogey" – where do they get the energy? – and it is so peaceful and so normal it is hard to believe there is a war on.

June, 1943

115

Good news for Collette. About time, too. Her Billy has been promoted to sergeant – we are all so chuffed. He's got a few days' leave and is going to spend it in Suffolk, and we are going up to see them and taking her dad with us. Jimmy says it's time we had a break, and I agree.

We've had some dreadful raids this year. Jack can't go to school because it was badly damaged again last month. Fortunately all the kids had gone home, not like that school in Catford. How those parents coped, pulling their dead children out of the rubble, is beyond me. Some nights I wake up with the sweat pouring off me just thinking about it. Trouble is you get frightened to let them out of your sight.

Anyway, a few days with Thirza and the others should put things in proportion again. It seems that we are really going to win this war, or at least that is what they tell us. The papers are full of victories here and victories there – but all we really would like to know is the question no one can answer, how much longer?

Everything is so short, I was reduced to making curried swede in the canteen the other day. Tess keeps catching rabbits when she goes in the park with Jimmy, even though she's not really supposed to, but Jimmy quickly wraps them in newspaper and brings them home. Definitely improves the home menu, and I make sure that Tess gets her share, of course. Poor little Biggles came in with a terrible abscess the other day. Jack reckons it's a rat bite gone bad. He's cleaning it and washing it with saltwater twice a day and it looks a lot better. Jack has always had a way with animals. Wish he would be as good about washing himself without me shouting at him. Ever since soap was rationed he's regarded it as a great excuse for not bothering.

We don't see much of Stan at the minute. I think there's a lot of stuff happening. I've only just got in from the canteen and for once I'm on my own. It really hits me how awful the house looks with the boarded-up windows and the damp patches on the wall where the blast from the bombs has knocked the plaster off. Then I go to switch the light on and there is no electricity again. I suddenly feel so down and worn out that I start to have a little cry. Feeling a bit sorry for myself, I suppose. Don't often have the time. Just as well, obviously.

I heard on the wireless this morning that nice Leslie Howard's plane was shot down yesterday. Missing. He's been going all over the place trying to get people to buy British films. Funny how you feel you know these people. We went to see him in a picture only a couple of days ago. Don't know why it's upsetting me so much. After all I didn't really know him. But it seems like the last straw, somehow.

Stan's voice makes me jump coming out of the gloom. "Hang in there, Lillian," he said with that lovely film-star accent he has. "There's lots I can't tell you about but we're winning, my lovely." Then he put his arms round me. "I can't believe how you people hold up," he says. "For my money you can have a little weep any time." Of course I stop then and go to get him some tea. But he's made me feel a lot better.

July, 1943

117

The journey to Suffolk seems to be taking forever. Jack and Jimmy have both nodded off to sleep and I'm quite worried about Collette's dad, Mr Deeprose, he looks so frail. The train keeps stopping and starting and if you open the window to get some air all the dirty old steam comes in and everyone starts coughing. Enough of that with Jimmy already, without adding to it.

Makes me realise how lucky we've been in the past with Marcus being in the taxi business, so we've been brought up in style. We were meant to catch the two o'clock train but it didn't get in until nearly three and now it's getting on for seven o'clock. I don't know how near we are because they've taken away all the station signs. Just hope I'll recognise it when we get there. If we ever do.

Jack is waking up and asking if there is anything to eat. I did some sandwiches for the journey, but they had those ages ago, so it's a good job I kept back some ginger biscuits. I open the packet and tell him not to wake his dad or Mr Deeprose, but Tess jumps up for a bit of biscuit and wakes them both. Biscuits all round, and a swig of tea from the Thermos. I must say I'm glad we managed to persuade Jack that Biggles would be fine with Mrs Smith or we'd probably have him with us as well. She is a brick, such a good neighbour. She's going to come in and feed the hens as well and when I told her to take any eggs she found she insisted that she would put them in the preserving bucket for when we got back.

We've stopped again. I believe we have finally arrived…yes, there's Thirza! Oh, how lovely to see her. We scramble down, all stiff and dirty, and Tess is first off, barking madly, closely followed by Jack. Jimmy and I help Mr Deeprose down and the guard is getting our bags off.

Thirza has got her little car, what a treat. I am not going to ask how she got the petrol in case I'd rather not know. We all pile in and it seems no time at all before we are home and Martha is hugging us and Father is shaking everyone's hands, and Collette has her arms round her dad and all the children have appeared and are dancing around. I can't believe how grown-up Cynthia is, but of course she's nearly fourteen now and as pretty as a picture. She says she's going to be a film star and she's certainly got the looks for it. Collette's Billy is already here, and her Gladys is home to see her grandad, but she has to be off in the morning. She's just joined the Land Army and is billeted somewhere in Lincolnshire. What a noisy lot we are!

The light is beginning to go so we all crowd into Uncle Jethro's cottage and the men get the blackout up. Martha has obviously been cooking all day and she's made a wonderful bacon pudding with loads of vegetables from the garden. Then when we are all fit to bust she brings in a bowl full of plums she bottled last autumn, and an egg custard. Nectar! We are sitting back with a nice cup of tea when there's a knock at the door and in comes Lettie. What a lovely surprise. Martha and Thirza pack the younger kids off to bed, and Collette takes her dad upstairs – it's been such a long day for him.

Then we sit chatting till nearly midnight and everyone agrees that we are winning this war. Billy reckons it will be over soon. I look round and see so much sadness under the gaiety. Thirza longing for

Marcus, Lettie for Timmy, Collette with half her family wiped out and all of us praying it will end before the rest of our children are old enough to be called up. And even up here listening with half an ear all the time we are talking for sirens and planes.

Collette says, "One thing I do know, when it is all over, and please God they start rebuilding quickly, we want something better than we had before." That's what William was saying the other day. "No more servants and masters, Mum, we are all going to be equal when we come out of this."

Jimmy and I look at each other and Father goes on looking into the fire. Uncle Jethro says what we are thinking. "I hope you're right, lass, but that's what they said last time and it didn't happen then." Thirza has been sitting listening quietly. "This time," she says, "we are going to make sure it does happen."

I have never heard her say that sort of thing so firmly and I am taken aback. Jimmy says, "Thirza, you are turning into a leftie," and everyone laughs.

Then she says, "Just wait, Jimmy Spencer, we've not gone through all this to see things go on the way they were."

Jimmy looks back at her for a minute. Then he says, "Good on you, girl. As our William says, 'Roll on, Sir William Beveridge and your Brave New World.'"

We finally pack up and go to bed. Back in Father's house, lying beside Jimmy, who is out for the count, I'm thinking about what they were saying and my brother Jack comes into my head. In the end it felt as if his life was just wasted. At least this time we know what the war is about. But I think they are right. When it is finally all over, perhaps we will find ourselves at the beginning of another fight.

I can almost hear Jack's voice. "Interesting times we live in, little sister, interesting times."

When I go downstairs this morning Jack and Father are already up and I can see Jack is busting to tell me something. He waits till I'm sitting with my cuppa, and then: "Mum – you know you keep saying I mustn't keep giving Tess titbits because she's getting fat?" In an instant I see where this is going, of course, but I'm not going to spoil his fun, am I? "Well...," long dramatic pause – obviously Cynthia is not the only one in the family with dramatic tendencies. "Grandad says she's going to have puppies!"

I must say I feel a bit of a chump not having noticed but I hadn't given it a thought so I act as surprised as Jack wants me to be. Then he rushes off next door to tell his cousins and Collette's Ronnie and Moira. Of course they all have to come into Father's garden disturbing Tess, who was having a snooze in the sun, and then Ivy comes down and has to be told the news, and she goes off to get Martha and Donald, and from the excitement you would think no dog in the whole world had ever had puppies before. Father goes out to calm them down and leaves Martha and me on our own for once.

Martha asks me if I've spotted another impending birth in the family. I think I know who she means. "Lettie?"

"Mm," says Martha. "I suppose it does make you believe in the future, doesn't it?"

I ask if Lettie has said anything, but she hasn't. Probably waiting for Timmy to get some leave so they can tell us together.

"Martha," I say suddenly, "I'm so glad you married Father." She looks quite startled and for a moment I think she is going to cry. I get up quickly and give her a hug. She is such a good person and always cheerful even though I know she must be worried sick that her Donald will be old enough for call-up next year. Young Ronnie will be as well. Please God, let it be over before Jack is eighteen.

Lots of goodbyes this morning. Jimmy and I have to get back but we've had such a lovely few days. Thirza had to go off early so we went for a walk together first thing. Marcus is doing so well, we were all over the moon when he got promoted to sergeant after El Alamein. And yesterday she had a letter from him telling her he's being sent to Alexandria for officer training. Our Marcus – an officer! But, as Jimmy said, he was always going to be officer material.

Jack and Tess are going to stay here and help with the harvest next month. Mr Nash popped down from the big house, I must say he does wear well, he doesn't seem a lot older now than he did when I was a girl. Anyway, he's offered to pay all the youngsters for helping, as he's so short of men, so of course Jack volunteered immediately. It's good for him to be with his cousins, he might even learn to keep his end up with Cynthia and Norma. What a bossy pair they are. Little Margaret is much quieter, always got her head stuck in a book so it mostly passes her by.

Jack and the girls have decided to walk to the station with us so we put our luggage in Father's old hand cart and they take turns to push it, with Tess running alongside and Father's two border collies bringing up the rear. What a circus we must look. A bit tearful when I hug Jack, but I'll be back for him in about six weeks and I think it's good for him up here.

On the train I have a little sniffle but Jimmy holds my hand and says, "Lil, do you realise this will be the first time we've been on our own for twelve years? It'll be like a second honeymoon."

"Yes," I say, "as long as Mr Hitler doesn't make us spend it with a few hundred other people on Penge East Station."

September, 1943

William is coming up to Suffolk with me to collect Jack as the schools start again next week. William has spent most of the summer helping to organise leisure activities. The council have been doing these Stay-at-home, Play-at-home holidays, and he's done everything from getting comedians to perform in the parks to organising full-length Shakespearean productions. One evening alone he had nineteen different things going. All the swimming pools have a gala on every week and he's got fairs and fêtes going at the weekends. And dances, of course.

Jimmy and I went dancing at the Crystal Palace several evenings when he was off duty. It was lovely, the bandstand is right in the middle of the lake and the music sort of drifts over the water. Very romantic, almost like the films. When you come back down the road after it's a bit of a let-down though. The tip-and-run raids have devastated the whole area. There are more gaps than there are houses. It said on the wireless the other day that Penge was one of the worst-hit places in the country. Something to do with dropping their bombs as near the centre of London as they can get and still fly back again.

Tilly is manning a searchlight at Biggin Hill. William is hoping she'll have some leave before Christmas. Poor kids, what a way to start your married life, hardly ever seeing each other.

Everyone up here is so pleased to see William. Even Father gives him a big hug. The main attraction at the moment is Tess and her puppies, they are so beautiful. Without any doubt their dad was a border collie. One with no morals, says William. Fortunately the kids don't know what he means but I give him one of my looks just in case. We've already agreed that Jack can keep one and the other two are going to stay down here and work on the farm.

Ronnie and Donald have received their call-ups and are both going for their medical next month. Wonder where they'll be sent? Billy is in Sicily. Thirza thinks that's where Marcus will be sent, but he should get some leave first. Second Lieutenant Marcus Osborne now. We are all so proud of him. I'm glad the boys won't have to go before Christmas. That would have made it even harder for their mums.

Martha has managed to do a wonderful spread for us as usual. No wonder Jack has filled out so much in six weeks. I tell them about the tins of whale meat that we've been getting in the canteen and how we all try to pretend it tastes like proper meat. It is very cheap, only 2s 6d for a pound tin and you don't need points, but Jimmy says he'd rather be hungry and on the whole I agree. In the canteen I dress it up and don't tell them what it is so it goes down all right. Eileen keeps singing

"Whale meat again" like Vera Lynn and gives me the giggles. Martha can't believe people really eat such stuff. There's no doubt that living on a farm means you eat better.

Jack is quite keen to get home now and see his mates. He asks me quietly as we are getting his things together if everyone is OK. I know what he is really asking me, of course, but all his friends are still alive, thank heavens. He's a bit put out when I tell him they've put up Nissen huts in the school grounds so the school is open again, but I have a feeling that underneath he's quite glad. He wants to know if the horse chestnuts are out in the park. Apparently the government are paying 7s 6d a hundredweight for them. I cannot imagine what they want them for, but it's too early for them anyway so perhaps he'll get some schoolwork done before they take over his life. Jack and his projects.

December, 1943

We are spending most of this Christmas in the canteen. So many people have got nowhere decent to go. Eileen and Mrs Smith and I decided to ask our families to pile in and see if we can make it really festive in here. They have agreed and so have Rose and Peggy, and several of the others. Rose was bombed out herself, but she's moved in with Peggy. With both their husbands abroad they're company for each other. Nice to have your sister so close. We've got the kids putting up paper chains and they've collected holly from the park, and we've been allowed extra rations for Christmas Day. We're still having to put some carrots in the puddings, of course, but between us we've rustled up a good Christmas dinner. We are going to be cooking and serving all day.

I keep remembering our miracle last year. Feels like I can give a bit back.

Perhaps next Christmas it will all be over.

January, 1944

Another birthday. Forty-four years old. Goodness. And William will be twenty-three in a couple of days. Tilly couldn't get leave but Jimmy has got the evening off and we are going to have a joint celebration. Glenn Miller is playing at the Empire and William managed to get us all tickets. Pity Stan isn't here, I know he's not American, but Canadian doesn't seem that much different to me.

Elsie Bryant has been showing us all in the canteen how to do this new jitterbugging. Jack had a go with her the other day and the next thing I knew Artie Shaw and his orchestra came on the wireless and the whole canteen were on their feet joining in. Mr Bryant grabbed me and there I was going over his shoulder. Mind you, I made him stop before he tried to throw me between his knees. "Mr Bryant," I said, "we are too old for this. Behave yourself." Would you believe, he just laughed and carried on dancing with Mrs Everton, of all people. Well, I wasn't going to be outdone so Jack and I had a go together. I must admit it is very exhilarating but I felt a bit creaky the next day.

A lovely birthday surprise. We are all getting ready to go to the concert when who should walk in but Marcus. He's got a few days' leave and wanted to give us both our birthday presents before going up to Suffolk. He looks so distinguished in his officer's uniform. We send Jack round to the Empire to ask if they can squeeze him in and of course they do.

Marcus has brought me a beautiful silky scarf. He says it came from a market in Alexandria. He's given William a tie in the same sort of exotic colours. William says he's going to save it till Tilly is home. She's hoping to have some time off next weekend and William is going to book them into a hotel. I've never stayed in a hotel. Must be nice. I think I could probably get used to being waited on. Those two deserve a good break.

As Jack says, the concert is fan-TAS-tic. Glenn Miller is such a nice man and the music sounds even better than on the wireless. He plays all his well-known ones including "String of Pearls", which is my favourite. We sing them on the way home. William and Marcus are both staying over so when we get in I rustle up some toast and dripping to go with our cuppa. This is the first birthday since 1939 that I've hardly thought about the war at all.

April, 1944

News from all quarters. Tilly is pregnant. I'm going to be a grandmother. I'm so excited. William is over the moon. The baby is due in September and Tilly is being discharged next month. Hard to remember now that I was so against their marriage. I can't even remember why. I'm so glad that I never said anything. And Lettie has just had a little boy. Timmy is going home for a few days on compassionate leave. They are going to call him Edward. Such a nice name.

There is a letter from Martha as well. Donald and Ronnie are both going down the mines. I don't know if the two lads think it's good news or bad but I feel pleased. Instead of being conscripted into the Army they are going to be Bevin Boys. I know there are dangers in it, and that the miners are not over-happy about the Bevin Boys, but at least they should be safer there than being shot at in some desert thousands of miles away. And they will be together. I bet Collette is relieved.

June, 1944

Tilly is spending a couple of days with her mum and dad and planning to do some shopping. She's hoping to get some things for the baby in the market. William is up to his eyes with getting the children's exam papers ready, so she's left him to it.

We all feel quite different since D-Day. Everyone is going around making the V sign and meaning it. They've been saying in the papers that what they call the battle of London is over. It is wonderfully quiet everywhere and a lot of the children who were evacuated have come back home. I really believe my grandchild is going to be born into a peaceful world.

It's not so busy in the canteen today and I ask Eileen if she would mind taking over so that I can catch up with Tilly. She popped her head round just now to say she and Jack were going down to the park to meet Jimmy and do a bit of window shopping on the way. She's come over today so she can be early at the Monday market tomorrow.

"You know what I am for a bargain," she laughs.

Jimmy will be pleased to see them. So will Tess – Jack's taking Puppy down with them. I do wish he'd give him a proper name, he's nearly as big as Tess now.

Eileen is quite happy to man the fort and I'm just hanging my pinny up when we hear this really strange noise. Like a motorbike in the sky. Then it stops. We all look at each other and I start to say "What…" when…*oh no, oh God, it's finished, don't do this, not now, not again…..we are ducking under the tables…there is the most enormous bang and the end wall of the hall blows in.*

Silence. Screaming. Screaming. Screaming. A man's voice calling, "Get help, get help, someone." I run out. There are bodies everywhere, some of them are moving. Jack, for God's sake, where are you, Jack? I call his name. I'm screaming: "Jack, Jack." A figure stands up and through the dust I can see it's Jack.

"Mum, Mum," he calls. "Mum, I'm here, I'm OK." I'm touching his face his arms his hair thank God – oh thank God – Tilly – oh my God – Tilly: "Where's Tilly?" She's not there…I'm calling "Tilly, Tilly," and I'm pulling Jack with me because I can't bear to let go of his hand and we are stepping over people and I can't find Tilly.

Then I do. She is so beautiful. Even with the dust still swirling round her and her head at that funny angle. I'm on my knees beside her. "Tilly, I'm so sorry, I'm so sorry, I'm so sorry." They push

Jack and I sit in the road. Someone is calling our names. It's Jimmy. He takes my hand. Tilly. The tears are streaming down his face. I can't cry. We are in the canteen. Strange. It's untouched except for that wall.

Tilly. I don't know how long we have been here. William comes in and I hold him as he sobs. Tilly. Jack comes up to me. His face is screwed up and he is cuddling something that is very still and lifeless. "Mum," he says. It's Puppy. Nameless Puppy. Finally I cry.

July,1944

That old joke came into my head this morning. The one about putting grit in your shoe so you forget your toothache. When this nightmare is over and we count up our dead will we be too numb to weep for them?

My mind screams Tilly's name a hundred times a day. And my grandchild. The grandchild that I shall never know. But there isn't time. There is hardly a house that isn't damaged. All of that big family in Blenheim Road killed outright yesterday, and while we were trying to dig them out another flying bomb hit the High Street. It's worse than the blitz because there is no warning. You just know that when the engine cuts out you've got about twelve seconds – to do what? You can't run because you don't know where it's going.

I need to get Jack away from here. But I can't leave William. Or Jimmy. The whole town is covered in this thick dust, you can't get the grime off your skin no matter how hard you scrub, and Jimmy never stops coughing. Mrs Everton insists on helping in the canteen but when I look at her I see again the look in Mother's eyes after Jack was killed. We're like robots. Going through the motions. Can't even feel the fear anymore. Only for our kids. And Tilly was Mrs E's only. No grandchildren for her. Ever.

August, 1944

Getting off the train in Suffolk this morning, for the first time I feel as if I am right to be coming back home. Not just running away. Only the basement of our house is liveable in and we are back to spending most of our off time in the station. I was serving up dinner in the canteen the other day and my hands started to shake so much I nearly dropped the plates. Eileen and the others said they could manage without me for a couple of weeks if I wanted to have a break. Probably glad to get rid of me.

Gives me a chance to get Jack out of the town as well. So here we are again. Jimmy is with us. He's been so bad that I made him go to the doctor yesterday. Dr Ewing is on the panel so it shouldn't cost too much, and he can't go on like this. He says Jimmy's chest was weakened in the last war – well, we knew that – and he's got an infection from all the dust. He's given him some of this new penicillin that we've heard so much about, and signed him off for a couple of weeks.

Father and Martha are making such a fuss of us though I can tell they are a bit shocked at the way we look. So am I when I look in the mirror. I'm learning not to do it too often.

All the news from abroad is good. The Allies marched into Paris yesterday. The wireless talks of nothing else. It must have been so dreadful for those poor people all this time. At least we haven't had Nazi soldiers in our streets. I know it must mean that we have nearly won, that it's nearly over, but something inside me can't really believe it.

Up here everyone's spirits are quite obviously high and there is a bubble of excitement that bursts out every now and again. I am conscious of struggling to share their optimism, because it would be dreadful to dampen it.

Jack, who has been so quiet since that dreadful day in June, has been dragged off by Thirza's girls and looks perkier already. Tess is running around yapping happily with the other dogs and this time we do have Biggles with us. Jack absolutely refused to leave him behind this time. He was convinced he would be blown up and how could I tell him for sure that he wouldn't?

We made a cover for my shopping basket and brought him on the train in that. I must say he was very good. No noise and no mess. Probably too scared to do either. Tess sat by the basket most of the way and I think that reassured him. Father has just given him a little bit of the rabbit Martha's preparing for supper. Makes me realise how much Father has mellowed in recent years.

William is coming down in a couple of days. He's been tying up some of the Play-at-home, Stay-at-home entertainments first. He didn't want to stop working. It's often easier that way. But he's been ordered to take time off now by his bosses. I suppose they've seen it all before. Too often.

William's train is late so I've been sitting waiting for quite some time. He's the only person to get off here and I give him a big hug. He's got so thin. "Thought a quiet walk back, just the two of us, would be nice," I say. He puts his arm round my shoulders briefly, then picks up his bag and we start to walk.

"Don't worry, Mum, I'm not good company but I'll do my best."

I remember my brother Jack and the hurt and the pain and I give him the only thing I can. Words. From the depths of my own grief. I tell him what Freddy told me all those years ago about those left behind having an obligation to live their lives to the full. And I tell him what I learnt when he was missing. That pretending that you are coping is sometimes the only way of doing it. And eventually you find that you are. "Like whistling in the dark," I say. We walk along in silence for a bit. Then we stop and I realise that we are both crying.

"Thanks, Mum," he says. And we go in to greet the family.

September, 1944

Jimmy has had to go back but I'm staying a bit longer. Jack wants to help with the harvest again and they do need all the help they can get, so we don't have to feel guilty. Sebastian came on a flying visit – what a daft thing to say about a pilot – it was wonderful to see him. Cynthia flirted outrageously with him, Thirza said she didn't know whether to be amused or embarrassed. She's fifteen going on twenty, that one. Sebastian has broken up with Linda. When I asked how she was he said it hadn't worked out between them. Later he told me that he thought their relationship put too much strain on her. She's just got engaged to another RAF-type, but this one is deskbound. He doesn't seem too cut up so I suppose it wasn't meant to be.

William has formed this really close friendship with Mr Deeprose. Collette says it's done wonders for her dad, and it's certainly done as much for William. Mr Deeprose can't walk far since the accident, so William made him this really strange wheelchair from old handcarts and prams lying around the farm. Collette said he'd never go in it, but she was wrong. William packs up some food and a Thermos and off they go on expeditions together.

Mr Nash lent them a book on wildflowers and the other night they brought back some wild roses and Mr Deeprose drew them. The picture was so good Martha's going to look out Ivy's old paint box for him. War makes very odd bedfellows. But it's taken both their wives, of course, and although I suspect they never talk about that, it's made a sort of bond between them.

Had a wire from Jimmy today saying that there haven't been any doodlebugs for three weeks. The harvest is in and it's time to go back. William has gone already. Beckenham has suffered such a lot of damage but the schools all opened on time. Jack is due to start there next week, the new boys always go a week later. William is teaching older boys now. He's pleased about that, and a bit relieved as he's not keen on having his kid brother in his class. Can't say I blame him.

Jack's class will be using one of the Nissen huts they've put in the grounds. Seems he can't get away from them. They always look a bit flimsy to me, so I hope we don't have a bad winter. Though Jack and his friends don't seem to feel the cold much. Just as well.

October, 1944

We've all moved into Thirza and Marcus's place for

now. Amazingly it has been untouched, even though the houses on either side are damaged. It was Thirza's idea, as William couldn't come back to us with only the basement habitable, and we none of us wanted him to stay here on his own. Means he and Jack can go to school together and Jimmy is just as near the park here.

Had a letter from Stan – he's hoping to come and see us soon. I quite miss him whistling around the place. Always cheerful. Could do with that. But the other day we were listening to *ITMA* in the canteen and I found that I was laughing. I mean *really* laughing. I suppose I've turned some kind of corner.

December, 1944

William has written a nativity play for the school. It's not like the ones they do with the young children, all sheep and "Away in a Manger". It's about a baby being born in an air-raid shelter and all the people rallying round to help the bombed-out parents.

Jack said could they have some animals in it and the headmaster said he didn't see why not as long as they behaved, so Tess is going to be one of three dogs who protect the baby Jesus.

In spite of these awful V2s the government has refused to close the schools and I agree with them. They come over with almost no warning, so I think well, if it's got your number on it…...… In the canteen we agreed that we are just too tired to run anymore. Even if there was anywhere to run to. Two fingers to you, Mr Adolf Hitler. We know you are almost finished. Kill us if you can, but we are not going to be bullied anymore.

The play is lovely. I had no idea that William could write stuff like that. All the kids who were in it are so good. It obviously means a lot to them and they're taking it very seriously. Jack plays a street urchin. As Jimmy says, typecasting.

Tess is a bit of a star. Once she understood at rehearsals that she had to follow the girl playing Mary and growl at all the nasty "officials," she had a lovely time. Never put a paw wrong. It's the border collie in her, she's so intelligent, bless her.

It's over and a lot of the audience are in tears. They are calling "Author, author," and the head calls William up onto the stage. He holds his hand up for silence and everyone looks expectantly at William. "Thank you so much," he says, then he pauses. "I should like to dedicate this evening to my wife, Tilly, who gave me the idea for the play." For a split second no one moves. They all know what happened, of course.

Then everyone stands at the same time and they start to clap and the young actors are clapping, and William just stands there and for a fleeting minute I can almost see Tilly at his side. Smiling.

It is an evening that I shall never forget.

We've decided to spend Christmas at the canteen again. Jimmy has been discharged from the Civil Defence because his cough is still bad. But it means he'll be able to help us this year. Eileen is going to bring her gramophone in and on Boxing Day we are going to play all her Glenn Miller records as a special tribute to him. We were all sad to hear he was missing. She says we must dance our socks off because that's what he would have liked us to do. I think she's right. And that is just what we shall do.

January, 1945

My three men are taking me to see Bing Crosby in *Going my Way* as a birthday treat. What is more, they've volunteered to do me a birthday tea. Probably a good job I have my dinner in the canteen. Eileen wanted to know if they've volunteered to clear up after. I haven't asked.

The film is *so* funny. And Bing is wonderful. I tell my lads that if we had a priest like him I'd convert immediately. "From what?" asks Jack. He sometimes has a knack of hitting the nail squarely on the head. It seems I only feel close to God when something really good or really bad happens. Perhaps He's not interested in the day-to-day stuff anyway. If He's there at all. But I couldn't bear to think there was nothing up there.

We have my birthday tea when we get home. I'm sat at the table like a duchess and not allowed into the kitchen. Jack is setting the table for the four of us and Jean Metcalfe's *Forces Favourites* is on the wireless.

Jimmy throws open the door with a flourish and in comes William with an egg and potato pie and then Jimmy follows with a dish of cauliflower and carrots. I don't have to pretend to be impressed, I definitely am. It tastes really good too. Takes ages to eat, of course, because I have to keep telling them how good it is and in the end we all get the giggles.

Then Elsie Bryant comes over on her bike with a trifle her mum's made and says it's instead of a cake, and I tumble to the fact that they've had a bit of help. I ask her to stay but she won't – she says it's good for us to be together.

I know she's remembering what is in all our minds. That it would have been William and Tilly's second wedding anniversary today. She's brought round a bottle of sherry from her dad as well. Jimmy finds some glasses and they drink a toast to me. Very formally. "To Lillian – to Mum."

So I get up as if we are at some big dinner and raise my glass. "To my smashing, clever family. Thank you." They stand up and raise their glasses and we drink but it is there, hanging in the air. So I raise my glass again and say, "To our lovely daughter, Tilly," and we drink silently. Then William says, "Thank you, Mum," and I know that I did the right thing.

As we clear the dishes we put the wireless on and they are playing "Swinging on a Star", which Bing sang in the film. We all start to sing along with it. Not such a bad birthday, after all.

April, 1945

We are going to the pictures again tonight, second time this week. They are showing Judy Garland in *Meet me in St Louis* and everyone says how good it is. Eileen went last night and when I ask her about it she says, "Yes, it's very good, Lillian," and then she goes quiet and her eyes fill up with tears.

"Well," I laugh, "I thought it was a musical, if it's that miserable I'll stay at home!"

She goes over to the sink and starts to wash up. The canteen has been ever so busy with breakfasts today. Without looking up at me she says, "There's other stuff

138

apart from the film." It must be the second feature. Perhaps we'll get there late and miss it if it's that sad.

There's a queue outside and Mr and Mrs Everton are here. They drop back and stand with us. Mrs Everton says they don't go to the pictures very often but they knew they must see this. I'm not sure what she is talking about and it must show on my face. "They're showing the newsreel of the German camps," she says.

I didn't realise. I've heard a bit of course. We were all so happy that the people held in the camps are free now. When we get to the ticket office the lady says do we want Jack to go in. I'm a bit taken aback but William looks at Jimmy and then answers for us. "He's fourteen next month, not a child any more." So in we go.

The second feature has nearly finished by the time we are in but you can see it's some silly American gangster film so we haven't missed much. Then the manager comes out onto the stage and tells us that the news will be at the end of the evening, after the film. Never known that before. As Eileen said, film is very good but we are all wondering about what is coming next, though some people there have obviously heard a lot more than me.

*Oh dear God. I never dreamt…*oh how could they…how could anyone…those piles and piles of bodies…not bodies really……just wasted into bones…even worse, the ghosts of people stumbling around…no flesh, no clothes, barely able to sit, let alone stand. Men, women, children, starving, filthy, and death, death, death everywhere. A figure, you can't tell if it's a man or a woman, holds out a hand to a soldier

139

who drops to his knees beside…This is what hell must be like. Corpses, some still living and breathing, everywhere. All around me people are crying but I am afraid that if I start I may never stop.

We leave the cinema in a silence broken occasionally by someone sobbing. We join the queue for the bus back to Norwood. William has his arm round Jack's shoulders. "Remember, Jack," he says, "that is what it's all been about. Don't ever forget what you saw tonight."

May, 1945

It's over. The whole country is going mad, every light in England must be blazing away and where the fireworks have come from heaven only knows. The church bells have been ringing for hours. All the houses that are still standing have got flags hanging from the windows, mostly Union Jacks of course, but anything goes, from a kid's skull and crossbones to a giant V chalked on a blackout curtain that, please God, will never be needed again. William has taken Jack up to Trafalgar Square and promised him that just this once he can jump in the fountain. From what I hear on the wireless they'll be lucky to get that near.

I walk down to the park and Jimmy and I sit in his hut. I feel too tired to celebrate but I know it will really hit me later. I'm thinking of Marcus and Billy, both in Italy still, and the war against Japan still not done. Jimmy reads my mind, as he always does.

"We'll have a big party when they are all home safe, Lil," he promises. We hold hands and look out at the pond and that bit of woodland on the far side. The bluebells are out.

Apart from the railings being gone you'd never know the last five years had ever happened.

June, 1945

I'm having a good old tidy-up so we can leave Thirza's house looking sparkling. Marcus is being demobbed and she is coming back tomorrow with the girls. We have managed to get our place habitable, though it needs a fair old bit of work done before it'll look anything like it did before the war. There isn't a single house in Penge that hasn't got some damage. There was a bit about it in the papers. Odd thing to be famous for...

Letter from Collette this morning. She's not coming back yet and possibly not at all. Gladys has fallen in love with country life, she says, and Mr Nash has a cottage empty, which he has offered them. He's going to send Gladys to agricultural college. Mr Deeprose is really firm that he never wants to go back. He says everyone he cares about is up there now. Funny to think of that family of cockney sparrows taking root in Suffolk while we are here in London.

My brother Frank has already been demobbed and he's gone to live with Uncle Jethro, who is getting so frail. Frank was engaged to such a nice lass before the war but he got one of those "Dear John" letters and she'd just got married to a GI. Frank was dreadfully upset at the time, they'd been courting for several years, but I think he's quite philosophical about it now.

Collette says he's helping her to paint her cottage. She's working in the village shop. Apparently Mr

141

Naismith is not such a bad old stick to work for but as soon as his Eric is demobbed he wants to retire. Collette's always got on well with Eric so she says that should work out OK. His wife is expecting their fifth – one for every leave!

August, 1945

It really is all over now. Japan has surrendered. The Americans dropped an atomic bomb on one of their cities and when that wasn't enough they dropped another. Thank God the rest of our boys will soon be home. On the newsreel they showed us some of them in the POW camps and you couldn't believe how awful they looked. Starved, beaten, tortured. When you think how well we've always treated POWs in this country you just feel that those Japs got what they deserved.

I don't fully understand what this atomic bomb is, only that it was big enough to finally put an end to the war. I don't want to know anything else.

Everything seems to be coming up roses. We've got our Labour government. We are going to have free doctors, and the kids are going to stay at school until they are fifteen, and they are going to give a weekly allowance to mums for their second child, and everything that we have hoped for is happening. No more of the nobs having it all their own way, not any more.

I feel sorry for poor old Mr Churchill, he must have been sure he would win the election. We went to see him when he was doing his election tour in Bromley. There were hundreds of us cheering him because we know he brought us through the war, but in spite of all the pink make-up he had on he looked so old and tired. It was difficult to realise that this chap in the old-fashioned clothes, barely bothering to wave to us, was the man whose voice on the wireless was so familiar to us. Of course, none of us had ever seen him before, except for bits on the newsreels. It was a bit of a shock to be honest.

On the bus going home Jimmy said what we were all thinking: "He's not one of us, really. He's never had to struggle where money's concerned, has he?"

We all think we've got the right man for job in Mr Attlee. What was it William said that night all those months ago – "Roll on, Brave New World." Let's hope so.

September, 1945

We are having a big party in the rec. A lot of places have had their victory parties already but we decided to wait till more of our chaps were back home. We did a bit of a celebration on VJ Day but nothing like this. Jimmy, William and Marcus have organised fairy lights and music as well as the tables and chairs, and us girls are doing the food. Or trying to, nothing is off the ration yet, but everything does seem to be getting better slowly. We've mustered up enough for a good old feast, anyway.

It is such a lovely evening, warm and calm. We've just finished the sandwiches and cakes and taken round some jelly for the kids. Nearly all the men have returned now, even Sebastian is here. Turned up this morning saying he felt like a good party.

We're sitting under the trees having a quiet smoke

and suddenly Maxy starts up with his squeeze box and a couple of others join in with their mouth organs, and everyone is on their feet Hokey-Cokeying and singing and laughing. That minx Cynthia has pulled Sebastian up to dance. Jimmy and I whirl past them in the foxtrot and it's good to see Sebastian enjoying himself so much. I must say he and Cynthia are a couple of very nifty dancers.

Thirza calls out: "What *am* I going to do with her?" as she and Marcus whiz by, but they are both laughing. Sebastian may be nearly old enough to be Cynthia's dad but he certainly doesn't look it. Mind you, I hope he's got her stamina because she's not letting him sit any out.

Norma and Jack are dancing together – a sort of not-very-proficient jitterbug. Pleased to see that Mr and Mrs Everton are here. Not dancing but joining in the talking. Elsie has gone over to talk to William. He does attempt to dance sometimes, just to be sociable, but it is difficult for him with his leg. She's such a thoughtful girl. Quite pretty, too, in a quiet sort of way. William said the other day that now the war is over she's hoping to finish training to be a teacher. I think she'll be good at that, she's always been very patient with her brothers.

Jimmy and I are sitting back under the trees watching them all. Jimmy can't dance too long or his cough gets the better of him.

"Do you know," I say to him, "I'm really beginning to believe it's over."

"So am I, girl," he says "so am I."

December, 1945

144

It's Christmas Eve and we are up in Suffolk for the festivities. The last time we spent Christmas here was in 1939, and that was only because of the war, but we know Martha is worried about Father's health and wants us to be with them this year. The kids have been out gathering holly and we have made each other presents.

Thirza and I walk down to help decorate the church. "Isn't it funny," she says, "this is what we did as children and yet the whole world has changed." It *is* like being in one of those films where time goes backwards. Our real lives haven't been here for such a long time.

Later, in church, my mind wanders during the sermon. I think of all the things that have happened since I was a child here.

I remember old Pastor Reynolds and his hellfire – a much milder vicar in the pulpit now – and going into service, and meeting Jimmy, and losing my brother Jack in the "war to end all wars." William being born and Mother dying. Jack being born and Thirza marrying Marcus.

The Christmases spent wondering where the bombs would fall next. The Christmas that William came back from the dead.

And Tilly. Always Tilly.

As we get up to sing the next carol Jimmy squeezes my hand. "They're all here with us, Lil," he whispers. How does he always know what I'm thinking? We stand shoulder to shoulder as the organist strikes up: "God Rest You, Merry Gentlemen", and I think he may be right.

Part Three: The Austerity Years

January, 1947

Talk about one thing after another. Looks like we are going to celebrate my birthday tonight by candlelight. It always seems romantic in the films but, as this is the second power cut today and our delivery of coal still hasn't turned up, I'm glad that Jimmy suggested we go round to The Queens Arms. At least they've got a fire here even if there's no proper light. It is so cold – I can't ever remember a winter as bad as this one, and they say there is more of the same to come. And they are much worse off up in Suffolk. Martha rang Thirza today and said they are actually talking about air-lifting food into the village if it goes on much longer.

Well, as it turns out, I'm having a really nice birthday. Just goes to show that you never can tell. Thirza and Marcus are here, and William, of course. Elsie's dad got Maxy to play "Happy Birthday" on the piano as I came in, and Jack jumped up on a chair and yelled, "Three cheers for Mum," and everyone hip-hip hurrahed like mad. I was quite embarrassed but I had to laugh. They've even arranged to lay on a bit of a spread. I don't know how they managed it with everything so short. I sometimes think the rationing is tighter now than during the war.

We are all sitting round the fire making the most of the warmth. Elsie says the coal lorries can't get through the snowdrifts and there is only enough coal for a couple more days. Mr Bryant and Maxy are having a good moan. "Here, you two," says Jimmy. "No grumbling on Lil's birthday, we're supposed to be having a party."

I turn to smile at them and say, "Anyway, cold or not, I am just so thankful every day of my life that no one's dropping bombs on us anymore. I don't think I'll ever complain about anything again."

"Quite right, Lillian," says Marcus, "I'm all for counting a few blessings. Takes your mind off the chilblains as well. And what about Collette and Frank? Now there's a bit of winter cheer."

He's certainly right about that. We had some really great news yesterday, the best present I could possibly have had. Collette and Frank are married. They did it really quietly, crafty pair. Sneaked off last week to the register office in Ipswich. Said they were too old for much fuss and they'll have a big get-together in the spring. So Collette is my sister now. Funny old world.

Frank's got himself a ready-made family, of course. Collette says Ronnie is the only one that she hasn't heard from. He and Martha's Donald are still up in Wales. They haven't demobbed the Bevin Boys yet. Seems a bit unfair, really, with everyone else getting back to civvy street.

Ronnie's best mate was killed in that big pit disaster, and Collette says he's changed a lot. He came home for two weeks last autumn and she couldn't talk to him at all. Says he was quite surly. Kept saying he shouldn't have been sent down the pits, that it wasn't fair. But as Collette told him, it was all done by ballot, even some of the real toffs went. But I suppose there's no glamour in telling the girls you spent the war in the mines, even if it was hard and dangerous. Mind you, Donald seems to really like it up there, but Ronnie says he has a girlfriend who looks like Jean Simmons, so I suppose that could make a difference.

Collette's letter says that Billy seems really thrilled about her and Frank. He's decided to stay in the army and make a career of it, so she doesn't see that much of him, but he sent a telegram and wrote as well saying how pleased he was. Mr Deeprose, Gladys and young Moira were their witnesses so they were in on the secret.

Gladys is finishing at college this summer and going to manage the farm for Mr Nash. Collette says she's done ever so well, got top-notch marks in everything. Mr Nash has been so good to her. After his wife died I think he was very lonely and watching Gladys take to farming like a duck to water cheered him up no end. Even before she went into the Land Army he was always taking her round the farm explaining things. He'll be glad to let her take over some of the running of the place.

Mr Bryant is calling "Time, gentlemen, please," so we're bundling ourselves back into our coats. Tess is curled up at William's feet pretending not to notice it's time to go. William is deep in conversation with Elsie – she qualifies this summer so they must have a lot to discuss. One thing for sure, she won't have a problem getting a job, there's such a shortage of teachers.

Jimmy takes my hand. "Happy birthday, Lil. Come on, out into the frozen wastes with us." No street lights, of course, the power still hasn't come on. "I knew all that practising during the war would come in useful," Jimmy says. "Let's get home and get to bed, it'll be warmer there." He's got quite a twinkle in his eye. Well, there are worse ways to keep warm on a winter night, I reckon.

July, 1947

Thirza came in today wearing a New Look skirt and jacket. She looked smashing. I told her I could feel myself going green with envy. The skirt is really long and full and the jacket is nipped in at the waist. Such a change from all our short, square utility clothes. I'm going to see what I've got that I can alter. I'm sure I could make a skirt like that out of one of my old dresses. Going to try anyway. One thing I'm really conceited about (though I shouldn't like anyone to know) is that I *have* kept my figure. I have still got a waist to nip in, not like a lot of the women round here.

Just heard on the wireless that Princess Elizabeth is going to marry that handsome young Prince Phillip. There have been rumours for weeks. Well, good luck to them, I say. We need some cheering up after all these cuts and the rationing. As Eileen said the other day: "If anyone else talks about 'tightening our belts' I shall throw the wireless out of the window."

But when you read the papers and you hear of the trouble all over the world you know we've just got to get on with it. At least we are at peace, and things *are* changing for the better. Just not as fast as we hoped.

I'm in charge of the canteen up in the laundry now and the pay is quite good so things are not too hard for us. And Jack's going to stay on at school. He wants to go to college. Says he's going to be a scientist. Imagine.

November, 1947

The papers are full of pictures of the wedding. The Princess looks so lovely and her dress is just out of this world, beautiful embroidery all over the skirt and a full-length veil. I think it really is a love match, she looks radiant and her parents seem so happy about it.

We went up to the Mall in the evening. They floodlit the palace and it looked like something out of a fairy tale. Elizabeth and Phillip had left before we got up there but the King and Queen and Margaret came onto the balcony. Everyone waved and cheered like mad and sang "God Save the King" and "Rule Britannia" and "Land of Hope and Glory" and oohed and aahed at the fireworks. *The Daily Mirror* said it was the biggest crowd ever seen in London – it was like being at an enormous party.

We caught the last train home and I noticed Elsie was asleep with her head on William's shoulder. I wonder…perhaps I've got weddings on the brain…but…wouldn't that be great?

January, 1952

Jimmy's cough has been so bad I'm insisting we go to see the doctor this evening. He says, "Not on your birthday."

"Jimmy," I say, "I am too old to worry about birthdays, but not too old to worry about you. We are going to see the doctor."

He's not really well enough to go in to work today, I'm sure it's not good for him being outside most of the time in this weather. I can't persuade him to stay at home though. I know how ill he must be feeling if he's agreed to see the doctor.

We haven't had much of a wait, only six people in front of us and two of them out quickly. Dr Marsh is calling us in. He goes all over Jimmy, tapping him and lying him down and then sitting him up, but he doesn't say a word. It seems to go on for ages. When I can't stand it any more I ask, "Is it another infection, doctor?"

He's quiet for a minute. Then he says that he'd like Jimmy to go to the hospital for tests. That really scares me. I start to ask him if it's serious, but Jimmy interrupts: "Lil, the doctor doesn't know. That's why I'm going to the hospital."

Jimmy's had more to do with hospitals than me, of course, because of what happened to him in the Great War, so perhaps I'm reading too much into it. I suppose I've been very lucky, because I've never had to go to a hospital for myself. Dr Marsh says we'll get a letter with an appointment, but he gives Jimmy a prescription for some cough medicine to keep him going. It can't be anything that bad if a bottle of cough mixture can make a difference, can it?

When we get home Jack is waiting for us. "Goodness," I say, "this is an honour – not down with Alan working on the monster, then?" He and his best pal are both motorbike mad and when they're not riding them they are taking them to bits in Alan's garden shed. He knows I'm only kidding and gives me a big hug.

"So how's my dad?"

We tell him what happened and he says he'll pop and get the mixture from the chemist on the corner and pick up some fish and chips for supper at the same time.

He is such a good lad. Got his twenty-first coming up this year. Still more interested in bikes than girls though.

There's a knock at the door and it's William. He's bought me a lovely picture frame with a photograph of little Rosalind in it. I am so touched. He says that Elsie sends her love and would have come round but Rosalind has just dropped off to sleep. They've hardly had a decent night since she was born so they are going to try to get an early night and hope she sleeps through. I tell him how much I like my present and that I'll pop round tomorrow to see Elsie and my granddaughter. Tired or not, it's so good to see William happy again.

Just settling down to the fish and chips and in comes Thirza. She's on her way to some posh dinner and is wearing a really glorious black and gold New Look dress. Marcus is going straight from his office, she says, but sends me his love. Since he's been on the council I sometimes think she only sees him at these do's. I know she enjoys it all though.

They've given me a real leather handbag – the first one I've ever owned. I tell her that I shall be frightened to use it but she laughs and says she'll be watching to make sure I do. Hugs all round and off she goes in her little car. I tease her about living the high life but they've both still got their feet firmly on the ground.

Jimmy and Jack have given me a bottle of Evening in Paris scent and some soap to match. It smells lovely. Money is a bit tight at the minute, and if Jimmy has to go on sick pay for a while it will be even tighter. But at least it's not like before the war when there wouldn't have been anything coming in.

Jack doesn't earn a lot yet but then he's done so

well to get himself apprenticed to J Arthur Rank. And they are paying for him to go to college one day a week as well. Day release, they call it. William knows some of his tutors, and he says Jack is doing ever so well.

Birthdays always make me think back and when we are getting ready for bed, I say to Jimmy, "We are lucky to have two such clever sons, aren't we?"

"Take after their brilliant parents, girl," he says. Hmm.

April, 1952

Jimmy's had to go into the hospital. They've done all sorts of tests, but they still don't really seem to know what the matter is. He couldn't get his breath the other day and nearly blacked out. I wasn't here but Mrs Smith had popped in to borrow a cupful of sugar and she called the ambulance. I am so grateful to her for acting so quickly. She must have absolutely flown down to the corner shop to use the phone. The hospital says if Jimmy hadn't got in there so quickly it would have been a lot worse.

Mr Cole, at the laundry, told me to take a few days off so I can be with Jimmy. Eileen can run the canteen as well as I can. "Always in your shadow, Lillian," she says, but laughing. We were a good team in the war and we still are and we both know it.

I'm sitting beside Jimmy and he sounds as if he's got a mouth organ in his chest. The doctor, who looks as if he should still be at school, comes in and pulls up a chair. "Mr Spencer," he says, "I'm afraid the prognosis is not good."

I've never heard the word before but I know he's

telling us something bad. And I'm right. He gives Jimmy's illness a funny name, something like Hammonds Rich Syndrome. I've probably got it wrong but that sticks in my mind because our landlady is Mrs Hammond and she's rich.

I realise that I am holding my breath because I'm frightened to hear what is coming next.

He explains that Jimmy's chest is being sort of cobwebbed and that's what's making him cough. And they can't get rid of the cobwebs or stop any more coming. He reckons it started with the gas in the first war and all the smoke and dust in the last one has just put the tin lid on it.

Jimmy looks at him. He's holding my hand tightly but he's firm as a rock. "How long?" he asks. For a minute I can't think what he means, then it hits me like a blow inside my head.

"If you're careful and avoid exertion, with luck you could have a couple of years. I am so sorry." He gets up and leaves us.

The curtains are drawn round the cubicle. I can hear the nurses moving around.

The world has just tipped sideways. "They might be wrong, Lil," says my Jimmy, struggling to sit up.

I pull up his pillow for him. "Of course they are. They don't know everything. And in two years' time there might be new medicines anyway." We sit holding hands until the nurse brings in Jimmy's tea, and visiting time is over.

I stand at the bus stop and make polite conversation with another lady. We've caught the same bus before. She works on the wards. Inside my head I'm screaming. Jimmy, Jimmy, my love, my life, don't leave me,

154

Jimmy, please don't leave me.

June, 1952

Jimmy is home. He looks quite good, considering how poorly he's been, and his cough seems a lot better. We never talk about what the doctor said that day. If we discuss it then it will become real. I don't believe it. Jimmy is getting better. I've never said anything to the family and I know he hasn't.

Elsie brought Rosalind round to see him today. He couldn't believe how she had grown. And Cynthia dropped in. Haven't seen her for ages, with all this modelling she does she's up in London a lot of the time. She brought this magazine in, with her on the cover. She said it's only a trade magazine but she got paid quite well for it and it could lead to bigger things.

She's home for a couple of days because she's been booked for a shoot up at the Crystal Palace among the dinosaurs. "As long as no one thinks I'm one of them," she giggles. Fat chance, she is so beautiful and bubbly. Jimmy wants to know if there is a special man in her life yet, she seems to have had so many passing through we've lost track. For once she goes a bit quiet. "Might be," she says. "I'll let you know when I've landed him." What a girl she is. Sometimes she reminds me so much of her mother at that age.

We went to see Gene Kelly in *Singin' in the Rain* this afternoon. Oh, it was so good, made you feel like singing and dancing yourself. And so funny. We did something we haven't done for ages, we stayed and saw it round again. When we came out there was a big

155

queue waiting to go in and I should have felt a bit guilty but I didn't.

When we get home Cynthia is in the kitchen and practically every towel we possess is lying around soaking wet – and so is she.

"Whatever is going on?" I ask her.

"Oh, Auntie Lillian," she says, "I've done the daftest thing." We make her wait while we conjure up some more towels and wrap her in my dressing gown and then she tells us what has happened.

She's up at the Palace modelling this horribly expensive mink coat and the photographer chap asks her to stand and pose on the creature at the edge of the lake. So up she climbs on it, feeling really hot because you're always modelling stuff in the wrong season. I remember she was doing swimsuits last January on some rooftop somewhere and went down with a terrible cold.

Anyway this photographer decides the light isn't right. So will she move to the pterodactyl, or suchlike, that is a bit further out? So she does. She's standing balanced on this thing right in the water when he asks her to pull the coat off her shoulders a bit, as if she's just taking it off. She completely forgets she's only got her bra and pants on underneath because of the heat, until someone who has stopped to watch gives a whistle and calls out, "Lovely, darling!" She's so flustered when the penny drops she steps backwards, slips and falls into the water. Ruining a coat that costs about a year's salary. "I'll never get another job," she sobs.

I know it's a crisis for her but it's difficult not to see the funny side and I'm trying not to look at Jimmy because I know I'll start to giggle. Anyway, I make her

156

a nice cup of tea and she starts to cheer up. Her agent has got her an interview with Rank next month and if she gets a contract with them and becomes one of those Rank starlets, well, the sky's the limit, isn't it? She won't care about the modelling anymore.

When she has gone we finally let ourselves have a bit of a laugh. Jimmy says he thinks she's got something she's not telling us up her sleeve – he reckons she's not as excited about the Rank interview as you would expect. When I think about it he may have something.

August, 1952

Jimmy had to go back to the hospital today and they were amazed at how well he is doing. The young doctor said if he wanted to he could go back to work. Of course he does want to, though I would much rather he didn't. Still, I think it must mean that they were wrong about what they said before. I am so glad we never told anyone. As we leave the hospital Jimmy says, "It's thanks to your cooking, Lil, they didn't know about that – Britain's secret weapon!" Please God, let it go on…

Had a note from Thirza this morning summoning us to her house on Sunday. Marcus will come and get us, she says, and Jack must come too. William and Elsie and baby Rosalind will be there. Family party. What's this about, I wonder? Not like my sister to play her cards so close to her chest. Very mysterious.

Well! I'm surprised yet I'm not. We should have seen it coming. Cynthia is engaged – and to Sebastian! They look so happy it shines out of them. He's bought her a beautiful sapphire and diamond ring. She tells me that there has never been anyone for her but him in spite of all the young men she brought home.

Marcus tells me quietly that when they came and told Thirza and him, a couple of days ago, he was quite shocked. Sebastian is fourteen years older than Cynthia after all. Then he said he thought about Father and Martha, and how well that had worked out and all the happy years they had together. "And, anyway," he says, "you couldn't stop them even if you wanted to, so you just have to cross your fingers and hope they make it."

I tell him the signs look pretty good to me and he gives me a hug. "I'm beginning to think so, too," he says.

Thirza said that when Cynthia was so quiet about being offered the contract with Rank, she sort of guessed, because of course they have to agree not to get married when they sign up. Anyway, looking at the pair of them, it's difficult not to believe that this is a marriage made in heaven. The wedding will be in October, and Norma and Margaret are going to be bridesmaids. No point in hanging around. Marcus says that Sebastian is something quite important in the City now, so there's no money problem. And Mrs Willett has met Cynthia lots of times and is delighted. I know she was starting to wonder if he would ever get married.

December, 1952

Thirza and Marcus have given us an early Christmas present and I can't quite get used to having it. I'm still not sure that we needed to have a telephone put in. It *is* nice to be able to talk to Thirza, and Cynthia, of course, but as I don't know many people who have one there aren't that many people I can ring. And when it goes, Jimmy and I both jump out of our skins. Never mind, I'm sure it will come in useful one day.

Collette rang me from the shop the other day. Billy and his wife are out in Aden and doing very nicely but she is worried about Ronnie. She says he's got in with a bad crowd in London and dresses like one of these Teddy Boys. He's a bit old for that, I'd have thought. Her Moira is doing fine, she's working in a shoe shop in Ipswich and spends most of her evenings in coffee bars. Don't think Collette sees a lot of her.

She and Frank seem very settled though I think she misses Martha not being so near. But we both think Martha was very brave to up sticks and move after Father died. She and Ivy are renting this pretty little cottage just outside the town and their little dress-making business is going well. They are going to spend Christmas in Wales with Donald and Angarhad and the children. Donald is a foreman in the mines now.

I was so grateful for the telephone last night. Jimmy started to cough, and then he just couldn't stop and he turned such a funny colour. I yelled for Jack and he phoned for the ambulance. I've just come back from the hospital. Matron said to come and get some sleep. I can't do that but I'll have a quick wash and change and get back. He's breathing through a mask. Please God, let him be all right.

I've just got back to the hospital and there aren't

any nurses around so I go straight down the ward – they must have moved Jimmy because the bed is stripped – and here comes Matron, she's coming to talk to me, and *no, no, no, no, no* – don't tell me that, it's not true, *no*, my Jimmy isn't, he isn't, he isn't – JIMMY…

They send for William. I can't leave my Jimmy here alone. They've put him in a bed in a little room by himself and he's not coughing anymore – I'm holding his hand and it's so cold – hold it tight – make it warm – no, you don't understand – I won't go, how can I leave him here on his own? – how can I go on without you? – Jimmy – Jimmy, my love – Jimmy…

The funeral is over. There were lots of people there. Lots of people who cared about him, who loved him. I've sent William home. He's got his own life to live and although everyone seems to want me to go and stay with them I know I've got to get used to being on my own.

I can't tell them the truth. I wanted to go with him. I understand how those Indian women are able to climb onto the fire where their husbands' bodies are being burnt. I wanted to hold his hand so he didn't have to do this dying thing on his own.

But I couldn't do that to Jack and William and Thirza and all the people I love. And who love me.

Jimmy, my love, my strength, how am I going to manage without you? I'm telling Jack that I'm fine and he's to go and sort out his precious bike with Alan. I tell him, with absolute truth, that's what his dad would have wanted.

Freddy said those who are left behind have an obligation to live life to the full. But I didn't know what

160

it felt like to have your life torn up and scattered to the winds.

Help me, God. If you're up there, help me. And look after my Jimmy.

January, 1953

William and Elsie were so anxious about me I could see I wasn't doing anyone any good not going to stay with them for a few days, so here I am. Another birthday done with. Today would have been my thirty-third wedding anniversary. I'm not going to think about it.

I helped Elsie to cook us all a special supper, as I said to her, I'd rather be doing something useful than just sitting around. She's got such a nice modern kitchen – everything is so colourful and easy to keep clean. Makes my old scullery and range seem very dingy. Jack's away on a course in Brighton but he rang me this evening at William's. He's going to the theatre with his mates this evening. I'm pleased about that, he's taken his dad's death very hard. It's a bit easier for William because he's not lived at home for so long and his life is here with his family.

Rosalind is toddling now. I think I can see some of her grandad in her, she's got his eyes.

June, 1953

Thirza is planning a big party tomorrow at their house. They've got a television especially so we can all see the Coronation as it is happening. I'm cooking all sorts of snacks to keep us going through the day. I've

161

only seen television a couple of times, once when I popped in to Thirza's and once in Elsie's dad's flat over the pub. It always seems to have what they call the test card on.

I said to Eileen, "I don't know what all the fuss is about, I'd as soon listen to it on the wireless." Though Jack says it will be much more exciting on what he calls the telly. I notice he's not going to be there, though, he's meeting someone in London. Says he wants to be part of the crowd outside the Abbey. I expect I would have done at his age.

I think I'm turning into an old grouch. I try so hard to be enthusiastic about stuff but I feel as if there is this glass wall between me and the rest of the world. Nothing quite reaches me. And I'm so tired of being brave, putting on a face, when inside I'm screaming, "I want my life back – can't you see I'm just going through the motions?" But I know they are all saying how well I'm coping. I wonder if this is what it is like for the Queen Mother. Watching her daughter crowned because her husband is dead. Smiling, and waving at the crowds.

August 1953

This 'mate' that Jack's always on about and going down to Brighton to see, this 'Harry' turns out to be a girl! An actress, no less. I can hardly believe he's only just told me. He's bringing her to meet me on Sunday. William and Elsie are coming round with Rosalind later. Going to pretend they are just dropping in. In fact they are as eaten up with curiosity as I am. What a dark horse my youngest son has turned out to be. Wonder what she's like? I feel quite nervous.

She's lovely. Her proper name is Harriet, and she's warm and funny and beautiful. Jack obviously adores her and she seems to care a lot about him. I can't believe my quiet, motorbike-mad son is going out with this girl who must have the world at her feet. She's in repertory in Brighton and tells us all sorts of stories about things going wrong, like scenery falling over and drunken actors and having to kiss people who've just eaten onions, but nearly all her stories are poking fun at herself, which I really like.

William and Elsie drop in as planned but they have a genuine reason. William heard yesterday he's got that headmastership he was hoping for at the new comprehensive. Two thousand pupils. I can't imagine a school that big but I know that both William and Elsie think these comprehensives are the way things are going. Harriet is telling them about the one at Stanmer, just outside Brighton, where her company has done a couple of what she calls watered-down Shakespeare plays. She says the facilities are amazing and reckons they ought to be able to inspire even the most unlikely kids.

I've done a special crab salad for tea, with rolls that I've made myself hot from the oven, and everyone tucks in. Harriet says she's never tasted bread like it and can she come again, please? We all laugh but when it's time for her to go I put my arms round her and say: "Please do come again, very soon," and I mean it.

Jack is going on the train with her back to Brighton and then coming home again tonight. He really is smitten. When they've all left I realise that I've had the first day since Jimmy died that I've enjoyed. Not pretended to, but enjoyed. I clear up, thinking about it all.

"Well, Jimmy," I say, "who would have thought? We always reckoned he'd find some nice Jenny Wren, and he's brought home a humming bird." I swear I can almost hear him chuckling.

January, 1956

I've had so many birthday cards today. I must say I rather like the way people send you pretty cards nowadays. Even the ones you don't see very often put a note in and it gives you a chance to catch up with them. Collette's Ronnie came over to see me this morning – such a surprise. I saw this car draw up outside and I couldn't think who it was. Lovely suit he had on and a big bunch of flowers for me. Said his mum asked him to drop them in because she knew he was working out this way.

When I asked him what he was doing now he was a bit shifty, though. "Ah, a bit of this and a bit of that," he said. Eileen says that's what crooks and conmen say. Gave me a big hug before he went on his way. I phoned Collette to say thank you and when she asked how he looked I just said, "Very smart," and I could hear she was relieved. I know she worries about him.

I'm round at William and Elsie's for supper. Rosalind is being allowed to stay up in my honour. She is such a monkey. Elsie is quite firm with her but she twists William round her little finger. She's only five, but she's reading really well already. When she started school they put her in the babies' class and then had to move her up after two weeks because she kept telling them she was bored. I don't think I would have known what bored was at her age.

Thirza and Marcus are here too and we are having a very pleasant evening. William drives me home in his little car. I'm rather tired now. I wish I didn't find birthdays so difficult. I'd rather let them go unmarked really, too many memories, but I can't tell them that. They mean well, bless them.

We are always careful not to mention that it is my wedding anniversary, because then we have to remember that it is also William and Tilly's today, and that might be difficult for Elsie and sad for William. Jimmy and I never made a big thing of it anyway, just a special kiss and cuddle and telling each other how lucky we were. So we were.

I look at the papers and it seems to me there is always someone at war. Korea, Palestine, this Mau Mau thing in Kenya, and now Cyprus. And the so-called Cold War with Russia. We were friends in the war, fighting on the same side. I'm glad neither of my boys is in the army, like Billy. But the two big wars combined to kill my Jimmy and sometimes, when I see couples walking along hand-in-hand or queuing for the pictures together, I can't help wondering, why us? Jimmy fought for his country and in the end his country killed him. I don't even get a war widow's pension. It's like none of it counts or has made any difference.

Mustn't let it get me down. I shouldn't like the boys to know how I feel. Next weekend should cheer me up. Jack and I are going to stay with Harriet for a couple of days. She's in Noel Coward's *Blithe Spirit* at the Theatre Royal in Brighton, and I saw the film some time ago, with Margaret Rutherford as Madam Arcati, so I'm looking forward to it.

And I am finally going to meet Harriet's dad. They've been engaged for nearly a year now and we've spoken on the phone but she usually comes up and stays with us so there hasn't really been an opportunity to meet. Jack says he's very nice. He was blinded in the Great War and after Harriet's mum died he went to live in St Dunstan's at Brighton. Harriet says he had several friends from his army days in St Dunstan's that he used to visit all the time so it seemed a natural thing for him to do. Her brother and sister are quite a lot older than her and married and moved away, so I suppose he didn't want to be rattling around all by himself in a big house. I must say I do wonder how I shall feel when Jack goes.

Harriet has got us one of the boxes. I feel very grand. It's not a very big theatre, not like the Empire, and there are only two boxes, one on either side of the stage. Jack and I are here a bit early and we're watching everyone come in – it's like being invisible, looking down on their heads. Jack is quite nervous but he always is before Harriet comes on.

The lights are starting to go down and I'm telling him to stop fidgeting and settle down (I do forget that he's twenty-five sometimes) when the door opens and in comes Harriet's dad with his dog. Jack jumps up and shakes his hand and I whisper: "Hallo, nice to meet you," but of course I can only see shapes in the dark and someone down in the audience goes: "Shush!" because the curtain has gone up and they've started. He whispers back, very softly: "And you," and we both have a *very*quiet giggle and I think: "I'm going to like you," and then the play is underway.

Harriet is brilliant, and even though I know we are prejudiced it's obvious that the rest of the audience love her as well and the play is just as good as I expected. We are still laughing when we get to the interval and the lights go up and I finally turn to greet Mr Curtis properly.

For a stunned minute I can't believe who I'm looking at, but he really hasn't changed a lot, even though it must be nearly forty years. He's standing and holding out his hand to me and I sit there feeling as if I've been winded.

There is a silence and Jack goes: "Mum…" then I hear this funny voice that doesn't sound like mine at all saying: "Freddy – oh my God, it's Freddy," and I get up and take his hand and put it to my face as if I've been doing this all my life, and he runs his fingers over my face and God knows how he recognises this wrinkled old skin but: "Lillian – I don't – I can't – Lillian – it is you, isn't it?"

And I pull my chair beside his, and his dog, who is called Berry, is licking my hand and we are both half-laughing and half-crying and trying to explain to Jack and trying to catch up and the years are being washed away. Freddy.

We are sitting in one of these new coffee bars that are everywhere in Brighton, waiting for Harriet. This one is very modern with red gingham tablecloths and lamps made out of wine bottles and a jukebox in the corner. Freddy orders us an espresso coffee each and some continental pastries. Someone puts some coins in the jukebox and it starts to play "Rock Around the Clock" and a couple of youngsters start to do this hand jive to the music. My feet are tapping too and I know instinctively that this will be one of those moments that are etched in my memory forever.

Freddy and I have been talking non-stop ever since the play ended. He had heard that Jimmy and I were married but he says, "I was still learning to be blind then, and not properly back in the world." He tells me how he didn't want to see anyone until he had learnt to cope on his own, and about his marriage to Beatie, which lasted for nearly thirty years until her death three years ago. I know a little bit about her because Jack met her just before she died, and I have always thought that our two youngest children comforted each other over the deaths of their respective parents.

I am relieved that Freddy seems as fond of Jack as I am of Harriet. When Harriet appears we have to explain everything all over again and she is amazed and delighted and it's more hugs all round. It is getting quite smoky in here as more and more people pile in. Brighton obviously has a much livelier nightlife than Penge – everyone is tucked up by eleven o'clock at home and it's nearly midnight now and the town is still full of people.

Freddy asks me if I am tired and to my surprise I find that I am not. "Let's leave these young people and go for a walk along the front," he says. So we bundle into our coats and walk through the Lanes and suddenly we are quiet. Not awkward quiet, just the quiet of two old friends. "How old were you when we last met, Lillian?" he asks.

I work it out. "Seventeen," I say.

"My God," he says and I know what he means.

We stop and look out at the sea and I find myself describing to him how lovely the moon is tonight, making a silver path over the water. Berry sits beside Freddy and I tell him about Tess and how much I miss her but how I haven't been able to bring myself to have another dog. We walk slowly back along the promenade and sit in the gardens at the Old Steine and for the first time I find myself talking about how tired I am of having to be brave, and how empty my life has felt at its very centre since Jimmy's death.

Freddy takes my hand. "The word is lonely, Lillian," he says. "Sometimes you feel it more when you are surrounded by people than when you are on your own. You can't tell your nearest and dearest that because it sounds like a criticism of them when they are trying so hard to help and coping with their own grief as well." He pauses. "My brother Raymond died, you know."

I didn't. I am shocked because Josephine told me he had come through the war.

"Stupid riding accident in '21. Survived so much to die chasing a fox. Always did think it was a damn silly thing to do."

I ask about Sophia and Isabel and learn they have seven children between them. They are still angelic children themselves in my memory and I tell him this.

"Both vastly overweight now, more elephantine than angelic."

I understand that he has deliberately broken the mood and we laugh together.

Dear Freddy, always wise, even as a boy. His stepmother remarried after his father's death and he

169

says that she spends even more time now lying on her sofa issuing orders. But at least she has the excuse of age nowadays. "I never forgot how cross you were at being renamed Ellen," he says. "Raymond and I were so indignant on your behalf when we heard."

I thank him, nearly forty years on, for the note he sent me after Jack's death. I tell him that his words have remained with me and supported me all my life. He is silent.

Then: "Oh, Lillian, I am so glad we have met again."

So am I. Oh, so am I.

April, 1956

Jack has been given a really big pay rise. He's earning £950 a year. That's more than Jimmy ever earned. He has done so well with all his exams. When his apprenticeship ended last year they still weren't paying him that much so he applied for another job. When he was offered it he went and told his present boss how much the others were going to pay him and they promptly gave him this rise to make him stay. He says it's a lesson well learnt because he knew he was worth it.

He's been moved onto a special project that he's quite excited about – something to do with putting black boxes in aeroplanes so that if they crash people will be able to find out what went wrong. Sebastian and Cynthia came over today and he is telling Sebastian about it. Sebastian says it sounds like a great idea.

Cynthia is much quieter than she used to be, she's so desperate to have a baby but none of the tests she's had show why she's not getting pregnant. I think she's found it quite hard because of Norma falling as soon as she got married and having twins. Norma and her Mike have decided to emigrate to New Zealand. They are due to go next month on one of these assisted passages. Thirza's got very mixed feelings about her grandchildren disappearing to the other side of the world, but, as she says, you can't stop them, can you?

I can't see Margaret having a family yet, she's still at Cambridge, the family blue stocking. I don't think she ever notices there are young men around. We tease her but she knows how proud we are of her. Especially Marcus. I think it gives him a real kick seeing his daughter get the education that would have been beyond his wildest dreams.

August, 1956

I'm rushing around like a maniac trying to get everything ready for Jack and Harriet's wedding tomorrow. Freddy says to calm down, the big advantage of being the mother of the groom is that the bride's family are supposed to shoulder the burden, but I don't like to leave it all to him. The wedding is to be at St Peter's, the big church right in the centre of Brighton, and they are having their reception at the Grand Hotel on the front.

I can't believe how posh it's all going to be. *Everyone* is coming – and I'm a bit embarrassed because there's stacks more of us than there are of them, but when I say this to Freddy he just laughs and says: "Lillian, be quiet, just between you and me I'm quite well off, you know." I suppose he must be. When

171

I think about it, the family must have been rich to have had so many of us servants. It's all so long ago.

The wedding is beautiful. Freddy came and sat by me after he'd given Harriet away. None of this nonsense with you on one side of the church and me on the other, he says. William is Jack's best man and Harriet asked Rosalind to be her bridesmaid. I was afraid that she might be fidgety but she was as good as gold. I well up in the middle of the service, so much happiness is almost too much, but Freddy passes me a hanky and I don't disgrace myself.

At the reception, after William's speech, Freddy gets to his feet and says he would like to propose a toast to the mother of the groom and everyone gets to their feet and drinks a toast to me. I stand and say "Thank you" to them and then sit down very quickly. Everyone knows I'm not one for speeches and they all laugh.

Then Freddy says that he would like them stand and raise their glasses once more: "To my wife and Harriet's mother, Beatie, and Lillian's husband and Jack's father, Jimmy, a brave man who I knew and valued greatly."

I am choked for the second time on this extraordinary and wonderful day. I look around the room. William and Elsie, Thirza and Marcus, Collette and Frank, Timmy and Lettie, Sebastian and Cynthia, Martha, and all our children and grandchildren. And, of course, Jack and Harriet. My family. We raise our glasses.

November, 1956

Margaret has been staying with me for a few weeks. I think it is a plot by Thirza and Marcus so that I won't miss Jack too much as she could easily have gone home to them. She's working for some MP in the House of Commons. Seems a funny job to me after all the studying. She says that she is grateful to be here as it's useful to be so near the station but I know that's an excuse. They are all so well-meaning that I didn't like to tell them I am better now than I've been since Jimmy died. Mind you, Margaret is good company, and I enjoy having her. Nice to have someone to cook for, too. I don't bother much with meals when I'm on my own.

We both got really upset the other night. She's got one of these short-wave wirelesses and we've been listening to it a lot trying to get news of all this dreadful trouble in Hungary. One of her friends from Cambridge, Maria, is Hungarian and I know Margaret has been very worried about her. Tonight we heard some people calling: "Help us, please help us," in English. Then there was lots of terrible noise and what sounded like guns and a voice called: "The tanks are coming, the tanks are coming, help us, save our souls, save our souls," and then there was something we didn't understand and it all went quiet.

We were both in tears – it sounded so desperate and so awful. Margaret phoned her boss and said he was an MP so what was he going to do about it? But although he talked for a bit it came down to nothing much.

I don't understand. Mr Eden rushed our soldiers off to Egypt because of this Suez business and yet the Hungarians don't seem to matter. I thought the last war was about stopping this kind of thing happening ever again. Sometimes I wish we didn't know so much about

173

what is going on nowadays. After all, if we are not going to do anything about it, what *is* the point?

December, 1956

Jack and Harriet have got this lovely house right on the seafront and I've come to stay for a few days. I wouldn't before because I wanted to give them time to be on their own. Freddy is coming round later and he's taking me out for supper tonight. How grand! I'm all dressed up in my New Look suit, nigger brown with white trimmings, and Thirza lent me her camel coat to go over it. Harriet says, "Lillian, you look wonderful," and Jack says, "Mum, I hardly recognise you," which I tell him is a bit of a backhanded compliment. But I know I look nice.

Freddy arrives early and we stay long enough to have a sherry with Jack and Harriet, then Freddy orders a taxi and off we go. The restaurant is quite small, and the waiters are all Italian. Freddy says the food here is wonderful and what will I order? So I tell him I haven't a clue, Lyons' Corner House is the poshest place I've ever eaten in, and he'll have to order for me. I like just about everything, anyway.

Freddy orders for us both and asks for some wine. One sherry can have me under the table so I'm going to be very careful. When the waiter brings the wine he says something to Freddy that I don't catch. When he's gone I ask what he said, and Freddy says: "He said that you were 'bellissima,' a beautiful lady." He reaches across the table and takes my hand. "Lillian, I was going to wait until after supper, but I find I can't. Do you think you could take on a blind old man? Will you

174

marry me, Lillian?"

I've known, just as I knew all those years ago with Jimmy, that he was going to ask me. I put his hand to my cheek. "Of course I will, Freddy." Then, because the combination of the sherry and the whole occasion has made me cheeky, I ask: "What took you so long?"

We decide to tell the family when we are all together at Christmas. We usually go to Thirza'a nowadays because she and Marcus have the most room. I still do the cooking, because I enjoy it. Freddy is already invited and is coming with Jack and Harriet so it should be the perfect time. I know they will be pleased for me.

Freddy is going to tell the matron at St Dunstan's tomorrow. There is so much to think about, all the practicalities such as where we are going to live. We won't set a date until we've sorted that out, but Freddy says, "We won't take long, will we?" and I reply that if it comes to it, we'll live in a beach hut, we are too old to hang around!

Freddy was right. The food certainly *is* wonderful but we are both so excited we hardly notice it. When we leave the waiter gives me a red rose. Freddy stops our taxi by the Old Steine and we go and sit on the same seat that we sat on that night in January. It's another cold but moonlit night and we sit holding hands. Just being together.

A thought occurs to me. "Oh, Freddy, what *will* your stepmother say?" Then: "I won't visit her unless she promises to call me Lillian." We are still laughing when we get back to the taxi.

Another Christmas. My goodness, there have been

good ones and bad ones, and strange ones but this promises to be a very happy one. As chief cook I'm never allowed to clear, Thirza and the girls are doing that.

Sebastian is telling me that he and Cynthia are going to adopt a baby. They have filled out all the forms and are waiting for something to happen. It doesn't usually take long, there are so many poor babies without a father. It must be an awful wrench for some of those girls, giving up their baby to a stranger. I know people say that they are no better than they should be, and not fit to be mothers, but they must have loved the baby's father in the first place. It always seems to be the girls that have the agony, first having the baby, then parting with it. The men just walk away. It would have broken my heart to give my baby away. If my boys had got some girl in trouble I'd have made them stand by her. Still, seeing how happy Cynthia looks, it's an ill wind...

I'm sitting by Freddy and we are all waiting for the Queen's broadcast. Rosalind, who is thoroughly over-excited, announces that she doesn't feel well and Elsie rushes her off to the toilet and what with one thing and another I really couldn't tell you what the Queen has said. I'm waiting for our own announcement, and I can tell from the way he's squeezing my hand that Freddy is too. We're drinking the loyal toast and are finally sitting quietly. Everyone's lit their cigarettes and relaxing and at last the moment seems right.

I say: "Freddy and I have got something we'd like to tell you," and all eyes turn to us.

Freddy says: "We wanted you to be here together for our news. I hope you will be happy for us. Lillian

176

has consented to be my wife." And he turns and gives me a hug.

Funny thing is, I thought they would have guessed. But obviously not. There's a kind of stunned silence, then Thirza says: "Oh, Lillian, that's wonderful," and she and Marcus and Cynthia and Margaret and Sebastian are kissing us and shaking Freddy's hand. And Harriet is dancing round with Rosalind singing: "I knew it, I knew it, isn't that super!" and Elsie comes and puts her arms round me and says: "Oh, Lillian, I am so happy for you."

But William and Jack are standing together by the fireplace and I realise with a shock that they are looking at me as if I've committed some sort of crime. There's a split second of silence as the others take this in, then Harriet pulls Jack over and laughingly orders him to give his mum a big kiss, which he does.

"Jack?" I query, and he mutters something about "a bit of a shock," and then I see that William is leaving.

Elsie goes after him and then comes back into the room alone. "Leave him be, Lillian, I'll sort him out later. Rosalind and I are going to lay the table for tea." And she covers the moment, bless her, and everyone begins to bustle about.

Freddy takes my arm and whispers: "Lillian, is it because I'm blind?"

"Don't be daft," I reply. "I don't know what it's about, but it's not going to spoil our first Christmas together." But it has, of course.

It's the day after Boxing Day and I've rung Elsie to make sure they are going to be in, because I'm on my way round to find out what is going on. When I get there Elsie has taken Rosalind into the park with her new doll's pram. She's a tactful girl. I'm beginning to think I'm luckier in my daughters-in-law than in my sons.

William opens the door and I haven't seen him looking so sulky since he was a boy. "Right," I say, getting straight into it without even taking my coat off. "What was that performance on Christmas Day about, William?" Then it comes pouring out. How can I have forgotten his dad, how can anyone replace his dad, how can I be so disloyal to his dad's memory?

Well, I'm probably not feeling very diplomatic, so I take a deep breath and take my coat off and give it to him to go and hang up, which gives me a minute to get my thoughts in order. I'm resisting the urge to shout at him and tell him how thoughtless and how selfish he's being. I want to make him see it for himself.

So when he comes back I remind him of how much he loved Tilly. And I ask him if he has ever stopped loving her. And he looks a bit startled but then he says no, of course not. And I ask him if he loves Elsie any less because Tilly was first and he says no, of course not, again. I point out that it must be a different love because they are different people, but loving one doesn't stop you still loving the other one. He's beginning to look ashamed now. Good.

Then I tell him, and I'm glad I'm so angry or else I might spoil it and cry, that his dad and I were together for thirty years and I'm not going to forget him or stop loving him any more than I would expect Freddy to forget his Beattie. But Freddy and I are right for each other, as he and Elsie are, and he is spoiling my joy at this totally unexpected and unimagined gift at this point in my life. "You, of all people, should understand," I tell him.

Then he's on his knees beside me giving me a hug and asking me to forgive him – which of course I do. Elsie comes back and I play with Rosalind for a bit. Elsie comes to the door with me. "Well done, Lillian," she says.

"Well done, you," I say, putting my arms round her.

"He only wanted to protect you," she says. I am sure she's right. Men!

Part Four: Better Times

January, 1957

Jack and Harriet have turned my birthday into a dual celebration. They insist that it's to be our engagement party as well. All protestations on our part that we are much too old for such festivities have, happily, been ignored and we are in the middle of such a delightful evening. They have been so extravagant but I think most of the family must have chipped in. Well, I hope so.

They have hired the Banqueting Room at the Royal Albion, on Brighton seafront. Freddy and I were ordered to arrive at seven p.m. in our best bibs and tuckers. Freddy looks so handsome in his tuxedo. A bit like Fred Astaire, I think. Though possibly a bit chubbier. Harriet dragged me off to the January sales last week to find my bib and tucker and I feel more glamorous than I ever thought I could. We found this wonderful full-length sea green dress in shot taffeta, and it fits as if it is made for me. And it has this little bolero so I don't feel undressed at the top, if you know what I mean.

I don't even know how much it cost because Harriet says it was all decided beforehand and is a present from her and Jack and William and Elsie. I don't argue. I know it is my two sons' way of apologising for the hiccup in our relationship and that I must accept graciously. So I do.

There is a splendid grand piano in the corner of the

room, and the pianist is playing some of the popular music of the century. Which is my lifetime, of course. When you are the same age as the year no one ever forgets how old you are. Bit of a drawback if I ever want to chop a couple of years off. Ivor Novello, Gershwin, tunes from some of the shows that I remember so well, even *Chu Chin Chow* – my goodness, what a long time ago that was! In another life, it seems. I read something once about the past being another country and I've only just really understood what it meant.

Charleston music now, which gets Thirza and Marcus a round of applause for an impromptu demonstration. Such energy. Just as the pianist starts on some Glenn Miller tunes, which bring a lump to my throat though I don't really know why, the waiter comes in with an enormous cake and then brings round champagne. The music stops, and Freddy stands and says, "To Lillian. Happy birthday, my love. And thank you for lighting up my life."

I am rendered quite speechless, of course, so I put my glass down and give him a kiss and then I turn to kiss Harriet and then everyone is kissing everyone and laughing and I think that never, in my whole life, have I had such a birthday as this.

March, 1957

I think we have found our house. We decided that we should like to live in Brighton. Freddy has so many friends here, and we will be near to Jack and Harriet. William and Elsie say that it may take longer for them to come down here to see us but it will be a lot more

181

fun than Penge. Elsie says they are thinking of moving a bit further out anyway. Rosalind definitely feels that a granny at the seaside is desirable. She is so excited and we have promised she can come and stay often.

The house is near the Dyke Road, on the outskirts of the town, and is called Sea View. Which it hasn't, of course, but never mind. It is Victorian, with three nice bedrooms and a lovely bathroom on the mezzanine floor. I have always wanted to have a house with a proper bathroom. We used to strip-wash in the kitchen at Penge and go to the public baths every week. Jimmy tried to persuade Mrs Hammond to have one put in but she always refused, saying that it was new-fangled nonsense.

There is an extra bedroom in the attic, which was for the servants, I suppose. It certainly reminds me of the one Josephine and I shared. I tell Freddy and he says, "I hope you are not going to hold it against me every time you go upstairs," and I reassure him that nothing could be further from my mind but anyway I know that he is pulling my leg.

There is such a pretty garden that runs right round the house, with apple trees and plum trees and shrubs planted in a delightfully higgledy-piggledy fashion. Not so enormous as to be a worry, but big enough for Berry to run in, and for family parties. The dining room has French doors that open onto a small terrace, and there is a good-sized sitting room at the front, facing south. And a really modern kitchen with built-in cupboards and a double sink and a most impressive gas cooker that has so many controls it looks as if it might be able to fly the Channel.

But best of all it has this amazing wallpaper

everywhere. It is flowers and ivy and beautiful swirling leaves in greens and reds and golds, and when I describe it to Freddy he says that it sounds as if the house still has the original William Morris paper. I've never heard of William Morris but Freddy says he was an artist and a poet in the last century and that his designs are famous.

He says, "You've fallen in love with this place, haven't you, my darling?" and I confess that just about sums it up. It feels as if it has been standing here forever waiting for us to come along.

"Then," says Freddy, "we shall take it."

"Gracious," I say, "how the other half live!"

"Lillian," says my lovely husband-to-be, "you *are* the other half now."

My goodness, what a thought. I must be careful not to get above myself.

April, 1957

Mr and Mrs Frederick Curtis took up residence at Sea View today. Actually, Freddy says we must change the name as, "Even for you, my darling, I don't think I can live in a house called Sea View that is at the foot of the South Downs with not a wave in sight." I think he's right.

We sneaked off last week with only Marcus and Thirza knowing that we were tying the knot. They were our witnesses and it was a simple ceremony in a register office. It just felt better that way. We spent three glorious days on the Isle of Wight staying at a hotel on the edge of the cliffs, and we sent postcards to all the family asking them to forgive us for wanting to do it so quietly. They have assured us they understand, bless them.

I am so happy that sometimes I want to cry with it. I never expected such happiness again. I have so much to be thankful for. Thank you, God, for giving me Freddy and this wonderful new life.

January, 1958

I've told Freddy that I don't want any fuss on my birthday this year and, of course, he understands. We came back from Suffolk after Christmas but Ronnie's death in that awful train crash has affected everyone. He was only thirty-one. He was always a bit of a tearaway but he'd just begun to look as if he was settling down. He took Marlene down to meet Collette and Frank in the summer and promised to spend Christmas with them. First time in years.

Ivy was dreadfully upset at the funeral, Martha told me that she always thought that she carried a bit of a torch for him. Of course they were all growing up together in the war years. It must have brought the children very close. The crash was so dreadful. They think it was caused by the fog, but no one is quite sure what really happened. Three trains packed with Christmas shoppers – and our Ronnie.

There are over 100 dead and the numbers are still going up every day. Marcus went to identify the body. Collette rang him as he was the nearest to Lewisham. He went and broke the news to Marlene, too. He hasn't spoken about it much but Thirza says he couldn't sleep for days. We all stayed on after the funeral so we could be near them over Christmas.

184

Gladys and her young man were there and Billy came home from Cyprus, but they both had to leave soon afterwards. Collett's got Moira, thank heavens, but especially since Mr Deeprose died she rightly thinks of us as her family, and I know Frank was grateful we were there. It's an awful thing to lose a child, against nature. Poor Collette, she has had so much loss. I don't know, we can send a dog into space (poor little sausage), but we can't prevent trains crashing into each other.

So we are going to the restaurant where Freddy proposed to me for a quiet birthday supper. We will have been married nine whole months. I feel almost guilty about being so happy sometimes, but I know that's silly.

William and Elsie came down today with such a pretty vase for me, and Rosalind carried the flowers to put in it and presented them to me with such ceremony. I cooked lunch for us all and they went back this afternoon. They had a big surprise for us. They say they are fed up with paying rent and are going to buy a house. I am a bit concerned about it but they are adamant that now Elsie is teaching again they can afford a mortgage.

They have found somewhere that they like in Orpington. They have obviously done a lot of homework, and have saved up £300 for the deposit, but I am still stunned to find that they are borrowing £3,000 and it will be a lot more by the time they have paid it back in twenty-five years. I don't know anyone else who is buying a house, but Freddy, who always seems to know about these things, says that only the other day Marcus mentioned that he was thinking of trying to buy their house in Norwood. So perhaps it is not such a daft idea. Marcus has certainly always had his head screwed on where money is concerned.

The restaurant is as lovely as ever and the waiters remember us. I think Freddy may have tipped them off but I don't let on. After supper he puts a small box on the table, and says, "Happy birthday, my love." I think it must be jewellery, of course, and open it expecting to see a brooch or something, but instead I find a small key sitting on a velvet cushion.

"What is it to?" I ask, totally bewildered.

"Wait and see. All is about to be revealed," says my mysterious husband. He calls the taxi, and as we draw up outside our little Victorian house, I see there is a car parked outside it with an enormous ribbon on it.

"Freddy," I start to stammer, but Jack and Harriet are there pulling me out of the taxi and Freddy is grinning and a kind-looking middle-aged man is standing by the kerb looking a bit shy and everyone is laughing, even me, though I haven't a clue what is going on.

"This," says Freddy, touching the shiny black bonnet of the car, "is yours, Lillian. And this," he puts out a hand and the man comes and grasps it, "is my old friend Barry, who is going to teach you to drive it. A selfish present, I am aware, but I need a chauffeur."

Well! For a minute I'm stunned and, I suppose, a bit scared. Then I think, OK. Thirza's been doing this for years, and I think of being able to take Freddy up to the Downs, or along the seafront, or to see the family, and I can feel this big smile spreading across my face.

"Thank you, Freddy," I say, and as I stand there grinning they all start to clap. My goodness, as quiet birthdays go, this is one to remember.

March, 1958

I'm not finding this car-driving as easy as they said it would be. I did have my doubts in the first place. I've had eighteen lessons and I still don't understand what the gears actually *do*, though Barry says I'm doing well. I drove along the Western Road into Hove yesterday, but I feel that although I'm doing all the things that Barry tells me I don't really know *why* I am doing them, so how will I ever be able to manage on my own?

Freddy is planning to visit some friends at St Dunstan's this afternoon. I'm going to beg off going with him so that I can ring Harriet privately. I don't want Freddy to know that I'm beginning to wonder if I will ever go in for, let alone pass the test. Barry told me that you should reckon to have one lesson for every year of your life. I'll probably be dead before I've finished at that rate. Harriet has been driving since she was eighteen and she's got a lot of her dad's good sense. If she thinks there's no hope for me she'll be honest. She's what she calls "resting" at the moment, which means not acting, so with any luck I'll catch her.

Bless her, two minutes on the phone and she's on her way round in her little car. We're out in the road and she's pulled the bonnet on my car up (I didn't even know you could do that) and she's showing me what happens when you change gears and explaining how you can have more control or more speed. We are going out in my car and she is going to sit with me. Not only clever and kind but brave too, I reckon.

Actually, that was amazing. I feel as if I've been given a pair of wings. For the first time I understood what I was doing. I'm going to ring up and book my test. And I'm going to pass.

April, 1958

It's Easter Sunday and I am driving us up to Marcus and Thirza's, it's the longest journey I've done since I got my licence. When we arrive they have to come out and admire my little Hillman Minx, of course, and Thirza whispers, "I'm so proud of you, Lillian," which makes me feel good.

Sebastian and Cynthia are here with Natalie and little Michael. Natalie is nearly two now and adores the baby. He was only two months old when they adopted him, a bit younger than Natalie was when they brought her home. Sometimes I find myself thinking how like Cynthia Natalie is, which is quite strange. But Marcus says the adoption people go to a lot of trouble to try and match adopting parents with their children. I suppose that is sensible, though Sebastian and Cynthia have made a point of telling Natalie that she is special and "chosen" right from the start.

William and Elsie are coming over later. Rosalind loves her cousins and is so patient with Natalie. I've been quite surprised at how good she is with them both.

Marcus has set up a screen in the living room because Norma has sent some ciné film of them from New Zealand, which I am looking forward to seeing. Margaret arrives in time for dinner with a rather scruffy young man. His name is Teddy and he has a beard and is wearing one of these duffel coats. But he has a very posh accent and lovely manners so I suppose that looking a bit unkempt is a sort of fashionable thing to do.

Over dinner Margaret tells us that they are going on the CND march to Aldermaston tomorrow. I've read about it all in the papers, of course, and I am pleased that someone from our family is going. I think these H bombs and A bombs are dreadful. When I see the pictures of what happened to those people in Japan it makes my blood run cold. It makes us almost as bad as they were. Freddy says that dropping it shortened the war and I know that is true, but please God, don't let anyone ever drop another now we know what they do.

It's funny, but because I sit and read the papers to Freddy in the morning, I find we discuss a lot of things that I probably wouldn't have thought much about before. It's like he's given me an extra pair of eyes, even though he laughs when I say that.

Norma looks very happy and settled in her new country. The children seem to spend all their time running around with next to nothing on and there is lots of film of them cooking on a sort of outdoor stove. Thirza says it is so hot out there they eat out of doors more often than not. I think I might have a problem with the insects but it certainly looks fun.

We've just got to the end of the film and I'm trying to keep Freddy in the picture, so to speak, with a running commentary, when Jack and Harriet turn up. We were only half expecting them as they weren't sure what they were doing today, but I can see that they are bursting with news.

Harriet has got a part in this big new show in the West End, *My Fair Lady*. One of the cast had to drop out and her agent rang this morning. She is over the moon – it's only a tiny part but it's her first in the West End. I do hope it doesn't turn out to be one of these shows that runs for three nights and then sinks without trace. Marcus says he's going to be in town tomorrow, he'll try and get us tickets. How exciting!

My goodness, it really is a wonderful, wonderful show. Marvellous music and dancing, and Julie Andrews is fantastic. I remember her as that little girl who used to sing with Archie Andrews on the wireless and she always had a lovely voice, but her acting is so good too. Rex Harrison is just right as Professor Higgins and, oh, it was "luverley" as Freddy put it.

I don't know when I have enjoyed a musical more – and our Harriet was perfect, of course. We hum the songs all the way home on the train, until Berry, who is lying on Freddy's feet the way he always does, sits up and glares at us.

"I think he's saying we're off key," says Freddy.

"Humph!" goes Berry, as he slumps down again. We take the hint and shut up. Such a happy evening.

June, 1958

We've come up to see William and Elsie in their new house today. It really is very nice, built just before the war, with three bedrooms and lots of space downstairs and a nice garden for Rosalind to play in. They have promised her that now they have their own house she can have a kitten. She's been on about it for ages, and I have to admit that I'm looking forward to seeing it. I do miss Biggles, even though he made it to a good age, and I'm afraid to have another one in case Freddy falls over it. But Rosalind says that "Granny can have a share in my kitten," bless her.

I must say that William and Elsie have done the house up beautifully, they told us they were decorating all through because it was a bit dingy when they bought it, but now it is really contemporary. They've painted most of the rooms a pale cream and wallpapered one wall in each room to make it colourful. In the living room they've put a red paper with black zigzags on it round the chimneybreast.

They've bought some new furniture, all very angular with straight lines and little legs on nearly everything, but their three-piece suite, which is red and black, is surprisingly comfortable. It wouldn't be my choice but I tell them with absolute truth that it all looks smart and attractive and inviting. And, as I say to Freddy when we are driving home, every generation should do different stuff. Now I have got used to the idea of them buying a house I must say I feel very proud of them both.

September, 1958

Moira's wedding today. I am so pleased that Collette has something to celebrate. We came up last night and standing in the village church always makes the years roll back. Moira looks beautiful and Neville seems a nice lad. Collette told me in strictest confidence – "not even Freddy, mind," that "there's a baby on the way but they wanted to get married anyway so no harm done and it'll just have to be a bit premature, won't it?"

"Mum's the word," I reassure her, then we both

191

realise what I've said and have a dreadful attack of the giggles. Nice we're not too old for that.

Frank looks very handsome, dressed in what he insists on calling a monkey suit, but I can see he's very chuffed to be giving his stepdaughter away. Gladys is her matron of honour, and Billy's two little ones are pages. Collette hasn't seen them for ages and they all have to go back to Cyprus next week, so she's making the most of them. I think she must have taken about a hundred pictures with her little Brownie. Billy has to keep loading more film in for her. Martha and Ivy are here, and Donald has come down from Wales with Angarhad and the children, so what with all of us, and Neville's family, the church is packed. Neither William nor Jack could make it, but, as Thirza points out, Moira doesn't know them so well as they were in London when she was growing up.

It's a lovely reception in the church hall, Collette got a caterer in and I have to admit he's done them proud. Most of the youngsters are dancing now and Freddy is deep in conversation with Donald. Collette comes over and we sit taking it all in.

"We've come a long way since I was a 'French' maid and you were the youngest cook in service, haven't we, Lillian?" she laughs. "I sometimes wake up in the middle of the night and realise that meeting you changed my life."

I am so surprised I can't think of anything to say. "Did it?" I stammer.

Collette puts her arm round my shoulders. "If you hadn't helped me after Sid was killed, and when Moira was so ill, I'd never have come up here. And now look at me, Lillian, married to your brother, one daughter a farmer, the other a real Suffolk girl. Why, I even have a Suffolk accent of sorts. But most of all, I have a family again."

I am so touched I can't think of anything to say. So I don't. I give her hand a quick squeeze and say, "Come on, you daft thing, introduce me to these kids of Billy's, I never can remember which is which."

On the way home, I tell Freddy what Collette said, and how I would have liked the words to tell her that her refusal to be bowed under by all her troubles, her cockney humour and her bravery, have been mainstays in my life. That she and Thirza and Martha have supported me through thick and thin and that for every give there has been a take.

He says, "Darling Lillian, that is called friendship. You have a great gift for giving and receiving it. Sometimes I think we men are not so capable of the honesty it demands. Cherish it, my love. I'm sure Collette knows how you feel."

I do hope he is right. But he usually is.

January, 1963

I've been invited to Buckingham Palace! I can hardly believe it. What a wonderful, exciting way to start the year. I've just opened a letter from Josephine and she's asked Freddy and me to go with her when she collects her CBE from the Queen in June. Of course, I'm on the phone in a trice telling her that we'd love to come.

Freddy is sitting at the table eating his toast, laughing at me and saying, loud enough for Josephine to hear, "She hasn't even asked me if I want to go," and it's true, I did sort of take it for granted. I've been so chuffed ever since we heard about her award, but it never occurred to me that she'd want us to be her guests. She's saying that as she's got no really close family left, her oldest friend is the person she most wants there. "And," she says with that giggle that takes me right back to 1912, "who better than my first employer to accompany her?"

I am dying to tell the family. They will be here later. Most of them only met her for the first time at my wedding to Freddy but they all know how proud I am of her. Josephine has just retired from the big hospital in Cheshire where she was Matron. We've managed to see a bit more of each other lately, which has been really nice.

And Harriet's baby is nearly due. She has never been one of these incredibly dedicated actresses and didn't want to put off having her children any longer. She says it will be good if she can pick up again but she is not pining for her career.

Last summer she was going up to London for an audition and she was sharing a carriage with this chap who looked a bit familiar and she got chatting to him. When she told him she was an actress, he said he did a bit of acting himself, so she told him not to lose heart and that he must persevere. "Even at my sort of level," she told him, "you can earn a decent living doing something you enjoy." As they arrived at Victoria she was saying goodbye to him when this woman pulled open the train door and said, "Sir Laurence, your car is waiting on the forecourt." Harriet claims to have been mortified but, as she's been telling the story ever since, I don't think she's lost any sleep over it.

I expect she'll try to go back later when the baby is a bit off-hand. As if your kids ever are. She is still taking private pupils for acting and public-speaking lessons so that will help them financially. Now Jack and Harriet are buying their house too I get the feeling that money is a bit tight sometimes, but they only ever give a mortgage on the husband's salary so Jack's must be enough. Freddy says that we could always help them out but I know Jack wouldn't have that.

Jack does look very tired lately. I wondered if it was going backwards and forwards to London every day but he says not. He goes on the Brighton Belle and eats his breakfast in the Pullman car and says by the time he's drinking his coffee they've arrived. Sounds very grand.

I can't help worrying about him and his work, though. I don't really understand what he does, but I do know that he had to sign the Official Secrets Act. He has to wear this yellow badge when he is at work and when it goes orange he has to rush off and shower and put on clean clothes and they burn all the ones he was wearing. William says that he must be working with radioactive materials but "they know what they are doing". Wish I was as sure.

William and Elsie and the children are coming down today and we are having a joint birthday party for him and me. Long time since we did that. It was Rosalind's idea because Freddy and I spent Christmas with his stepmother. Poor old girl is nearly ninety and *can't* get off her sofa now, but as she never did anyway I can't see it matters that much. Freddy says I'm heartless, but I know he doesn't mean it. He teases me sometimes by calling me Ellen. Life is so strange. I would never have believed there would be a time in my life when that would make me laugh. But on Freddy's lips it always does.

William and Elsie have caught us on the hop. What with all the excitement and phoning Josephine we are still in our dressing gowns and I can hear their car pulling up outside. We throw open the door and it's hugs all round and hoping the neighbours can't see us. Though, even if I say it myself, we do have very smart dressing gowns.

Rosalind is so grown up, eleven years old and nearly as tall as me. Even little Andrew is coming up to four. How quickly childhood goes. Though mercifully not as quickly as in our day. We leave them to make a cuppa and go up to dress but I can hear Jack and Harriet arriving and Elsie letting them in and all the noisy greetings going on. They always behave as if they haven't seen each other for months when they meet, even though the two girls chat on the phone every week.

"It's like the Viking invasion all over again," jokes Freddy. "Good job my family is not as sociable as yours." I point out that Harriet is actually his daughter and we have a giggly moment before joining them.

It's dinnertime and Thirza and Marcus have arrived to complete our party, and we are telling them about Josephine and going to the Palace. Thirza says we must make a date to go shopping for an outfit for me. What fun.

We are having a snacky dinner, just soup and sandwiches because we are going to have supper at a new restaurant on the seafront. I will never get used to all this luxury. I didn't realise just how well off Freddy was until after we were married. Sometimes, if his blindness makes him drop something and he gets irritated with himself, or he gets a bit frustrated and grumpy, I tell him that I only married him for his money. It always makes him snap out of it. He knows it's my upside-down way of letting him know how much I love him.

Such a nice evening. The food is lovely. English cooking at its best and the sort of varied menu you couldn't have dreamed of a few years ago. Even the vegetables cooked properly, not all slimy and done to death. Over coffee Marcus tells us that Margaret is hoping to stand for parliament at the next election. More excitement. Wouldn't it be great to have an MP in the family?

March, 1963

Harriet has just phoned to say can I come straightaway, the baby has started and she can't get hold of Jack. I've phoned for the ambulance but I am trying to get to the house before it arrives.

The ambulance is drawing up outside as I get there. I park the car all sticking out from the kerb and run over to them. Harriet is having four-minute pains and her waters have broken but the ambulance men are calm and capable and before we know it I've collected her bag and we're being rushed to the hospital. Harriet asks if I can stay with her and although they don't usually let anyone in the labour room who isn't staff they say that I can. I've left Freddy trying to get hold of Jack, but they never let the husbands come in until it's all over anyway.

Harriet is moaning and my stomach is churning in sympathy as she grips my hands. I swear I'm feeling the contractions with her and the sweat is running off us both.

Then – "There's the head," the midwife exclaims, and I'm shoved out of the way and it's all happening and suddenly there is this loud cry and…

There is something wrong. Everyone has gone quiet. I am pushing Harriet's hair off her face and wiping her forehead and she is holding out her hands to see her baby, and they are tucking it into blankets and looking at each other and not at Harriet and not at me.

"Go to sleep, dear, you can see him later," says the midwife.

Harriet struggles into a sitting position and demands, "Give me my baby," and the silence is a tangible presence in the room as they reluctantly pass her the swaddled figure.

Her hands are shaking as she kisses the top of his head – lots of dark hair, I'm thinking, but the silence is growing louder – and then she pulls the shawls off him and she makes a sound that is between a scream and a sob…oh no, oh God, how can you go along with this? – our baby has…our baby has no arms and no legs.

April, 1963

Little Frederick died two hours after he was born. Such a short life. They say it was the drug Harriet was given when she had all that morning sickness. Thalidomide or something. Meant to help. No one knew it had side effects. Like death.

Harriet has been offered a contract with the new

198

Royal Shakespeare Company and is starting work next week. Jack says he can't get her to talk about it, she is pretending it didn't happen. I know, for the moment, that it is the only way she can cope. I have no words that can help them through the horror of what has happened.

May, 1963

Thirza and I are meeting Harriet in Swan and Edgar's for a shopping expedition. I am so pleased she is coming with us. We are going to look for my Buckingham Palace outfit and it is the first time in too long that I have seen Harriet look quite animated. We have a gossip over coffee and cakes, just talking the way women do when they are on their own, and Harriet tells us about this new actor at the Royal Shakespeare Company who she says is going to be very famous.

"Looks, talent, and personality," she laughs, "what more does he need?"

At that moment this chap who looks a bit like Cary Grant comes up behind us and says, "Harriet, darling, I hope you are talking about me."

Harriet turns and throws her arms round him. "Gerald, meet Lillian, the best mum-in-law in the world, and her lovely sister Thirza," and we get up to shake hands, but he's kissing us without a by-your-leave, but it is somehow OK. Well, these theatricals, they are a bit different from the rest of us, I reckon.

He takes Harriet's hand and says, "Darling Harriet, you are looking better every day. See you tonight," and then he kisses us all again and disappears.

Thirza says, "Harriet, is he stuck on you?" and, to

my surprise, Harriet goes into the biggest fit of the giggles.

"Oh, Thirza, I don't think he much cares for young ladies."

I don't know what she means, and I am not sure that Thirza does either. I must ask Freddy when I get back.

I think I must have tried on twenty different things. None of them looks right. Or if Thirza and Harriet think they do, then I don't. Just as I am giving up hope of finding anything the assistant comes up with this pale blue and white suit in this new material called Courtelle, and it fits like a dream and I feel elegant even in my stockinged feet, and we all agree it is perfect. It is fifteen guineas and I nearly have a fit but Harriet reminds me that Freddy said I was to buy whatever I wanted and I take a deep breath and count out the money. I can't believe I am so extravagant. Thank heavens it doesn't take long to find me a hat, and I already have some shoes that will do and I've had enough anyway.

When I finally get home I go over the day with Freddy, and recognise that the very best thing was not finding the clothes, but seeing Harriet laughing again.

June, 1963

This is certainly a day to remember. Josephine looks extremely smart in her navy blue dress and jacket. Mind you, she is so nervous that before we go in she is shaking and I have to hold her hand very tightly. *I'm* quite nervous, and I've only come to watch.

When the Queen pins the award on her I think that I

200

am going to burst with pride. Josephine says that she felt enormous, because the Queen is so small. She says the Queen knew all about her work in both wars, as well as in the hospitals. After the ceremony, Freddy marches us along the Mall and we have tea at the Ritz.

Can you imagine? Tea at the Ritz! Me?

As Josephine says, "Who would ever have thought that we would all be here, together, on such an occasion?"

Freddy raises his teacup to her. "Who, indeed?"

November, 1963

We have just heard on the evening news that someone has shot President Kennedy. I burst into tears and then think, "Don't be daft, you didn't even know him." But then Jack and Harriet come round and they are as devastated as we are. In spite of all the bad things in the world he seemed like a kind of omen for good. We all felt as if we knew him.

The world seems a darker place tonight.

January, 1968

Thirza has been a bit off colour lately. I don't think there is a lot wrong, though I do hope I'm not tempting fate thinking that. Marcus says that she takes on too much, and I agree. She is always up to her eyes in some voluntary work or other. Freddy reckons she is just tired out. So we've dragged her off for a few days' holiday, and are celebrating my birthday with her and Marcus in Suffolk.

We are staying in this swish hotel and the idea is

that we pamper ourselves and don't lift a finger for five days. We shall visit the family, of course. We came up in Marcus's big car. Since that Dr Beeching axed the branch line it's the only way you can get around. But now Marcus has finally sold the taxi business he can be more flexible. Mind you, he seems to spend even more time on his council stuff, but then we all know that's where his heart is. And since Margaret became an MP Thirza says it's politics morning, noon and night in their house. She's ever so proud of them both really.

We are meeting Martha this morning at her little shop. Martha and Ivy have made quite a name for themselves in the fashion world. Cynthia says a tee shirt or scarf with "Miva" on it costs a small fortune. We are having coffee in the back room and Martha is making us laugh telling us about their accidental discovery of tie-dying when Ivy dropped a shirt they were making into some purple Dylon, and it came out ruined but interesting. Ivy is up in London today talking accessories with Mary Quant, would you believe? Thirza says, "Martha, I never saw you as an icon in the world of fashion," and we collapse into gales of laughter, and a customer who was browsing round the displays scurries off looking very startled and that starts us off again, of course.

Martha's granddaughter, Donald's daughter, Nerys, is coming to London to start her nursing training in September, and Martha asks if she has been in touch. She knew that Nerys was wondering if she could stay with Cynthia while she looks for a bed-sit of her own. Thirza says that Cynthia and Sebastian are delighted at the idea, especially as Nerys has volunteered to do the occasional baby-sit for them. Donald has already rung

Cynthia to discuss it and they suggested that she might like their attic room. Nerys said, "Yes, please!" so it's all settled.

Martha is very pleased, she says Nerys has grown into a lovely girl, and that living in Knightsbridge will be very handy for the hospital. I think she feels that Cynthia's presence will be some protection from the temptations of "swinging London" as well, though she doesn't say that.

Martha and Ivy are coming to the hotel for dinner with us tomorrow, and so are Collette and Frank, and Timmy and Lettie. My goodness, it will be just like old times – though rather better, I think. Dress designers, politicians, teachers, a scientist, even an actress in the family. The sky is obviously the limit nowadays. Wouldn't my brother Jack have been pleased?

It has been what Rosalind would call a "fabulous" evening. I don't think we have drawn breath. Talking about the past, the present and the future. Sometimes it is so good to relax with your own age group and share the memories and the hopes. I tell them about Rosalind, a self-proclaimed "hippie," alternating between her mini skirts and her caftans and her long-haired young men who all look the same with their droopy moustaches. Fortunately she doesn't seem to take any of them seriously as far as we can see, though she insists that she is deeply in love with John Lennon.

She went to the flower-power festival at Woburn Abbey last August and bumped into Timmy's boy Edward, who plays the drums in a rock group. Seems they had a high old time there. I wonder if Timmy and Lettie had any greater insight into what the papers call the "youth culture," but they seem as bemused as the rest of us.

Collette says that Gladys and her husband are thinking of having one of these music festivals on their farm in Shropshire. They were hit quite badly by the foot-and-mouth epidemic last year and think it might help them to recoup financially. It would all be too noisy for me, I think, but I must say I enjoy seeing these youngsters having a chance to be youngsters, even if I do worry sometimes about the drugs thing. You just have to hope they are too sensible to get caught up in that.

April, 1968

Great excitement in the family. Mr Wilson has offered Margaret a post in the Home Office. It's a big step-up for her. She thinks she owes her promotion to her heroine, Barbara Castle, who has been such a help to her during these last three years. It was all a bit daunting for poor Margaret to start with, everyone assumed she was someone's secretary, but Barbara found her trying to find the ladies' toilets on her first day and took her under her wing. Apparently there weren't any as no one had ever anticipated women MPs. Isn't that awful? But our Margaret is obviously making her mark. Thirza reckons that Marcus might explode with pride if he's not careful.

The phone is going and it's Jack. "Guess what, Mum!" he says. "Who do you think is coming to see us?"

Well, what a daft question. "Haile Selassie," I say.

"Don't be sarcastic, Mum. But it is someone

204

coming a long way."

"Oh, for heaven's sake, Jack, just tell me," I exclaim.

"It's Stan! Coming over with Lena to show her 'little ol' England' and the people he met over here in the war."

Well! It certainly is a surprise, but what a lovely one. We've kept up with them, always writing a long letter at Christmas, and I know Jack has written a bit more often, but I never expected them to come over. They are going to be here early this summer and will stay with Jack and Harriet for a few days before going up to Scotland to see Stan's friends up there. It will be so good to see Stan again.

June, 1968

Do you know, Stan has hardly changed at all. A bit greyer but I would have known him anywhere. Lena is such a nice person, really warm and friendly. Both their children are grown up and off-hand (isn't that incredible – it only feels like two minutes since we were looking at Stan and Lena's wedding pictures), and they decided if they didn't come over now they never would.

Freddy is getting on famously with Stan, they went for a long walk along the seafront together this morning. I think Freddy wanted to show off Goldie as well. He's been a bit down since we lost our darling Berry, but last month he was given Goldie and I can see that I am no longer first in his affections.

There is some cricket on in Preston Park this afternoon and Stan wants to go. He says it is a last attempt to understand the rules of this mysterious game. I tell him I gave up trying years ago.

We are all sitting in the park and Rosalind has come down with her latest beau, Nicholas. She wanted to meet this Canadian she's heard so much about. They've got a transistor radio playing softly between them on the grass and I hear Nicholas say, "Oh no!" We all turn toward him and he says "Robert Kennedy's been shot dead."

We are stunned. The world is going mad. First President Kennedy, then Malcolm X and Martin Luther King, now this. Stan puts his head in his hands. The cricket is going on, no one has heard yet. Stan comes and sits beside me.

"When is it going to end, Lillian?" he asks. "We thought that we were fighting for peace, but we go on ricocheting from disaster to disaster all over the world. Look at this awful business in Vietnam. What are the Americans doing there, for heaven's sake? Lena and I went to Paris, France, on our way over here and got caught up with hundreds of students rioting against the Vietnamese war. And just over the border from where we live there are race riots, and violence in the streets, and Ku Klux Klan crosses burning some nights. And now your Enoch Powell is trying to stir up that kind of hatred over here. It goes on and on and there doesn't seem any way for decent people to stop it."

The cricket comes to an abrupt halt. Over the speaker a voice announces the news of another Kennedy death. "Play will be resumed in half an hour," says the voice. We stay for the end of the game but the day is dimmed.

This evening Stan is insisting on treating us to a

fish-and-chip supper. He says that he can't bring Lena to a British seaside town without her partaking of this national delicacy. Hmmm. We warn him it can be a bit variable.

Freddy and I meet Jack and Harriet and Stan and Lena at a fish-and-chip shop in the Lanes, which has a good reputation. It is also one of the few to have its own restaurant, which is just as well because we've refused point blank to walk along the prom eating them out of newspaper. Stan has affectionate memories of eating chips this way during the war. My misgivings are happily wrong. The fish comes in a batter that is golden and delicious and the chips are crisp and not soggy. As Freddy says, our culinary pride, such as it is, is intact. Lena is properly impressed.

As we leave the restaurant three Americans come in, two men and a woman, talking loudly. Goldie, who is still under training, manages to take Freddy slightly off course and he bumps into one of them. As Freddy starts to apologise, the American, who is obviously a bit drunk, says in a very loud voice, "Damn British, think the world owes them a living." While the rest of us are standing dumbfounded at this rudeness Stan goes up to this chap and says, "Buddy, watch your mouth. I was here during the war. The whole world *does* owe this country a living."

The other man in the group is obviously as embarrassed as we are, but the woman comes forward and takes Freddy's hand. "I can only apologise for my companion," she says. "Would you be forgiving enough to have a drink with us?" Put like that it is a bit difficult to refuse, so we reluctantly troop back in.

The woman's name is Shirley, and her husband is

Maurice. The drunken one sulks at the end of the bar and we never do find out his name. But in the end we have an unexpectedly delightful conversation with Shirley and Maurice, who have come over to try to find out about what they call their roots. When we eventually part company, Maurice says, "Your Canadian friend is right. The whole world does owe you a living. Don't let anyone ever tell you differently."

As we are undressing for bed, Freddy says, "What an extraordinary day it has been." It sure has, as our new friends would say.

September 1968

We are spending the day in London with Sebastian and Cynthia and the children. Nerys arrived last week and it is so nice to see her again. We haven't seen her since Moira's wedding nearly ten years ago when she was still a child. She is such a stunning-looking girl, a bit like Twiggy with enormous eyes and long blonde hair. And legs that go on forever, which is a definite advantage in these mini skirts. I think they are getting shorter and shorter and I am very relieved that all the girls wear these thick matching tights underneath.

Natalie and Michael obviously adore her already. She's hoping to specialise in children's nursing eventually. Her brother David, who is nearly twenty now, went down the mines as soon as he left school of course. Never considered doing anything else but following in his dad's footsteps. Funny, the different ways the war changed people's lives. Donald would probably have been on a farm in Suffolk if it hadn't been for Mr Bevin and his schemes.

It's been a nice, but long, day and we are on our way back home. I've left the car at the station in Brighton. Freddy is really tired tonight. He gave himself such a bump the other day on the corner of the garden shed. He is so good at finding his way around it shook us both a bit. He's got a massive bruise on his temple, so at least it's come out. But he's quieter than usual. When I ask him if he's OK he says, "Are you suggesting that I'm normally noisy?"

"Well," I say, "certainly very bossy."

"Wasting my time with you, then," he says and we both have a giggle.

Soon be home.

January 1969

Freddy woke up early this morning and I could hear him taking Goldie round the garden. It's one of those lovely winter mornings. Thin but determined sunshine leaking through the curtains. I'm so glad we decided to live here in Brighton. Freddy laughs at me but I always feel that the sun is brighter and the air fresher here. He says that's because I'm married to him, and it's possible he's right, of course.

There is a frightful noise going on. I get out of bed and draw the curtain and Freddy is standing under the window making a noise like a seagull. At least, that's what I think it's meant to be. As soon as Goldie sees me she gives a bark and Freddy goes into a noisy rendition of "Happy Birthday" accompanied by Goldie. They've obviously been practising. I am so convulsed with laughter I can hardly get down the stairs to hug them both and receive a full-scale face wash from Goldie.

We all go into the kitchen and I switch the kettle on. When I've made the tea Freddy gives me a little wooden box. I open it to find a tiny silver Victorian locket, shaped like a heart with leaves engraved on it. I throw my arms round his neck and give him an enormous hug. "Oh, Freddy, it is so beautiful," I say. "I'll wear it every day." And so I shall.

Then Freddy says, "Lillian, my love, the rest of your birthday present is being delivered tomorrow. Today we have an appointment in London and then I will tell you what your other present is." What a secretive old romantic. He does love surprises. I meekly go and get dressed. I'm not going to spoil his fun, am I?

It appears we are going to Harley Street. "Freddy," I ask, "what is going on?"

"Just wait, Lillian, darling. Nothing but good, I promise you."

So I relax a bit. We go to this very posh house and I see from the brass plaque outside the door that we are visiting a consultant optician. Freddy seats me in the waiting room and disappears.

After a very long hour I am called in to the consulting room. The receptionist, who has been plying me with coffee and biscuits that I can't swallow, because by now I am so nervous, gives me a reassuring smile as she holds the door for me. Freddy is sitting with an enormous grin on his face and Goldie at his feet.

As I enter he gets up and holds out his hands to me. "Lillian," he says, "I have not dared to tell you in case it wasn't permanent. I have some peripheral vision back. I can see shapes again. And if you come very close, my darling, I can just make out your beautiful face."

I almost don't dare believe him.

But the consultant is nodding and smiling too. "A sort of minor miracle, Mrs Curtis," he says. "Freddy remembers sustaining a hefty knock to the head last autumn. It may be that blow has reactivated some nerve-ends that were dormant, rather than dead. I was told that Mr Curtis wanted a second opinion before telling you. But without doubt, there is some restoration of sight and no reason to believe that it is transitory. My colleague, who saw Mr Curtis at St Dunstan's, is of the same opinion. I am so happy for you both."

I do what I always do when I am overjoyed – I burst into tears. Dear God – what is it they say? – he giveth and he taketh – thank you. Thank you.

I'm itching to get home and tell the family. We are going round to Marcus and Thirza's tonight for supper but I can't wait. I'm on the phone to Thirza before I've got my coat off. She is almost as thrilled as I am. Then I hand the phone to Freddy and say, "See if you can catch Harriet. You must tell her yourself."

She's obviously there because he's on the phone for ages. Then he comes into the kitchen where I'm making us a pot of tea and puts his arms round me. "Guess what!" he says. "Had some news from Harriet, too. Just think, Lillian, I'll be able to see this baby."

It takes me a minute to understand and then I'm nearly in tears for the second time that day. I had given up hope of them trying again after little Frederick. I am almost overcome with all this happiness.

July, 1969

I sometimes think my birthday present from Freddy

211

this year was a double-edged sword. I never particularly wanted a television and there was certainly no point when Freddy couldn't see it. But now he can make out enough to follow what is going on and is well on the way to becoming an addict, I reckon. Hooked on *Coronation Street*, for heaven's sake. But it is so wonderful for him to be able to see it and for me to watch him enjoying it, how could I begrudge it him? And it does mean that I can go to the shops with Thirza or Harriet without feeling guilty at leaving Freddy alone.

Harriet's baby is due any day now, and all seems to be well. The midwife thinks she might be having twins but we're not banking on it. As long as we've got a healthy baby that is all any of us cares about. Jack had a stack of leave to use up because he's been working such long hours and he's taking it all in a big lump so he can be with her. That will give him a chance to get to know the baby, as well as to help Harriet.

Most fathers hardly seem to see their children except at weekends. I suppose I was lucky seeing so much of my father, it was different growing up on the farm. And Jimmy worked shifts, of course. But with Jack commuting to London, the baby will probably be in bed when he gets home, so this time is precious. It's a pity dads don't have a sort of "paternity" leave when their children are born, but I don't suppose that will ever happen. Though they do talk of career women having maternity leave one day. I don't know how that would work out.

We are planning to stay up tonight and I think the television might finally come into its own. They are expecting these three Americans to land on the moon.

Can you imagine that? I can't quite believe it will happen but I don't want to miss it if it does – and both Jack and William say it will.

It was incredible. Almost unbelievable. And absolutely awe-inspiring. They did it. They really did it. Neil Armstrong came out first, then Buzz Aldrin joined him, and they were picking up stones and stuff and then they planted the American flag. On the moon! Actually up there, walking on the moon. Neil Armstrong said, "One small step for man, one giant leap for mankind."

William and Elsie had let Andrew stay up to watch. The phone went at 4.30 in the morning and it was our excited grandson. "Nana, Nana, did you and Freddy see?" I was so glad I was able to say yes. Perhaps it was a good birthday present after all.

August, 1969

It's twins and they are fine and beautiful and healthy – and oh I am so relieved! I know there was no reason for anything to go wrong but just the same... They've both got lots of dark curly hair and *very* good lungs. They are going to call them James (which I am so touched by – Jimmy would be delighted) and Sarah. Twins. What fun!

And we heard today that Rosalind has won a place at Oxford. What a year this is turning out to be.

January, 1974

Margaret rang today to say that she's been selected to stand as a candidate in the next general election.

213

She's a glutton for punishment, I reckon. But I do admire her persistence. When she lost her seat last time I must say I thought that would be that. Especially as since then she's made such a name for herself on the radio and the television talking about politics. She's carved out a real career as a freelance political journalist and she's got a weekly column in the *Daily Mirror* now as well. The press have dubbed her "the glamorous guru," which she thinks is a hoot. She's been doing a lot of work for CND as well. But I suppose she feels parliament is still where the most influence is.

Freddy jokes that he had no idea he was marrying into a family of lefties and I suppose in a way that's what has happened. But, as I say to him, my generation didn't think so much about all this stuff, we just took it for granted we'd go and be servants to people like him. If one good thing came out of two world wars it was that the working classes learnt they were worth something. Mind you, it's really old fashioned to talk about the working classes now. We are all supposed to be middle class, whatever that means.

Freddy and I are going to see *The Sting* tonight. It is such a treat to be able to go to the cinema again. It has all come up quite new to Freddy as when he lost his sight he had never seen a film. Not many cinemas in 1917. He's given me a beautiful cashmere jumper for my birthday, it's in a soft green colour, and I shall wear it tonight.

We have had such an enjoyable evening. What a clever film. All those ragtime tunes we both remember so well, and a good story. We were well and truly fooled at the end. "All that *and* those two handsome young men," I remark when we get home.

"How dare you notice that, wench!" he answers, and then he gives me an enormous hug. I must say, getting to seventy-four doesn't feel anything like as old as I thought it would.

April, 1974

I am completely exhausted. Jack and Harriet are here with the twins today. They are wonderful, but *such* hard work. I don't know how Harriet manages. They are just into everything. Poor old Goldie is so good with them, she lets them roll all over her and brush her, and then when she's had enough she goes and sits behind Freddy. It is a lovely sunny day so I suggest we take them out. Self-defence, really, it's always easier to keep them amused that way. We walk up to Dyke Road Park and go into the little café there. Amazing how ice cream can magic up some peace. Even if it only for five minutes.

The grown-ups are dying to talk about Margaret's programme on the television last night. She was discussing Mr Wilson's new cabinet and she did interviews with Denis Healey and Anthony Wedgwood Benn. Then she had Jeremy Thorpe on, talking about why the Liberals wouldn't go for the coalition with the Conservatives that Edward Heath suggested before the election. It was all so interesting. Margaret seems to be able to get so much out of them. More, you sometimes think, than they really intended to say.

We were all so disappointed for her when she didn't get elected, but Jack reckons that she is such an excellent political journalist and commentator that she has more influence than she would have in parliament. I think he is probably right. It might be different if we could hear some of the debates on the wireless, but although they keep talking about doing that, it just doesn't seem likely to happen. Margaret reckons it's because the MPs are afraid the House of Commons would sound like an unruly bear garden. "Because that's what it is most of the time," she says. Obviously a miracle that anything is ever achieved.

Everyone agrees that Mr Wilson is going to have to call another election soon as he hasn't got a proper majority. Still, he has put an end to the miners' strike by paying them proper wages. I think some of these trade unions get a bit above themselves and ask for too much, but Nerys told us that the conditions the miners live in would not be tolerated down here in the South. I don't think you can pay miners too much for what they do.

Nerys has just got engaged to her childhood sweetheart, Ivor. She's promised to bring him down to meet us all soon. He's a miner, of course, all the men in her village seem to be. She started working as a district nurse last month and she is loving it. She always said she was going to specialise in children's nursing but Sebastian says that Natalie and Michael cured her of that. I think he's only joking!

August, 1974

It seems we have a national treasure in the family. Well, that was how someone described Margaret on the wireless the other day. "She makes politics accessible and even compulsive." There you go. Marcus is quoting

216

it to everyone. A very proud dad. Quite right, too.

Margaret's been covering that awful Watergate business from America and she was the first with the news of Nixon's resignation. Never did understand how they could have elected him, he always looked shady. Marcus says that privately she thinks this Gerald Ford is what she calls a non-event, though. Let's hope that at least he is an honest non-event.

Rosalind is coming to stay with us for a while. She is going to spend what she calls the long vac working in an animal sanctuary near Patcham. I had no idea that training to be a vet would take so long. She has always loved animals and it does seem the perfect career for her but it's a good job that William and Elsie can afford to keep her at college.

I suppose vets have to do so much studying because the animals can't tell you where it hurts, can they? And there are so many different kinds to cope with when you think about it – everything from birds to elephants. Not that we have many elephants round here.

She told me on the phone that she had something she needed to discuss with me. "I do hope it won't make it difficult for me to stay with you, Gran." I am consumed with curiosity. Freddy says she's probably pregnant by an African pygmy and is going to ask us to bring up the baby. I sometimes wonder about his sense of humour...

Definitely *not* an African pygmy, though as I said to Freddy, I am sure they are charming people. Well, I need to keep him in order, don't I? No, Rosalind's big secret is that she doesn't eat meat anymore. "Not," she tells me, "that I'm a vegetarian, because I do eat fish sometimes. It's just that ever since I was about ten when I try to eat meat it turns into sheep or cows or pigs in my mind. Then I can't seem to swallow it. I think it is because I'm so silly about animals, they are like people to me."

I understand absolutely, of course. I know if we lived in a place where they eat dogs or cats I'd find that impossible, so it's not hard to make the jump. The thing is, if you say you don't eat meat people think you go about in plastic sandals waving a large banner, and as she says, she doesn't mind other people eating meat, it's just that *she* can't. I think Freddy is quite relieved that he doesn't have to forsake his roast beef, but I'm already thinking I shall quite enjoy a new cooking challenge. Might even end up a veggie myself.

September, 1974

Freddy is threatening to go and live in the greenhouse. We have been invaded. Andrew rang to say could he come down for a few days. I checked that William and Elsie were happy about it, after all he is only fourteen, but he had already asked them and got the go-ahead to ask us. He was planning to cycle down by himself but the A27 is quite busy so I suggested he came with Cynthia's Michael. Michael is that bit older than Andrew and a lot more sensible, I reckon. And I know they are very good friends.

Today they turned up, worn out from the ride, and Natalie is with them as well. A last-minute decision, they say, and Cynthia was going to ring us. I expect we were in the garden and didn't hear the phone. Truth to tell, we don't mind a bit as they are all smashing kids, but we weren't quite prepared for the noise factor. They've all got electric guitars strapped onto the bikes and it appears they are a group. They call themselves Dawn till Dusk and are hoping to become pop stars in about three weeks' time.

Freddy says he thinks it may take a little longer. Rosalind says it's quieter at the sanctuary where there are twenty-four dogs and as many cats as well as the odd donkey and parrot. I have a strong feeling she may be right. They've all gone to a beach party tonight and we've promised to go down later and see the bonfire. For all the hassle, they make me feel quite young again.

December, 1974

We are having a special family Christmas. I'm not sure who had the idea in the first place but it was such a good one. We've hired a house in the Cotswolds big enough for the entire family. William and Elsie are here with Andrew, and Rosalind is here with Steve, her latest beau. Jack and Harriet arrived just now with the twins, and Thirza and Marcus managed to get here before everyone and have been making up beds and stuff. Cynthia and Sebastian are coming tomorrow with Natalie and Michael, and Margaret is getting here on Christmas Eve with a mysterious someone. She's always been so determined to succeed in her career there haven't been many someones, so we are all madly curious and have got our fingers crossed he'll be extremely nice and a bit more permanent than the others have been. As Freddy says, "It's part of the natural order for people to be in pairs." I couldn't agree more, I tell him affectionately.

219

Collette and Frank are spending Christmas with Gladys and her family. Collette is so excited. It will be Billy's first Christmas at home for years, as he's out of the army now. Billy's eldest, Phil, will be following in his dad's footsteps, and going into the army next year, so heaven only knows when they'll all be together again. We shall get to see them, though, as us retired ones, as Marcus puts it, are staying on here till the New Year and Collette and Frank are coming to join us for that. And Martha and Ivy are coming, and Ivy's friend Paula. Donald and Angarhad are staying in Wales with her family, but Nerys and Ivor will be here after Boxing Day.

Freddy is poking the enormous wood fire and sending sparks all over the place. He keeps saying, "A real Dickensian Christmas, egad!" The twins are already examining the boxes of tree decorations Thirza and I have both brought with us, but Andrew is telling them very firmly that tree decorating has to wait until everyone is here. We have brought so much food with us we could feed an army, but looking at the size of the range there is not going to be a problem. It reminds me a bit of Christmas in the war, though we are certainly not economising now. No carrots in these Christmas puddings, thank heavens.

I think this must be one of the best Christmases ever. New Year's Eve today and our last day here. We have eaten and drunk and laughed and played games and oohed and aahed over our presents. We filled up the little village church at the midnight service, and sang carols as we walked home, and, incredibly, snow fell. The children were enraptured and Natalie and the

220

boys pretended for the twins that they could see Santa Claus on his sledge. James and Sarah's eyes were like saucers and nearly popping out of their heads as they searched the sky for Santa. Then, very high up, a plane went over with the moonlight catching its wings and they screamed, "Look, look, we can see him too!" It was a truly magical moment.

Then, when we got back to the house, we let Goldie out in the snow. She dashed round and round like a maniac, then she rolled over and over in it. Then she jumped up and down trying to catch the flakes. She was obviously captivated by this wonderful white world. We were all aching with laughter at her antics by the time we got her back in. The children insisted on hanging her stocking up over her bed but they had put some dog-chocs in it and she blotted her copybook by eating them and then the whole stocking during the night. Ah well. She didn't even look repentant. Or ill, fortunately.

On Christmas Day we were "entertained" by Dawn till Dusk. Mind you, they are improving in spite of what Freddy says. And when the youngsters were finally in bed we sat round the fire and indulged in reminiscences. Of course.

And the big news – Margaret's 'someone' is called Richard and she married him in America last week after a whirlwind courtship. I think Thirza was a bit stunned (well, so were we all) but she and Marcus rallied quickly. He seems lovely, an American divorcé with two children. Margaret says she has met them and they are charming. He's a writer, apparently quite a successful one. Margaret says they are going to live in both places, here and America. Atlantic commuters. I can hardly imagine doing that.

We are agreed we shall try to do this again next year at Christmas. It would be nice to think we shall. But I have reached an age where I know that you must live in the present. Who knows what this next year will bring us all?

January, 1976

I never thought that I would miss Martha so much. When I think about it, I'd known her all my life and sort of took it for granted that she would always be around. When we were small we used to hide in the haystacks together at harvest and listen to the grown-ups talking. Not that they ever said much, it was just that it felt deliciously wicked to be eavesdropping. A shared secret.

Her family was even poorer than ours. She was so impressed when Father made us a table and we sat round it for meals. Mother used to invite her in sometimes so that she could sit at the table with us and have a piece of bread and dripping. She loved that. She asked Thirza and me if she could be our pretend sister, and we laughed and said yes, but now I realise that it meant a lot to her and I'm so glad that we did say yes.

When she married Father I suppose I had mixed feelings, after all she was younger than me. But she made him and my brothers very happy. In fact, everyone she touched seemed to gain from knowing her. When she died so suddenly last year there were obituaries in most of the national papers for this woman "who had so much influence on modern fashion."

Dear, lovely Martha, I hope you are in heaven

roaring with laughter at that label just as you did down here.

April, 1976

Freddy has been forced to eat his words. Dawn till Dusk are getting what they call gigs, so often that they are actually making some money. We are staying with William and Elsie for a few days and Andrew is full of it. Collette's granddaughter, Moira's eldest, Samantha, is their singer. Collette had told me she was making quite a name for herself locally and she met up with the other three when she came down to London for an audition. She stayed with Cynthia – as Freddy says, "Doesn't everyone?" – and, although she didn't get the record contract she was after, they asked her to do a club date with them and apparently it went really well. They've got several more paid bookings, which Andrew says "Can't be bad, Gran." Privately, Elsie thinks it's all a flash in the pan, but better to let them try than spend the rest of their lives wondering what might have been. Quite right, too.

Rosalind and Steve are here for the day. It's good to see them both. They are working for the same veterinary practice in Bromley now and hoping to start up on their own soon. They are looking at the possibility of buying a house large enough to convert some of it into a surgery, but obviously they need to be very careful about where they go. No point in looking at places where there is already an established vet.

Rosalind's speciality is small domestic animals, especially cats and dogs, and Steve's is more agricultural, cattle and horses and large animals, so it looks as if a semi-rural practice would suit them. At the moment they are looking in East Kent, around Canterbury, as house prices are not quite so high there. They think they may have found a village that fits the bill. I hope they will be careful. I do worry about the amount of debt these youngsters take on.

One of William's neighbours popped in just now to ask if he could borrow their lawn mower. He said that he got his out for the first time this year and it seized up solidly. While William was getting it out, I was surprised to hear Rosalind introduce Steve as her "partner."

"I didn't realise that you had already started a business," I say.

Rosalind laughs, but I notice that she's not looking me in the eye the way she usually does. "No, Gran, I meant my life partner."

I take a moment to digest this and then have to tell her that I haven't a clue what she means. "Well," she says, and I see her look at Elsie as if she will come out with something that will clarify things for me, but Elsie is resolutely looking the other way. Then the penny drops.

"You mean that you are like these pop stars? Living in sin?"

"Oh, Gran, no, it's not a sin, it's just that we don't really believe that a bit of paper will make any difference to us, and we love each other and want to be together."

Freddy has been listening with great interest. "It's not the bit of paper," he says, "it's the promises you make to each other. And the commitment which stops you running off the first time living with another person gets difficult. Which, believe me, sooner or later it always does." Hmmm. This is turning out to be an interesting conversation. I'll take that one up with him later.

Then Steve cuts in: "Freddy, believe me, there is no greater commitment than a joint mortgage." Do you know, I hadn't thought of it like that. They are right, of course, and we tell them so. But I'm still glad I come from a time when you stood in front of your friends and family and swore to try and stay together forever. But it's their decision and I'll have to get used to it, I suppose.

Later, Rosalind and I go for a wander round the garden and she asks if I am shocked. I find that I am not, but: "Make sure that this is really what you want, Rosalind," I tell her, "and if it is not don't be afraid to tell Steve." Something in her face tells me I may have rung a bell somewhere. And, seeing as I seem to be in the mood for laying down the law, I add: "And promise me that you will discuss it very carefully again before you start a family. Children need to feel secure."

She puts her arms round me and gives me a big kiss. "I promise," she says. And we go indoors.

That song keeps going through my head – "Times they are a-changing". Indeed they are.

August, 1976

It is so incredibly hot. I can never remember anything like this. Everywhere the grass is brown and great cracks are appearing in the earth. We are all supposed to bath with a friend, not flush the toilet too often, never water the garden and a clean car makes you

225

socially unacceptable. I gather that Andrew is very keen on the idea of bathing with a friend, especially a young and nubile female one. Elsie says that as far as she is aware there have been no volunteers yet. But he lives in hope.

As always, there are the Jonahs who are swearing it will never rain again. The newly created Minister for Drought announced that they would probably have to introduce permanent water rationing before Christmas. Ridiculous, I reckon, for heaven's sake, this is England. Whatever would we talk about if there were no more rain?

I can't help feeling a bit worried about Marcus. He's put on a fair amount of weight lately with all these official dinners and I am quite shocked at how puffed out he gets. They came with us for a walk over the Downs with Goldie last weekend and he couldn't make it up the hills, had to sit and wait for us to get back. I didn't think it was entirely due to the heat, either, though I'm sure that didn't help. He's younger than Freddy, too. Thirza made light of it, but later she told me she's been trying to get him to see a doctor.

September, 1976

I knew it. It's been raining non-stop for a week. Feel like ringing the Minister of Drought and saying told you so, but I expect he's just lost his job anyway.

January 1979

We went up to Thirza's today and I was stunned at the chaos everywhere in London. It's bad enough down in Brighton, but all these strikes have made a disgusting mess here. There is rubbish wherever you look on the streets because the dustmen aren't working. We had a terrible job finding a garage that had any petrol – at one point I thought we were going to be stranded. Someone said that some gravediggers out Dartford way had refused to dig graves and bodies were piling up over there. That is just going too far. How could they do that? I don't understand half of what it's about but I'm sure that once again it comes down to money.

Margaret did a really good programme on the radio. She reckons that as soon as a Labour government gets in the unions start asking for the earth and inevitably the government falls. She thinks Mr Callaghan is on his way out and I must say I agree. The papers are calling this the "winter of discontent." It is so awful that the very people who should be backing the government are probably going to finish it off. Incredibly short-sighted.

I'm glad Thirza has decided to sell up. The Norwood house is much too big for her to be rattling around in on her own. I think she was right to wait a bit after she lost Marcus, before making any decisions, but it's been nearly eighteen months now and she seems quite sure. It's worked out for the best, with Sebastian retiring this year and wanting to move out of London. With what they get for the two houses they will be able to afford something really nice in Brighton and the granny annexe is an excellent idea. It will be good to have her so close again.

May, 1979

Margaret Thatcher won the election. I suppose it

was inevitable. There is a bit of me that is delighted to see a woman as Prime Minister. I certainly never thought it would happen in my lifetime. But I am sad to see the Tories back in power. William says that Mr Callaghan only lasted so long because of the Lib-Lab pact, so it wasn't a real Labour government anyway.

It all seems to have gone wrong somewhere. Mr Attlee did so much for us all and in such difficult times. Trying to put this country back on its feet while also supporting the very people we'd defeated. But we couldn't see them starve to death, could we? Most of them are just people like us, though Sebastian always says that a lot of them were expert at turning a blind eye while the Nazis were murdering millions of their fellow-citizens.

And, of course, we had to start paying back that enormous debt to America the minute the war was over. They lent us the money so that we could go on fighting the war, and then helped to make getting back to normal really difficult by demanding repayment while our country was still reeling. Margaret says that, with the interest, it will be 2006 before it's all paid back. I think that is dreadful. If we hadn't beaten Hitler they would have had to fight him all by themselves.

But even with all that to deal with, we still have the National Health Service, and decent schools for everyone, and we all live so much better now. A lot of that seems to me to be owed to socialism, but Freddy says it would have happened anyway. I don't know. Perhaps this Mrs Thatcher will be all right. I do hope so.

I am so proud of my family. You are always hearing

how unruly youngsters are and that there is no discipline, and that they are all punk rockers, whatever *they* are. Well, James and Sarah have been doing all sorts of odd jobs, and they have rounded up a lot of their school friends to help them. All to make money to send to those poor people in Uganda. That dreadful, murdering Idi Amin has finally been overthrown but of course the country has been left in a dreadful state.

Harriet told Elsie what they were doing and Andrew announced that he wanted to do something as well. He persuaded Natalie and Mike to re-form Dawn till Dusk, which was doing quite well as a support group until they decided they wanted to concentrate on their proper careers. And Samantha, who is making a bit of a name for herself – she was on the television the other night – agreed to help.

When word got around about that, they got quite a lot of publicity, and one of the national newspapers ran a story about it, which was very exciting. Pictures of them all, even James and Sarah, as the instigators, so to speak. Anyway, the upshot is that between them they have raised nearly £1,000! They sent the cheque off last week and James has just rung to tell us that they heard today that their money is buying two cows and the equipment to start digging a well, as well as planting a coconut grove in one village. Very essential things in this devastated country. Freddy and I are unapologetically puffed up with pride in our lovely, generous, grandchildren.

August, 1979

We are up in Oxford Street today on a sort of

shopping expedition. Nothing we can't get in Brighton really, but Harriet gave us tickets for the play at the National Theatre, *Amadeus*, which has had wonderful reviews. She says it is time we had a look at our National Theatre as it's been open for nearly four years and we've been too lazy to make the effort until now. She's right, of course, and we decided to make a day of it. So here we are wandering round Selfridge's looking at all sorts of grand things that we neither need nor want. But it's all quite interesting. Freddy wants us to go down to the basement where all the radios and televisions are, so we take the lift down. He still has difficulty negotiating some steps.

As we come out of the lift I can see an enormous television and on the screen are people in tears. We stop to watch as it looks like a trailer for a film. But – oh, no. Oh, no. They are carrying a body on a stretcher. This is no film. A voice is saying that it is Lord Mountbatten and he has been blown up on his boat. Two teenagers with him – dead. And others badly wounded. We stand frozen to the spot.

He was so well loved. A good man, by all accounts. The IRA, they are saying. How can this make people think they might have a case? How can killing children and old men achieve anything? A crowd has gathered round us watching the television. I hold Freddy's hand tightly. A man's voice behind us says, "God have mercy on his soul." Another voice adds: "And may the bastards who did this rot in hell."

September, 1979

Our darling Goldie has to be put to sleep today. Her

230

back legs have been unsteady for a while. We know that she has reached a good age, but that doesn't make it any easier. We've asked Rosalind to come and do it. Goldie knows her so well, she isn't at all upset or frightened. She lies on her bed with her doggy smile on her face and Freddy and I are holding her front paws. Steve digs her grave at the bottom of the garden. We are planning to plant a golden rose on it. Soon. When we are strong enough.

Steve and Rosalind tactfully drive off and leave us to have a good cry together. We are going to miss her terribly. Freddy doesn't need a guide dog anymore and we don't know if we should have another one at our age. We just know that there is already this big Goldie-shaped hole in our lives.

But as Freddy says: "It was a good way to go, Lillian. I shan't mind if I can do it with you holding my hand and a smile on my face."

January, 1981

A week after my birthday last year the Greek cargo ship, Athina B, washed up on the beach and it was such a dramatic start to the year. Practically the entire population of Brighton turned out to see her once we knew the crew were safe. Standing shivering and looking up at that enormous hull made you appreciate the fantastic job our lifeboat crews do.

The extra bonus for me was that it made the family forget that I had reached eighty. And I thought that my father was ancient when he was half my age. I suppose it's all a question of perspective. Freddy, of course, is even older than me. We tell the children that we are going to make it to the Queen's telegram. Mind you, our children are getting on a bit themselves. Freddy often jokes that they are actually older than us, which causes some people to do a double take. Not everyone appreciates his sense of humour.

But, with my fingers crossed, we *are* blessed with extraordinary good health. A combination of Dr Brighton's air and having to walk Rufus every day, we reckon. When Rosalind found him for us we thought that having a six-year-old dog would mean he had quietened down. Huh. I think her estimate of his age may be a bit generous. But he has filled a large vacuum in our lives as well as keeping us fit. He is of very dubious origin but reminds me a little of Tess. Found tied to some railings in Ashford. He has already had two homes where he didn't settle. Or perhaps the people didn't have enough time and space for him. All he really needed was a garden big enough to chase a ball in and work off some of his energy. And to be spoilt rotten. So now he is ours. "For our sins," blusters Freddy, who adores him.

March, 1981

Harriet has got a part in a new soap opera and she is ecstatic. She has been teaching with various children's drama groups for some time now and tells us that you could have knocked her down with a feather when her agent rang and told her she'd been invited to audition. She didn't want to tell us until she knew she'd got the part. She's playing the head nurse in the accident and emergency department of a big hospital. It means that she will have to commute backwards and forwards to

London, but Jack's been doing that for years and at least now they can go together.

The twins are nearly twelve (incredibly) and Harriet has always had a knack of finding excellent au pairs, largely because she treats them so well, I think. So it should all be manageable. And of course, we can always help out if there is a problem with James and Sarah. She starts work next month and the first episode goes out in September. My goodness, it is *so* exciting. Our Harriet a telly star!

Nerys and Ivor are down to stay for a few days. They are hoping this new deal for the miners will put paid to the strikes. Mrs Thatcher's U-turn, the papers are calling it. They are such a delightful couple. Nerys says her dad only works in the office now. Martha would have been pleased to hear that, as she never really got used to him being down the mines.

Nerys is wearing a boiler suit. It is bright pink and in a kind of silk. Freddy says it reminds him of Churchill, but she looks wonderful in it. It's one of Ivy's designs, and is apparently selling like hot cakes. Ivy has taken Paula into partnership with her now and they do seem to produce some stunning clothes together. I say that I think it's a pity Ivy has never married and after a bit of a silence Nerys says, "I think she's quite happy as she is, Auntie Lillian." Well, of course she is. I just like to see people in pairs.

July, 1981

Prince Charles is marrying that pretty Lady Di today. We walked Rufus early, made piles of sandwiches, and sat in front of the television to watch.

233

It was lovely. She looks like such a nice girl. I can't help feeling he's a bit old for her, after all, she's still not much more than a child. Elsie says she's just a "brood mare" and as long as she produces an heir to the throne the royals will make sure she's inconspicuous and does as she is told. It doesn't sound much of a life put like that, so I hope she is wrong.

But I do enjoy all the ceremony and pomp and music and the sheer grandeur of it all. You don't have to be a royalist to know that we do this better than anyone else in the world. We needed a bit of cheering up after this awful year – riots in Brixton, President Reagan shot, the Pope shot, all this trouble in Ireland. The world certainly doesn't get any more tolerant.

September, 1981

First episode of *Call Ambulance 999* goes out tonight and we are round at Jack and Harriet's to watch it with them. The critics have already reviewed it and are being enthusiastic and Harriet is coming in for a lot of praise. I expect we are prejudiced but we think it is brilliant. James and Sarah are so excited. Sarah gives Harriet a page from her exercise book and asks her to sign her name on every line.

"Whatever for?" asks Harriet.

"So we can sell your autograph at school tomorrow, of course," says James. Jack is trying so hard not to laugh he has to go outside, leaving poor Harriet to remonstrate with these two young entrepreneurs.

November, 1981

Josephine and I are having what seems to have become our annual meeting today. It's always a big day out, lunch at Fortnum and Mason's and a good old gossip. Josephine invariably chooses somewhere posh because she says it reminds her of how far we have come. I tell her that I think I have only got there because I married the boss, so to speak. Freddy has opted out. Says it's a girls' day out and he'll keep Rufus company. Girls indeed! Actually, Josephine is finally starting to look her age, but she is probably thinking the same about me.

As usual, we choose a table right at the back where it is a bit quiet and try to condense our year's events into a couple of hours. We are just debating whether we can possibly manage a second coffee each when I glance over and spot Harriet sitting on the other side of the restaurant. I'm about to get up and wave when something stops me. She's with that chap who plays the married doctor that she secretly loves.

He is holding her hands across the table and I watch, quite unable to look away. Josephine follows my gaze. "Ah," she says, "Lillian, don't look." She's right. I tear my eyes away. Josephine gathers up her bag and hands me mine. "Come on, we are going."

She settles our bill and fetches our coats and then we leave through the rear exit so we don't have to go past Harriet. I find that I am shaking. Josephine steers me through the shop and out into Oxford Street, just beginning to warm up for Christmas.

"I expect I'm making too much of it," I say, trying to laugh at myself. "These luvvies!"

Josephine doesn't say anything for a minute. Then: "We didn't see anything, Lillian. Whatever was going

235

on there, we didn't see it."

No, we didn't. Oh, how I wish I hadn't. Don't let Jack find out. Or Freddy. Oh, Harriet, my lovely Harriet, how could you?

December, 1981

Elsie took some of her pupils up to see a play the Royal Shakespeare Company are doing at the Aldwych, and she thought it was so special she's insisting on taking the family as a Christmas treat. Apparently it is very difficult to get tickets but Harriet managed to wangle some for us. It's such a long time since we've all been out together – William and Elsie and Jack and Harriet and the twins.

Freddy nearly had a fit when he learnt the play is nine hours long but he recovered slightly when he heard that there was a two-hour interval to eat in. We are going to leave Rufus with Cynthia for the day, he likes going there. We are all going up on the train together. It feels a bit like a Sunday-school outing. I find I keep watching Harriet with Jack but she doesn't seem any different. Perhaps I imagined the whole thing…

The play is quite extraordinary. No wonder it's a sell-out. It's an adaptation of Charles Dickens's Nicholas Nickleby. I remember my brother Jack reading it to me when I was a girl and I have always loved it. The music is haunting and evocative, and although there is no scenery there is this big revolving platform on the stage that the actors seem to be able to turn into anything they fancy at the drop of a hat.

By the interval we have laughed and cried so much

I am exhausted and, as my Freddy says, definitely in need of sustenance. We stagger over to one of the new cafés in Covent Garden. Last time I was here it was a fruit and vegetable market and I am very impressed with all the smart little shops. Not so impressed when I look at some of the prices, though.

Harriet knows the actor who is playing Nicholas, Roger Rees, who she says is charming and actually didn't want to take the part because he thought he was too old, but we all agree he is perfect. As, indeed, is every single one of the actors, most of whom are playing several parts. When we get back to the theatre, the actors are mingling with the audience as a lot of the action takes place in the auditorium.

Suddenly the play starts again. I didn't know that the theatre could be as exciting as this. We all yell and boo and call out as if we are part of the play as we are plunged back into Nicholas's story. At the end, and believe me there is not a dry eye in the house, even Freddy agrees it didn't seem a minute too long.

Part Five: The Final Years

January, 1983

My boys came over today, bless them. Both took the day off work to be with their mum. We walked up to the park with Rufus, and Jack had a bit of a rough and tumble with him and his ball, which he adores. The twins are so good at coming over after school and playing with him. Jack says they love doing it, and I think they really do, so I don't have to feel guilty. Mind you he really has calmed down a bit at last. About time too.

I think he misses his dad. Well, of course he does. We both do. More than anyone will ever know. Or perhaps they do. The trouble with getting old is that all the people that you love keep dying off. Collette gone, too. Poor Frank, alone again. Unique, sparky Collette. Who went from being the cockney sparrow with the fake French accent to a beloved sister. Still, at least she didn't have to see her grandson come home burnt and disfigured after that awful Falklands War. She had more than her share of tragedies to cope with, I reckon. I'm glad she was spared that one.

Dear, dear Freddy, who transformed my life so totally. Darling husband and friend. Who was able to make me laugh right up to the end. We talked a lot about religion and God and all that, especially after we knew he'd got cancer.

Freddy reckoned that God didn't want much to do with organised religion, he thought that it just caused a lot of trouble. And I've often thought that if I'd been born somewhere else I'd have grown up being a Moslem, or a Buddhist, or whatever. It sort of depends where you are. This is supposed to be a Christian country but all the different churches are always going on as if they are the only ones that know anything. All claiming to have a special hotline.

I think I do believe in God, but that may be because I can't bear to think that this is all there is and I'll never see Jimmy or Freddy again. But if He is up there, there's a lot of stuff I'd like to ask Him about. If I was God, I'd make people happy.

Thirza is coming over this evening with Sebastian. Cynthia is at some fund-raising do for the Greenham Common women. Thirza says she and I should go there for a few days and show solidarity. I know she is right but…

I've told her that I might go if it's a hot summer, but not in this weather. No point going and then getting ill, they don't need a couple of sick old girls on their hands. It'd take me out of myself, anyway, even if it doesn't do much good. Perhaps I'll turn into an elderly militant.

Oh, Freddy, I do miss you. So much.

March, 1983

Thirza is moving in with me today. Sebastian and Cynthia suggested that I come and live in their granny annexe with her, but with both of us living there, there wouldn't have been room to swing a cat and Thirza has two of those, Sophie and Darcy. We agreed that it was better this way round.

I didn't want to move from here anyway. I love this house and it has so many happy memories. Sea View. We never did change the name, incongruous though it is. We often discussed it but couldn't agree on an alternative. We usually outdid each other in coming up with sillier and sillier suggestions until we were worn out with laughing and then it got shelved again. It's Sea View forever now as far as I am concerned.

Thirza is bringing various pieces of her own furniture over. Of course I understand her wanting that, and I've given some of mine away to make room. We've decided to leave Sebastian organising everything and go out to lunch. Rufus is with the twins and having a lovely day, I expect. We'll fetch the cats when the removal men have gone. They know Rufus well from all the times Freddy and I left him over there, so they are good friends already. They've always got on well, though the cats do boss Rufus about a bit.

It'll be funny to be living with my baby sister again. Just like old times.

April, 1983

We are at Greenham as part of the human-chain protest. When Thirza told me that ninety-two-year-old Lord Brockway was going I couldn't make any more excuses. I have to say that I am very glad that I came. Julie Christie is here, and Bruce Kent, and thousands and thousands of people who think with us that nuclear weapons are terrible and wrong. After all, if we are not going to use them, why have them? We are spending the night here and going back tomorrow. I have got so many layers of clothes on I think I must look like the Michelin Man.

We are on our way home. Thirza is driving – she says that I'm getting erratic and she is probably right. I shall be glad to get in a hot bath. How do those women do it week after week? What's that word Sarah uses? Wimp. Makes me feel a proper wimp.

June, 1983

Election time again. We sat up to see the results coming in but it was all very depressing. Margaret Thatcher is back in power. A landslide. She went from being the most unpopular Prime Minister ever to being a national heroine when we won in the Falklands. I don't know what to think about that whole dreadful business. All those youngsters on both sides dead or wounded. Brave people doing their job.

But friends of William's were teaching at the school in Port Stanley and they said that Lord Carrington had been out there several times trying to persuade the Falklanders that it would be sensible to hand the islands back to the Argentinians. They got the impression that the government regarded them as an unnecessary expense and would be glad to get rid of them.

So you can't help feeling that the Argentinians just jumped the gun and if they'd waited Margaret Thatcher would have handed them back on a plate. Sebastian reckons they did the islanders a favour. Perhaps they did. But all those lives…

September, 1983

We are in Amsterdam, would you believe? On a boat going down a canal at the minute and it is such fun. I mentioned to Thirza that I had never been abroad and almost before you could say aeroplane I was on one and here we are.

She fell in love with this city when Marcus brought her here years ago and says this is the time to be here, not in the spring when everyone is walking around with bulb catalogues. All the Dutch seem to speak English, which is a blessing as I don't think I would be very good at learning another language. Though you never know.

This is such a fascinating city with the canals, and the houseboats moored along the sides, and the big tall houses towering over everything. I wondered why so many of the houses seemed to have poles sticking out at the top, but Bertha, our room maid, tells me it is for when people move house. They haul the big items up on the outside and take them in through the windows. Most of the houses are so narrow that makes a lot of sense.

We get off the boat and sit by the canal and a man appears on the deck of a large houseboat moored near to us. He is beckoning us over. "English tourists?" he asks, grinning at us. Laughing a bit ruefully, we didn't realise it was that obvious, we agree that we are. He invites us onto his boat. It is enormous and seems much bigger inside than out. At the far end (oh dear, is that the prow or the stern? – the front bit, anyway), under the window, is a grand piano.

"You would like some music?" our new friend asks. He seats us in two luxurious armchairs and with a flourish begins to play. We are transported. I recognise some of the music that Freddy used to listen to on the radio. I loved it but never really knew what it was. It is by turns haunting and thrilling and vigorous.

When he has been playing for about an hour, I look round and see that other people have come aboard and that there are more sitting on the towpath outside. A lady comes up quietly and gives us cups of wonderful Dutch coffee with some delicious almond biscuits and then sits with us. I am engulfed by the music. Our impromptu concert carries on for nearly another hour, then our host stops, turns and bows to us. There is deafening applause from the by now very large audience and he actually thanks us for listening!

Thirza and I are at loss for words. Even English ones. We try to stammer out how overcome we are, how grateful we are, but nothing we say seems adequate. It has been an overwhelming, magical experience. The coffee lady helps us ashore. She is the maestro's wife and quite charming. She hopes we have not been bored. We reassure her. Fervently.

Later we find that our pianist is world famous, and that he is well known and loved locally for his free and spontaneous concerts. And we have achieved a sort of fame ourselves for inspiring one of them. Isn't that great?

Today we are at Anne Frank's house. I thought the house where she hid all that time would be sad and haunted, and yet what I am conscious of is her joyful spirit. I read her diary to Freddy and we always intended to come here. We just never got round to it.

I love this city. Freddy would have too. Thank you,

my dear sister, for bringing me. How lucky I am to have you.

It has been a wonderful few days but, my goodness, we are agreed that it is good to be home again. Sebastian and Andrew fetch us from the airport. I must say this flying business is easier than I expected. I didn't tell Thirza but I was quite nervous about it.

Andrew is looking very smart. He's just started working in the City. Translated for our benefit that means dealing with money and stuff on the Stock Exchange. He says he's expecting to get very rich very quickly. Good luck to him, I say, though I hope he has other ambitions as well.

Cynthia, bless her, is waiting for us at home with Rufus and Sophie and Darcy. Rufus is ecstatic when we arrive but the cats are distinctly humpy with us. We shall no doubt have to pander to them like mad for a few days in order to get in their good books again. If there is anything in this reincarnation business, I am coming back as a cat.

January, 1985

William has decided that it is high time he and I shared a birthday celebration again, so we are on our way up to Orpington this afternoon with Cynthia and Sebastian. It's to be quite a big party tonight with all my grandchildren and my beautiful new great granddaughter.

Rosalind and Steve have decided to call her Phoebe, which seems a wonderfully old-fashioned name to Thirza and me. What goes around, comes around, as they say. Jack and Harriet and the twins are coming later and Andrew is actually leaving the City early for the occasion. Nerys is coming down for the day, which is lovely as I haven't seen her for ages. She's in London with one of the women's groups trying to raise support for the miners. This strike is a dreadful thing.

Elsie has done the most delicious spread, really inventive buffet food, as there are too many of us to sit down at once. Lots of clever non-meat things for Rosalind, though Sarah is a veggie now as well. I can never quite get used to not doing all the cooking myself on these occasions so I've made some vol-au-vents and sausage rolls and some of my cheese straws. Elsie has got the plates all ready for them.

"How did you know I'd bring them?" I ask her.

"Because I know you so well," she says with a laugh and gives me a big hug. When Jack and Harriet arrive with the twins I am delighted to see that Sarah has brought a tin full of biscuits that she made this morning. Gratifying that one of my grandchildren has inherited my love of cooking.

Andrew and Nerys arrive together and it's obvious that they are being a bit distant with each other. William takes Andrew aside and I can see that he is asking Andrew what is the matter. Andrew is shrugging in that non-committal manner that he specialises in. I love all my grandchildren but I sometimes feel that Andrew's conviction lately that he is always right makes him the least likeable. He didn't used to be like this.

There is a lull in the buzz of conversation round the room and we all hear Andrew say quite clearly, "Bloody miners should be back at work, not sponging on the public."

Nerys is like a whirlwind. "How dare you!" She is across the room and facing up to him before anyone can intervene.

"Sitting in front of your stupid computer all day playing with other people's money. You've never done a proper day's work in your life. What do you think it is like, seeing the papers and the television calling us 'the enemy within' as if we were some kind of terrorists, and telling lie after lie about us? The police act as if we are criminals, law-breakers. It would be funny if it wasn't so awful. Do you know, a woman in our village was arrested for using the word 'scab'! Just what is that about? The lives of our whole communities are at stake. Mining is what the villages do, all they know, all there is. My father, my brother, my husband. All miners, all good hardworking men who don't want to see their livelihood go down the drain, or spend years on the dole. If pits are closed for short-term gain, this country will live to regret it. It may be cheaper to buy Polish coal now, but it won't always be. And it will be too late then to get back what people like you are carelessly throwing away."

It is the longest speech I have ever heard Nerys make. Without thinking, I burst into applause and Thirza joins in. Andrew whirls round on us. "Well, you two have always been a couple of commies." This is so patently absurd that I am tempted to laugh at the picture conjured up in my mind, but fortunately I resist the temptation.

William says, "Andrew, apologise immediately, please. To everyone."

There is a moment's silence. Then, "I apologise,"

says Andrew. "This is not the time, the place and especially not the company for a serious political discussion."

Hardly a resounding apology. But nobody wants to sabotage the party any more than it has already been. Elsie beckons Nerys into the kitchen and Cynthia joins them. Everyone is studiously avoiding Andrew. A diversion is created by the arrival of Natalie and Michael with their respective partners and things sort of settle down again.

I'm just hoping the atmosphere will recover when Rosalind jumps on a chair and calls for order. "Steve and I have an announcement," she calls. "We are getting married in June, and you are all invited, of course. Even Andrew, if he behaves."

There is a roar of laughter and congratulations all round and Andrew finally looks a bit sheepish and goes and kisses his sister and then I see him go and give Nerys a hug and the crisis is over. Thank heavens. It turns into a splendid party.

When Thirza and I are finally back home in the small hours, putting our feet up and having a cup of tea, I say to her, "All these years and I've never realised how divisive politics can be in a family."

"That," says my clever sister, "is because you never think of it as politics. You just do what you think is right, like me. But nowadays, everything is politics. That's what Margaret says, anyway. And she should know."

"Come on then, fellow-commie," I say, "time for bed."

Nice to know we are not too old to giggle.

March, 1985

We had a call from Donald this morning. The miners are going back. We watch them on the television, marching, heads held high. I don't know when I have felt prouder of them. Margaret Thatcher is calling it a great victory, but there has been one of those inexplicable swings in opinion. As if what they call the media has been shamed by this show of courage. So they should be.

June, 1985

Rosalind and Steve's wedding and it is such a joyful day. They decided on a register office, and I was quite pleased about that as a church wedding with your baby in the congregation seems a bit bizarre to me, though I know they do that all the time now. They are having the reception in their garden in a huge marquee. Luckily it is warm and sunny, one of those perfect June days. There is a band playing unobtrusively but pleasantly, and some very efficient waiters serving a delicious four-course meal and it is all very grand and quite delightful. I ask William if he and Elsie are paying for it but he says luckily not, these vets do OK, and they are insisting on paying for it themselves. Just as well, I reckon.

Timmy and Lettie are here, they have photographs of Edward's three kiddies to show us. Timmy a grandfather. Well. There you go. Edward's eldest is a teenager now, so Timmy could be a great grandfather soon. That is almost as ridiculous as me being a great grandmother.

Frank is here too. He is such a darling. I asked how he was coping without Collette, and he said he'd been on his own for so long before he met her that he just counted himself incredibly lucky to have had so many happy years with her. "When I get a bit down," he says, "I just think that my whole life might have been like this and I count my blessings." I shall remember that next time I feel sorry for myself.

Elsie looks so pretty in a peach coloured dress and jacket. "Been dying to be the mother of the bride for years," she whispers to me.

Rosalind said it was all right to bring Rufus along so we put a big white bow on his collar, and he behaved impeccably. In fact, he did a fantastic job clearing the crumbs off the grass. A very public-spirited dog.

July, 1985

Today has been a most extraordinary day. The twins told us they were going up to a big concert in Hyde Park and to look out for them on the television. There were thousands of people there and we never glimpsed them at all but we were so glad we watched. It was all to raise money for Africa. We saw the newsreels of those starving children, of course. Belsen all over again. But not deliberate malice this time, just neglect. Just "I'm all right, Jack, sorry you're starving but there you go, nothing I can do". Then this one man, this Bob Geldoff, sees it and actually does something. Doesn't ask permission, doesn't think it's such a big a problem there's no point in trying to help, doesn't think it's nothing to do with him. They say it's raised over £40,000,000.

Television really does bring these things home – well, *into* our homes, I suppose. Makes it very personal and you know you have to try and do a bit to help. We enjoyed some of the music, but most of it wasn't really to our taste. But the faces in the crowd – now there was something. Joy on those faces. Not just for the music. Joy for being there, and joy for knowing they were part of something bigger. And something good. It was a privilege to be part of it, even by proxy.

I hope the Queen makes him Sir Bob. And I hope he accepts. You never know with him.

November, 1985

Barely had my first cup of tea and Jack is on the phone. "What are we going to do for William, Mum?"

"Sorry?" I say.

"He's retiring at the end of term, and I thought we should make a special thing of it at Christmas."

Oh my goodness, so he is. I'd quite forgotten, what with Rosalind's wedding and everything.

Jack says, "Harriet has had a word with Elsie and obviously they are having a big farewell do at the school, but we wondered about trying to get in touch with some of his early pupils. The twins are keen to get a video film together. What do you reckon?"

I think it is a marvellous idea and promise to ring Eileen, who I hear from every Christmas, and ask her if some of them still live near her. When he's rung off, I wake Thirza and inform her that we have a project. I must be incredibly old to have a son on the verge of retirement.

This is turning out to be rather exciting. Eileen has given us the names of several of William's pupils from his early days as a teacher and I've managed to speak to them all and they are more than happy to co-operate. We've even found one lady who was at St John's when he was doing his teaching practice in 1939. She's in her fifties now, but William taught her daughter, and now her granddaughter is at the comprehensive where William is head. The whole family are going to be in the film. The old hall is still standing and Eileen is going to arrange for us to meet there and for the twins to "interview" everyone.

Such a memorable day. Jack drives us up this morning, and it is quite a squash in the car with Harriet and the twins and Thirza and me. Good job none of us are very big. Funny to be in Penge again. I haven't been back for ages. Eileen's got some lunch all ready for us, then off we trot to the hall. Talk about the years rolling away.

Jack's old friend Alan, who lives in Croydon now, has heard what is going on and comes over. He reminds us that he was in that wonderful nativity play that William wrote during the war. James and Sarah are thrilled because he still has his script, all dog-eared and scruffy, but he holds it up to the camera and quotes his three lines from it. So many people have turned up with stories of how William helped and encouraged them that Harriet takes charge for a bit and directs the action. James may be intending to go to film school but his mum still has a lot more experience. We film and talk, and talk and film, for most of the afternoon.

Eventually, with the last memory recorded and the

last message to William safely on film, we thank all these old friends and promise that we'll come back next year and show the film. With the proviso, of course, that we are still around to do it.

Alan says, "Mrs Spencer, you are going to live forever," which makes us laugh. Funny to be called Mrs Spencer, but nobody here really knows me as Mrs Curtis and it doesn't matter. Back here, all my memories of Jimmy, never far away, come rushing back.

December, 1985

Cynthia and Sebastian insisted on us all coming here for Christmas so they could put the screen up in their big sitting room and not reveal it till after dinner. We were determined that William wouldn't have a clue as to what was going on. It was worth all the planning. I have never seen him so – what is that word they use nowadays? – "gobsmacked." The twins, aided and abetted by Jack and Harriet, have done a wonderful job.

They even have a special surprise for me. They've found some old ciné film of Elsie's, and by some mysterious process managed to make it part of their film. And there I am. Helping William to take a party of kids round the Festival of Britain in 1951. My goodness, I do look young.

There's film of us outside the Dome of Discovery, and on the Treetop Walk (I'm looking a bit harassed there) and oh, do look – there we are with Ivy the polar bear and her beautiful cub, Brumus. I'd forgotten all about that day. There is a really funny piece with William obviously telling two boys to behave "or else"

252

and I can see myself in the background looking just about ready to drop. I think it was the first and last time I ever volunteered to help on a school trip.

When the tape is finished, we make the twins take a bow, and then Jack takes the tape and presents it to William with a flourish. "For you, big brother," he says and actually gives him a hug. They've always been close but I've never seen it demonstrated so publicly before.

I think everyone is a bit choked. Rosalind and Andrew are looking at their dad with new respect. Elsie is probably the only one of us who fully understood what a good teacher he was. The twins asked her to do a winding-up speech and she said, "Darling William, you achieved what every teacher hopes for – you inspired your students – and you were loved by them."

What a sentimental lot we are. Hankies out all over the place. How proud Jimmy would have been. What a lovely, loving family I have. What a great Christmas. Happy retirement, my son.

January, 1987

When I was younger I thought that talking about dying as "going on before" was a load of nonsense. Perhaps it is. But when I heard this morning that Josephine had died, that was actually how it seemed. Her funeral will be in Suffolk and, of course, I shall go. A last farewell to my old friend. Or till we meet again. Who knows?

Thirza insisted on coming with me. I tell her she is becoming very bossy and that being six years older than her does not mean that I have lost my marbles and become incapable. As I point out, she is no spring chicken herself. Then we both giggle. Of course, she knows that I am grateful for her company. And although she didn't know Josephine well, she thought she was a lovely lady. We are going to stay with Frank for a couple of days, which will stop us getting too gloomy.

The church is packed. I somehow hadn't expected so many people to be here. How well respected and loved she was, borne out by the many tributes to her from nurses and doctors and colleagues. Her only surviving brother, who I haven't seen in seventy years, is there and actually recognises me. Josephine had asked for money to be sent to her favourite children's charity rather than have flowers and I believe a sizeable sum will be sent off. Mind you, I'm glad that I had flowers when Freddy died. I asked for them to be brought back to the house, and seeing and smelling them helped to ease the pain. Knowing that they were all sent with love.

After the funeral her brother comes up and passes me a small packet. "She left this for you," he says. "Had to promise that I would see you got it." When we are back at Frank's, I open it. It is her medal. Her precious CBE. The letter says:

Dear Lillian,
Wanted you to have this if I go first. You can leave it to one of your delightful grandchildren and tell them about us. I don't want it to end up in a second-hand shop with no one knowing who I was. It was the proudest moment of my life, and I am so glad you and Freddy were there to share it with me.

254

Love from Josephine.
PS See you soon!

Bless her – she was always able to make me laugh. Even through my tears.

March, 1987

Andrew is getting married next month. I rather thought he'd be too modern for that, but apparently Davina, for all she works on the Stock Exchange with him, is just an old-fashioned girl at heart, and wants the white dress and the full regalia. Good for her. William says it is going to be a *very* posh do with loads of money on her side of the family and Andrew, by all accounts, careering towards his first million.

A lot of these youngsters seem so money conscious. Natalie tells me that, as a not terribly well paid social worker, Andrew makes her feel like a total failure. "Yet, Auntie Lillian, I love what I do and I make enough to live quite well."

I tell her that, for what it is worth, I think having enough money does matter (I've been too short too often not to know how hard that is) but after that, doing what you get satisfaction from is very important. And that enough money is usually nothing like as much as you think it will be.

Samantha is going to sing at the wedding. She's made a good career for herself on the cabaret circuit, and goes away entertaining on cruise ships sometimes. She's got a couple of French songs she sings. That Edith Piaf one about not regretting is one of them. Every time I hear her do it I remember her gran, when I first knew her, pretending to be a French maid for Mrs Willett. Dear Collette.

The wedding is certainly very grand indeed. There is a master of ceremonies at the reception who keeps things whizzing along at a great pace. Michael is Andrew's best man and makes a really witty speech reminding everyone about Dawn till Dusk, and then Andrew thanks everyone from the bridesmaids (Davina's two sisters) to William and Elsie, and Rosalind for being such a great sister. Then to my surprise, he says, "And a special thank you to my lovely gran, for always being around when I needed her." I didn't know that I had, but I'm very touched.

Wicked Thirza whispers, "He's forgotten that we are a couple of commies!"

June, 1987

Another general election. The only bright spot was that demented man on the television with his swingometer or whatever he calls it. At least that gave us a laugh. We really didn't need anyone to tell us that Mrs Thatcher would be back. Almost all the papers cheering for her and the Labour Party still in disarray. A landslide. Again. A feel-good factor in the country, they say. Tell that to the unemployed. Jack says that unless the opposition get their act together she could go on forever. Labour has still not really recovered from Shirley Williams and the other three going off to form their Social Democrats. What a waste of time that was.

I don't understand the thinking behind half of this government's policies. All this selling off nationalised stuff to the people. I thought it belonged to us anyway. Looks like just another way of taking from the poor and giving to the better off to me. I expect I'm missing something. I hope so.

Jack is looking a lot better. I've been really worried about him ever since he came back from Russia. He looked so peaky. That Chernobyl explosion last year was dreadful – why he volunteered to go out with the team who were measuring the radiation fallout was beyond me. Seemed like asking for trouble. He said it was important to find out what was going on and how to contain the plant. That it might make a difference between life and death for a lot of people.

"Think of it like the war, Mum. Doing what you have to do."

I'd still rather he hadn't gone, and I know Harriet felt the same. But I am proud that he is so brave and so respected. I've never begun to understand what he does. A physicist. However did Jimmy and I produce a physicist? Such clever children and grandchildren. And a great granddaughter now. I wonder what Phoebe will grow up to be.

So lucky to have them all so near. I know how Thirza wishes her lot were, though she never dwells on it. Hard for her, Norma and her kids being over in New Zealand. All the photos and films and phone calls can't really make up for only having seen them just that once when they came over here in the '70s. But at least she knows they are well and happy. And now Margaret spending so much more time in America. Thank heavens Cynthia and Sebastian are just down the road, so to speak. And Natalie and Michael are a constant joy. It does make me count my blessings, though.

October,1987

Except for during the war I've always managed to sleep like a log, so when I realise that Thirza is shaking me awake in a panic and it's the middle of the night and there is this terrible noise going on outside, the memories come flooding back and I know straightaway what has happened.

"They've dropped the Bomb, Thirza," I yell, doing what passes for a leap out of bed nowadays. "Quick, into the cupboard under the stairs."

Thirza is only in her nightie and the temperature seems to have dropped alarmingly so I grab my dressing gown and am just about to go into her room to fetch hers when all the lights go off. For the first time in years I wish I hadn't given up smoking. Not even a match in the bedroom and it really is as black as pitch.

"Let's stand still till we can see something," Thirza says and I'm relieved to hear she's calmer. Not like Thirza to flap. She's always so self-controlled. Suddenly there is this enormous crash and we see this great tree from next door fall across the front of the house and hear the downstairs window go.

"That's it," I say. "Come on, Thirza, into my bed," and we both climb into my bed and pull the covers over our heads just like when we were kids. "If we are going to go, we may as well go together and in comfort," I say and wonder if we should try a prayer.

I'm just about to suggest this when even with all the noise going on I can hear the phone ringing. Only the phone is downstairs. But it might be the last chance I have to speak to Jack or William. I'm wondering what to do when the phone stops and there is a lull in this awful howling noise and I think I must be hallucinating because I am sure that is Sebastian's voice answering it.

I hear him say, "I'm just going to check, hold on," so I call out, "Sebastian, is that you?" and then there is a torch waving around on the landing and I realise that we must be virtually invisible under the blankets so I sit up and call him.

He appears in the doorway. "Are you all right? Are you both there?" and up pops Thirza's head. "Oh, thank God," he says. "We have been so worried. I had to come on foot through the storm because there are trees all over the roads."

By this time I am beginning to feel slightly foolish. I think they may not have dropped the bomb after all, and although that is obviously a relief I feel some face-saving might be in order. I dig Thirza firmly in the calf with my foot, and say, "It is a bad storm, isn't it? Thirza and I thought we should shelter from flying glass."

The first glimmer of dawn is starting to give us some light and we are finally able to go downstairs. I can't believe the mess. The garden is devastated, the greenhouse and shed have just disappeared, and all the downstairs windows are smashed. I suddenly remember Rufus and the cats – how could I have forgotten them? But then I spot the tip of a furry tail and call their names and the three of them come wriggling out from under the sofa and start sniffing around their very changed landscape. The biggest shock is realising that we can't even make a cup of tea, but the animals are already queuing for their breakfast and at least we don't need electricity for that.

In no time Jack turns up and he and Sebastian get a

little fire going in the garden with some of the wood that is lying around. Lots of branches blown down and bits of shed and what appears to be a whole fence panel. God knows how far that has travelled as we've certainly never seen it before. They boil some water in a saucepan and make our cuppa. At least the taps are working. Cynthia rings to say she is on her way over and, although no one seems to have any power, their house appears to be undamaged. Looks like the granny annexe for us for a bit.

Everywhere is so deathly quiet and still. We sit in the garden having a make-do breakfast with Jack and Sebastian and there is not a bird singing anywhere. Even the seagulls are silent. It feels uncanny, especially following all that unearthly noise.

We find some batteries and get one of the radios going. All the news is of the hurricane that has swept through Southern England. Casualties everywhere, but miraculously, almost no one killed.

I look round the wreckage of my lovely little house and I want to cry. Then I remember the war, and all the people who were bombed out, and sleeping in the station, and never knowing who would be around the next day. "Pull yourself together, Lillian," I tell myself. We collect up a few clothes and Rufus, pop the cats into their basket in the wheelbarrow, and start the slow march to Sebastian's house.

Refugees, indeed.

November, 1987

We are back in our house. Sebastian and Cynthia have been wonderful, but there really is no place like home. I am so grateful to the insurance people who came down the day after the hurricane and told us to do whatever was necessary.

I think my new kitchen is rather splendid. The old one had needed doing anyway, so it's an ill wind...no, that's not a very good phrase to use. It is so sad going into the town. We drove past St Peter's last week and all those majestic elms are still lying there like felled elephants. It's the same everywhere. Sevenoaks lost six of the oaks that gave it the name. Whole buildings were swept away. Lots of people still without power. But for most of us the worst reminder is seeing the hundreds of trees waiting to be cleared away. Will our green and pleasant land ever look quite the same again?

William and Elsie lost a couple of windows, but that was all. Jack and Harriet were untouched, but the house next door to them was almost destroyed. Isn't that weird? Like in the blitz. Rosalind and Steve have come off worst, I think. Their surgery was blown into the ground, and they are operating out of a temporary cabin. But they've been thinking for some time of opening a sanctuary adjacent to the clinic, so perhaps this will be the time to do it.

It seems that we have an unexpected casualty in the family, though nothing to do with the storm. William tells me that Andrew and Davina are in big financial trouble.

Obviously we had heard about the Stock Market crash, but I didn't realise the implications for them. William tells me that Andrew has admitted to him that between them, he and Davina are not only jobless but have debts amounting to nearly a quarter of a million pounds! And that is not counting their mortgage.

I am shocked. I can't see how we can possibly bail them out even if we all get together. And Jack and Harriet will soon have the twins at college so they won't have much spare, even if they feel inclined. How could those two possibly have incurred so much debt?

We are having a house-warming party to celebrate being home again. Our guests are William and Elsie, Jack and Harriet, and, of course, Cynthia and Sebastian, for carting us off and putting us up at a moment's notice. And putting up *with* us, if you see what I mean.

I worked out a special menu, my spinach and green-pea soup garnished with my own homemade horse radish sauce, followed by roast duckling with an orange salad, crisp roast potatoes and sweet corn sautéed in butter, and to finish, Thirza made a cream ice and we filled the centre with lychees. We did a simple cheese board as well, but no one had room for any. They insisted on providing the wines. I have to admit I don't know much about wine so I am always happy for them to do that. We did most of the work the day before. It was splendid to do so much cooking again. I had forgotten how much I enjoy doing a special-occasion menu.

We talk until well into the evening. We have kept a coal fire in the sitting room, and we sit round it, with just the lamps on, talking about the family and all sorts of other things. William says that Davina's family are helping Andrew and her with the money they owe, and obviously he and Elsie are weighing in too. I say that Andrew and Davina should bear some of the responsibility for their debts. Neither of them has found other jobs yet. They ought to be prepared to take anything to help themselves. Sweeping roads if that is all there is. I think Elsie agrees with me.

Jack says the twins will finally go their separate ways next year. Sarah is hoping eventually to go into medicine. She's been talking about doing this since she was small, of course, so it's hardly a surprise. Just fancy, a doctor in the family. And James has already been told he has a place at film school.

Thirza tells them that there is a possibility that Norma might come over for a month next summer. I do hope she can manage to, I know how Thirza would love that. If she does, I'll try to get Margaret over here so my lovely sister has all her girls together again.

Reluctantly, our party winds down and it's time for everyone to leave. When they've all gone we decide to leave the clearing up till the morning. Sitting in the middle of the debris, having a bedtime cup of tea, I say to Thirza, "Do you know, Sebastian is finally starting to look his age. I always forget he is so much older than Cynthia." We work out how old he is. Seventy-two. A mere youngster, we agree.

January, 1990

I am ninety years old today. Isn't that ridiculous? Inside I am about thirty. Of course, I have had such good health all my life. I can never remember having so much as a cold. Jack says that if we could market my antibodies we would make a fortune. But it does seem to take a very long time to climb the stairs nowadays, so I suppose everything is wearing out, antibodies or not. The Queen Mother is ninety this year too – 1900 must be a sturdy vintage, I reckon. She certainly still looks pretty good.

This year I didn't wait to be asked how I wanted to celebrate. I told them no party, but Thirza and I would love to go and see *Cats* in the West End. We have heard so much about it and it sounds such fun. We go to the matinees at the Theatre Royal sometimes but it's not the same as going to a London theatre. And since our dear Rufus died, cats have become even more important in my life. Sophie and Darcy are so loving, we sit in the evenings with one on each lap, and I'm not sure if it's their purring or the telly programmes, but we are usually all asleep in minutes. Hope I don't go to sleep at the show tonight.

It is a real treat, quite splendid. I couldn't have asked for a more enjoyable birthday. Harriet has got us seats on the revolving bit of the auditorium and I think she had tipped off the cast as a lot of the cats come down and make a fuss of us during the performance – including one very beautiful tom.

Thirza hisses in my ear: "Very tasty!"

"I can't take you anywhere," I hiss back but we are both giggling in a most unseemly way for two geriatrics.

We are familiar with the music but it makes it even nicer, seeing it in context. And the dancing is truly amazing. Afterwards Harriet takes us backstage and everyone makes a great fuss of us. Then, when the auditorium is empty, they put two chairs on the stage and the entire cast files back on and sings "Happy Birthday" to me! I tell them truthfully that I have never heard such a thrilling rendition of it – and that I am lost for more words. Except thank you. A wonderful (and moving) finale to a magnificent evening.

On the way home, Harriet tells us that she is finally leaving *Call Ambulance 999*. She is the only one of the original cast still in it and she has had enough. She says that she thinks they will probably "kill her off" as they have told her she will be going out with a bang. I glance at Jack, who is driving and there is something about his expression. In that instant, I realise that he knew about Harriet and that actor, and also that it is long over.

Later, at home, I tell Thirza about the day in Fortnum's. I've never told anyone before. She agrees that Jack probably did know but was also aware that any kind of confrontation might mean that he would lose Harriet. "Clever boy," she says. "Turned a blind eye and trusted in her love for him, and his for her, to win out eventually."

I think she is probably right. I find it comforting that, even in this age of disposable marriage, there are still people who love each other enough to survive a bit of human weakness.

March, 1990

It seems I have achieved a sort of minor fame! I have felt so angry about this wretched poll tax that I decided to write to the Argus. They rang me up to say they were publishing my letter and could they send someone round to take my picture? So there I am, on the front page— "Ninety-year-old protestor says 'I will not pay'". Then a television company rang up and said would I do an interview? They sent a charming girl round and we did it in the sitting room, and I told her that I couldn't imagine what the government was thinking of and that although I knew I was lucky enough to be able to pay it, that didn't make it right and anyway millions of other people couldn't afford it. We watched it on the news in the evening and I must say that I thought that both the sitting room and I looked rather good. But what was really nice was that today we went along to Sainsbury's and people kept coming up to tell me that they agreed with me, and then the Manager came up as we were leaving and gave me a bunch of flowers "on behalf of all your fans". Well! And then Andrew, who has surprised me by starting up his own catering company and doing rather well – he's nearly cleared his debts – rang me up and said, "Saw you on the telly, commie Gran, I felt very proud of you." Quite made my day.

One's grandchildren are a constant surprise. Sarah, always such a sensible girl, with ages to go before she is qualified, has got engaged to a vicar. Well, a curate, but he will be a vicar eventually. She is bringing him to meet us at the weekend. Whatever does one talk to a vicar about?

Actually, Ben seems like quite a nice chap. Not especially handsome, but pleasant-looking with nice blue eyes. I think he was nervous of meeting us. Have I become formidable in my old age? Surely not. But perhaps the prospect of being paraded before the two ancient matriarchs of the family is more daunting than I realise.

Anyway, once he relaxed he proved to have a good sense of humour and didn't mention God at all. Thank heavens on both counts, if that's not blasphemous. Sarah is obviously head-over-heels in love with him.

They are not planning to marry for some time, but say they wanted the public commitment of an engagement. Given his profession, I suppose they can't do this living-together bit. Or perhaps an engagement makes it all right even in the Church. Who knows?

Sarah told me that he had been in some trouble in his first parish for championing some travellers who had moved into a stretch of land adjacent to the by-pass. Apparently he told the congregation that there were parallels with nomadic Abraham and his smelly old goats. So I must admit by the time we met I was predisposed to like him.

He nearly blotted his copybook. He started to tell me earnestly that nowadays women expected to have a career, not stay at home to look after the children, like my generation. I told him in no uncertain terms that I had worked for most of my life, along with a great many of my contemporaries, at everything from cleaning other people's houses to washing their clothes. And, when I was lucky, as a cook. The fact that there was very little, if any, training and even fewer opportunities didn't mean we didn't work. Money was so short we had no choice. It just meant that we took our kids along with us and did low-paid, menial work, which we were mostly glad to get.

Then I said that I rejoice that my granddaughters are able to have proper careers, if that is their choice. But having that choice is the real difference. He went very quiet. Perhaps I came on a bit strong. To a vicar, as well.

May, 1990

I never know what my family are going to do next. Jack is taking early retirement this year, and he's just told me that he and William are buying a boat together. I had no idea they were even interested, though I remember that William and Elsie had some boating holidays when the kids were small. He says they have been talking about doing it for a couple of years and they went to see this little motor cruiser on the Medway this weekend, and they've bought her.

Thirza and I are invited to go out on her in a couple of weeks, when they've got her all spick and span. Her name is *Butterfly*. How exciting. I *am* looking forward to it. Harriet and Elsie have both been on the phone saying they expect they will become boating widows, but they don't sound too worried about it. Glad to get them out from under their feet sometimes, I expect. Well. William and Jack. Both retired. And messing about on the river. Together. Still boys at heart, I guess.

June, 1990

I insisted on taking a picnic on the boat. I wanted it to be a party. A surprise early, early retirement celebration for Jack. Thirza and I really went to town. Smoked salmon sandwiches, of course, crustless on wafer-thin brown bread, Cornish pasties, made the day before, and wrapped in white napkins, devilled chicken, tiny sausage rolls made with sausage meat rolled in herbs, English tomatoes cut in half and dipped in basil, and a grape salad.

We followed this with large plates of fresh strawberries soaked in sherry and sprinkled with a tiny touch of castor sugar, served with thick cream. Our own strawberry bed has finally come good after all these years of doing nothing much. So much nicer if you grow them yourself. We found Freddy's old picnic basket and piled everything into it. Harriet was in on the secret and had the champagne and good white wine in a chiller bag when she picked us up.

It is the most fantastic day. Hot, but with a cool breeze, and the river is calm and the boat is delightful. Not very big, but it somehow seems to absorb its crew and guests with ease. And there is a lovely thick padded seat long enough for three to sit on at the end of the deck. We're moored under some trees and have just finished the picnic, which has been a great success.

James is here, and Sarah with Ben, and Rosalind and Steve and little Phoebe. Andrew turned up on his own, he wants to know the recipe for the Cornish pasties! Lovely to have another cook in the family. I was a bit sceptical when he told me he was going to do a catering course, after the Stock Exchange fiasco, but he's really made a go of it with his Food for Living snack bars, and is planning to open another one soon.

He says Davina is still not working, she is suffering from depression and having counselling sessions every week. Hmm. Once upon a time you told people to snap out of it. I can't quite get to grips with all this cosseting. Of course you are depressed if you lose your job. As you are if you lose someone you love. But I can't help feeling that knuckling down and getting on with your life puts you back on track again more quickly than endlessly discussing how difficult everything is for you. All seems a bit of a self-indulgent wallow to me. But I don't say any of it to Andrew. He'd only say that I didn't understand. And he'd be right.

Rosalind has brought her enormous wolfhound along. His name is Wilfred and I think he knows that I am deeply in love with him. When he stepped on the boat it rocked very precariously but he's settled down at my feet now. Such a gentle giant. I feel very honoured. He turned up at the sanctuary, found shivering on Whitstable beach, and they never did find his owner. Makes you wonder – surely no one could willingly have abandoned him?

Rosalind is very quiet. Not quite herself. I shall ring her tomorrow. I am an interfering old woman. I don't care. Elsie has got one of these little CD players, and she's playing the music from *Showboat*. What else, indeed?

Even the most perfect days come to an end, and this one does when the midges appear. Big hugs all round, especially from Jack, who says, "I didn't know it was going to be a party, but thanks, Mum. It was great! And you still make the best picnic in the world." Back in the car I have a quiet smile. It used to be bloater paste sandwiches and Swiss roll if we were lucky. Nice to know he remembers it so affectionately, though.

Oh, I do like having a boat in the family.

I ring Rosalind this morning and ask her straight out what is the matter. I find that age gives me quite a lot of privileges, one of them being that I no longer find it necessary to beat about the bush. Well, let's face it, I probably haven't got time to.

She hedges a bit and then: "Things haven't been going too well, Gran. We've had an offer from someone who wants to buy the practice and keep the sanctuary going, and we are thinking it might be a wise thing to do. We don't know how much longer we can keep our heads above water if we keep losing patients at this rate. We're losing staff at a rate of knots as well. And we have no idea why."

I am speechless. The practice was successful almost from the day they took over and their reputation has grown and grown. Only a year ago they were talking about expanding and taking on a couple more vets. I make useless commiserations, and on the spur of the moment ask her, "Do you still have that Jillie working for you?"

"Yes, she does reception. I know you don't like her, Gran, but we feel sorry for her. When she turned up here last year she was recovering from a breakdown and couldn't find a job. Confidence gone, I suppose. She's all on her own and always saying how grateful she is. She's been with us nearly a year now."

I tell Rosalind that I love her and to give Phoebe a hug from me and we ring off.

It is true that I have never taken to this woman. She's in her fifties, with long grey hair that gives her a witch-like look, and she speaks with a cut-glass accent that you recognise immediately as put on. But my dislike is based on something more tangible than her unprepossessing appearance.

Not long ago Thirza and I were over at Rosalind's and I wandered off to have a look at the animals in the sanctuary, which is quite one of my favourite pastimes. I can easily lose a couple of hours chatting to them all and often go and sit in the runs, especially with the cats. Some of the dogs can get a bit boisterous for an aged visitor.

It was a warm afternoon and I dozed off with Fifi

the large white Persian on my lap and a couple of others on the bench with me. I woke with a start and it took a moment to get myself together. As I got to my feet I reached for my bag and then realised that I had left it under the counter in reception. I normally do that, as it is quite heavy. Like most of us I carry everything except the kitchen sink with me (actually Freddy used to swear that was in there as well). So I trotted back through to reception. At first I thought there was no one there, but when I went behind the counter, I found Jillie on her knees, going through the contents of my bag.

Well, of course I was very angry and asked what she thought she was doing. She made a series of lame excuses about not knowing who it belonged to and having to check and how everything had fallen out of it onto the floor, but we both knew she was lying.

Later I was reasonably certain I was a ten-pound note short and positive that some photos in my purse had been touched and that a couple of letters I always have with me had been unfolded and read. One was from Jimmy when I was in Suffolk during the war and the other from Freddy just before we got married. It made my blood boil to think of that woman reading them. I tried to tell Rosalind but she said, "Oh, Gran, I'm sure she was just trying to find out who had left it there." Hmm. A likely story.

Soon after that incident one of the nurses at the practice gave notice. I was very fond of her and made a special point of going to say goodbye and tell her how sorry I was that they were losing her.

"I can't work with that vicious woman anymore, Mrs Curtis," she said. For a minute I thought she meant my gentle Rosalind but then she said, "You tell

Rosalind to watch her back with that Jillie. I've tried but she won't listen. She's a wicked, jealous cow and I've heard her say awful things about Steve and Rosalind. This used to be a happy place to work, but it's not anymore."

With all this in my mind, I run this morning's phone call with Rosalind past Thirza while we have breakfast. Then I tell her about this niggle I have that Jillie might have something to do with their present troubles. Thirza suggest we ring Sebastian and ask if he thinks I'm putting two and two together and making five.

Sebastian listens a bit cynically. "Tell you what," he says, "I'll ask around and find out what I can about this woman. Mind you, there probably isn't anything *to* find out."

If anyone can dig up anything about Jillie, it is Sebastian. He has had such a successful career in the City, I think he knows everyone who is anyone, as Cynthia says. We can't ask for more. And we haven't got any other ideas.

Well! Three days on and would you believe it? This Jillie is a conwoman! She's been in prison twice for fraud and embezzlement and Sebastian says she leaves a trail of employers who were too busy rebuilding their businesses to prosecute. Just wanted her out of their lives.

"At least one suicide amongst her victims," he says grimly. "Not content with stealing from her employers she spreads malicious slanders about them. And if she can break up a marriage as well as destroy a business she's in her element."

A psychiatrist friend told Sebastian that Jillie is a

prime example of something called Narcissistic Syndrome. People whose belief in their own superiority is all-important to them and who are threatened by other people's success. He says they usually make up illustrious pasts, and that their whole life is a constant lie.

The following day we ask Rosalind and Steve to come over and Sebastian tells them what he has found out. Rosalind confirms that Jillie claimed she had been a doctor before her "breakdown" and also that she had once been "horsewoman of the year" at Olympia. Among other things. "All nonsense, almost certainly," says Sebastian. My goodness.

Rosalind and Steve have confronted her. She denied everything and flounced out. Afterwards Rosalind found all the petty cash had gone with her. Rosalind, very bravely, then confronted a "friend" who has been behaving oddly toward her. This person started to scream at Rosalind that she knew what an awful person Rosalind was, and how she knew that Rosalind had been "persecuting" Jillie for months. "Because Jillie had told me all about it." Poor Rosalind was horrified. The form the persecution was supposed to have taken remains a mystery. As does the reason that anyone would have believed such rubbish.

But at least now they are beginning to understand what has been behind their troubles. Rosalind says that, with hindsight, all sorts of odd things fell into place. "How can anyone be so wicked?" Rosalind asks. "We took her on to help her. We thought she was fond of us."

When you come up against malevolence like this, I

have to say it does shake you. I feel I have never seen pure evil so close to me. I hope I never do again. But William phoned this evening. "Clever old Mum," he says. "Ninety years old and still coming out fighting, eh?" I must admit, I do feel pleased with myself.

November, 1990

Margaret is over on a flying visit. She's staying with us, which is nice, but we've hardly seen her. The reason for her trip is the increasing speculation that Margaret Thatcher is about to be jettisoned by her party. The Americans are totally in thrall to Britain's first woman Prime Minister. Margaret says that they even watch Prime Minister's question time on the television over there. They cannot believe that she is not regarded with reverence and adulation here, like the Queen. I tell Margaret I don't know too many people who feel like that about the Queen, let alone Thatcher.

I don't believe she will go. I think she has bricked herself into Number 10 and will stay there forever. Margaret has become very American. When I say this to her she looks at me with her jaw dropping and I have to tell her that I am joking.

Thirza sees more of her daughter on the television than in the flesh. She is on the news nearly every night. I ask her what she thinks of Mrs Thatcher and she says, "She knows how to work the media." That's a bit too cryptic for me.

Thirza is so thrilled just to have her in England. We haven't seen her since the summer a couple of years ago when Norma came over and Thirza had them all together for the first time in years. That was very special. Funny how alike they all looked. It doesn't really show in photos, perhaps it's more mannerisms. Like the way they all hold their heads slightly to one side when they are talking. All such attractive women, too. Like their mum.

So the speculators were right. She's gone. Mrs Thatcher. I can hardly believe it. After eleven years. Toppled. At last. By her own party. They've always been good at the swift knife in the back. I could almost feel sorry for her. But not quite. Politics should be about more than personal affluence. I'm fed up with seeing people think that success is only measured by how much you earn. Wonder who will follow her? Margaret thinks it will be John Major.

It is John Major. The man who has made the swiftest rise through the ranks ever, I should think. Seems a bit of a nonentity to me. On the television Margaret described Major as the only man who has ever run away from the circus to become an accountant. He was briefly Foreign Secretary under Thatcher, and then, for not much longer, Chancellor of the Exchequer. As far as I can see, he made a mess of both jobs. Obviously he has hidden talents. Well hidden as far as I am concerned. Mind you, Thatcher, who backed him, made a remark about being "a good back-seat driver" and you should have seen his expression when he heard it. I shall watch with interest. As always.

December, 1990

What a difficult year this has been for William and

Elsie. Andrew has just told them that he and Davina are getting a divorce. They are both very upset but it's hard to believe they can have been that surprised. I told them that I thought divorce was better than being locked into an unhappy marriage for life. I would probably feel differently if there were children to consider, but under the circumstances it seems quite sensible to cut their losses.

Elsie says she thought I would be shocked. Funny girl, I don't suppose there's a lot that can shock me anymore. Saddened, because of all those wasted hopes and dreams, but they are both quite young enough to start again.

And talking of starting again, they say Rosalind and Steve are having an uphill struggle. That wretched woman started rumours that they were illegally selling on some of the drugs used in the practice. Even worse in Rosalind's opinion, she told people that they ill-treated and neglected the animals in the sanctuary. Steve has spoken to the police, who are aware of Ms Jillie's shenanigans, but slander is not a criminal offence, just a civil one, and very hard to prove.

An amazing amount of people were obviously happy to believe this nonsense in the face of everything they knew about Rosalind and Steve. And it seems that there were others, who did realise the truth, but were not prepared to stand up and be counted. Rosalind says some people have even said to her, "Oh, poor woman, how unhappy she must be." Right. Never mind her victims, with their devastated lives.

But as I said to Rosalind when she told me, that remark is a wonderful way of absolving yourself from doing anything. So Jillie will probably carry on lying and stealing and ruining lives. What is that old saying? Something about evil succeeding because good men stand by and do nothing. But anyway, Rosalind and Steve are determined not to let her ruin them, and everything they have worked so hard for, and the practice is slowly picking up again.

We are all going to spend Christmas with them. A bit of family solidarity will be good for their morale. The pair of them always work over Christmas, as they like to give the sanctuary staff a proper break, so we shall share the cooking and stuff between the rest of us. I shall probably wear my apron that Sarah gave me last year, which says "Chief cook",and sit in the kitchen giving orders. Like one of those TV chefs. With Wilfred (un-hygienically) at my feet. Good job it's a big kitchen.

I sometimes think I should have taken up bossiness earlier in life.

January, 1992

Still around. Well. There you go. Or not, in my case. Big party yesterday and I must admit I am quite tired today. It seems that reaching your nineties is so momentous that every birthday is celebrated as if it is your last. Of course, it probably is.

I know really that I am lucky to have such a loving family. It must be awful to be in a care home somewhere with a duty visit from a distant relation once in a while. There is an old people's home near us, and although the staff is excellent, nothing can disguise the fact that, with the best will in the world, it is just a job. Thirza and I started to pop in and say hallo to some of the residents last year and now we do it as a regular thing. Our children are vastly amused and make jokes about geriatrics visiting geriatrics, but we know that we are on the same wavelength as a lot of them and we enjoy it as much as they seem to.

Amazing how everyone wants to talk about their war. I suppose it was such an intense experience. Joan, who is even older than me, told me the other day that she never felt so alive, before or after, as she did in the war, and that she missed that feeling when it was over. I think that reaction was probably more understandable if you didn't have people you cared for to worry about.

I could barely believe it last year when we went to war again. Desert Storm. Dire forecasts of germ warfare, hospitals setting up isolation units, then wham – all over. Thank God. Our main casualties seem to have been from "friendly fire" according to the papers. Which means the Americans killed our soldiers by mistake. I am sure that was a great comfort to their families. And this Saddam Hussein is still there, tyrant and torturer, still in power. So what was it all about? It is sometimes difficult not to despair of the human race.

April, 1992

I'm worried about Jack. He's lost a lot of weight lately. I thought first of all it was all the preparations for Sarah and Ben's wedding. Vicars seem to have to invite their entire congregation to their wedding, political necessity apparently. And then there are all Sarah's medical colleagues, so it is going to be a mammoth shindig.

But yesterday he came over to cut the grass for me

and he had to sit down half-way through. I could see that he was drenched in sweat. When I asked if he was all right he said, "Just a bit tired," but he didn't meet my eyes and I know something is wrong. So I'm on the phone to Harriet.

"What's the matter with Jack?" There's a pause, and suddenly I can hear my heart thumping and I start to feel sick. "Harriet," I say sharply, "please don't patronise me. Jack is my son and if he is ill I want to know what is wrong."

Harriet says, "Lillian, I'm coming over. We need to talk. With you in half an hour," and puts the phone down.

Thirza is over at Cynthia's today. I wish she was here. I think I am going to need a hand to hold.

Jack has cancer. Harriet says they found a tumour last week. He's not been feeling well for some months, but his doctor kept telling him there was nothing wrong. Not big on diagnosis, obviously. But the tumour is small and they are planning to operate next week. She says the prognosis is good. I reach for her and we grasp each other tightly. We are both remembering Freddy. My husband, her dad, who fought this awful disease so bravely but lost.

Not again, dear Lord. If we can barter, could you take me instead? It must be nearly time. But not Jack. Please, please, please, not my Jack. Not my son.

May, 1992

The operation is a success. They say they have removed the tumour. No complications. They do not

280

believe there will be any recurrence. He is home. Gaining weight. Looking good. Thank you, God. Oh, thank you!

September, 1992

I am wearing a very glamorous lilac coloured dress with a slightly darker coat for the wedding. And a purple hat. Like in that poem. I feel rather exotic. Grandmother of the bride for the second time. Harriet looks wonderful, of course, in a very dramatic emerald green velvet suit with an ankle-length skirt (reminds me of the New Look – how we all loved that fashion).

And our Sarah…well, words fail me. She has chosen a cream coloured muslin empire-line dress and looks as if she has just walked out of a production of one of Jane Austen's novels. It suits her beautifully. Simple and elegant, with her hair piled up and flowers wound into it. And she is radiant. And so beautiful. I want to cry when her handsome and healthy father walks up the aisle with her. Little Phoebe is walking in front of her carrying a posy. They decided not to risk her holding Sarah's train, which sweeps along very prettily on its own.

The men are totally transformed by their toppers and tails. Funny, marriage is supposed to be becoming a thing of the past, but weddings seem to get bigger and bigger. James is filming the whole thing, of course. Nice to see Andrew here with his new lady. She's a very down-to-earth lass, the complete opposite to Davina. Rosalind and Steve are all smiles. They are back on an even keel and the practice is thriving again, though Elsie tells me it has taken real strength of character on their part to dig in and pick up again.

We are lucky with the weather, and the reception has toppled out of the marquee and into the delightful grounds that surround Ben's church. Not often we have all the younger members of the family together like this. What a good-looking bunch they are. Come to think of it, you almost never see a plain youngster nowadays. I wonder why? There were a lot in my day. Perhaps it's because they are encouraged to make the most of themselves. Pastor Reynolds would definitely have called that sinful vanity.

Cynthia comes over and gives me a hug. "Well, Auntie Lillian, it looks as if I have to make the most of this excuse to buy a special wedding outfit. My lot just aren't obliging." She's laughing, but I know she'd love it if either of her two tied the knot. We look across at Natalie and Mike, with their partners and children. "Perhaps this will inspire them," I say, but we neither of us believe it. Still, they appear to be very settled and happy, and when all's said and done you can't get married just to please your parents.

James wants to film Thirza and me, so we do a stately walk through the guests pretending to stop and talk to everyone. Unfortunately Phoebe is getting a bit tired and over-excited and comes rushing up to me and, as I bend to speak to her, she knocks my splendid purple hat over one eye. Captured for posterity looking squiffy, and I've only had half a glass of champagne. So much for matriarchal dignity.

Sarah is planning to be a GP eventually. She says they are bottom of the pile in the medical world, and it tends to be regarded as the job you do if you are not good enough to specialise. But it is what she has always wanted to do – to be in the front line, she says. Good girl. Seems a most laudable ambition to me.

One of Ben's church wardens has come up and is asking her, slightly aggressively, whether she will be able to spend much time helping Ben in his job. Cheek. She's a rather formidable-looking lady with brogues and an incongruous feathered scarlet hat on. "Not the kind of millinery women of taste, such as ourselves, would wear," I whisper to Thirza.

Sarah tells her, very sweetly, that she and Ben "hope to be mutually supportive to each other in their personal and professional roles." Not altogether mollified, the pillar of the church moves off. I look at Sarah and say, "You knew someone would ask that – you were all ready for it!"

"Too right, Gran," she giggles.

That's my girl.

November, 1992

James has invited us to his flat to show us the film of the wedding. Apart from the hat incident I think I looked pretty good. Afterwards, I asked if he would show me what they mean by this "surfing the net" everyone is on about. My goodness, what fun it is. You type your questions into a little box and it gives you simply *thousands* of answers. Of course, none of them are what you were looking for but the whole thing is quite fascinating. I wonder if I am too old to become a computer buff?

Sarah rang this afternoon to tell us that the Church of England Synod has voted in favour of having women priests. She and Ben are over the moon. Ben is one of the more enlightened vicars and he has been campaigning for this for several years. He has told us how very shaken he was when he realised how much bitterness and prejudice there was inside the Church. Somewhat naively he had supposed it was just a few old-fashioned stick-in-the-muds making a disproportionate amount of noise because of their high positions.

The Church of England is desperate for more vicars anyway so it took Ben a time to realise that these people really believed that "God would be mocked" if women were ordained. When he was at theological college he wrote an essay about the women who acted as deacons in the early church, and apparently his tutor tore it up. Described it as subversive. Very Christian.

I've a lot of respect for young Ben and his beliefs but I think I'll stick with my intermittent, but definitely one-to-one relationship with God. I am pleased about the women priests though, even if does seem long overdue to me. Thirza says she reckons that old Pastor Reynolds is spinning in his grave. It's probably wicked but we catch each other's eye and start to laugh. That'd bring his hell fire down on us. I don't think laughter figured high in his scheme of things.

January, 1995

I've just pulled out from under the bed the wooden chest that Father and Jack made for me on my twelfth birthday. I've been putting my "precious" things in it for years but it's ages since I looked through it properly. It's full up with all sorts of stuff.

Right on the top are photographs of *Butterfly* with just about every member of the family on it at some time or other. What happy times we have on that little boat. It's like stepping into another world when you are chugging along on the river. Not that I ever go very far, but dozing on the seat at the back (Jack says will I please call it the stern) has become one of life's great pleasures. And all these wedding photographs. I really should get round to putting them in an album.

Here are the cards and letters loads of people sent when my Freddy died. I still can hardly bear to read them but having them means so much to me. As do the ones that people sent for my Jimmy. How lucky I have been to have loved, and been loved by, two such wonderful men.

Here is Josephine's medal, and the tie-dyed scarf that Martha gave me before she became famous. And talking of fame, here is Samantha's best-loved CD, which is called *Collette* and sold well enough to keep her in luxury for the rest of her days. This one is signed and she has written on it "To my gran's dearest friend, Lillian."

And here is Goldie's name tag, and Tess's and Berry's. Rufus used to lose his all the time. I think we gave up on it in the end.

There seem to be stacks of newspaper pictures – two Silver Jubilees, George V and the Queen. The coronation, of course, and Princess Diana marrying the Prince of Wales. That seems to have all gone wrong. Poor girl.

I've just found the programme for *Cats* – oh, and for *Nicholas Nickleby* – and, goodness, I'd forgotten this was here – the programme for *Chu Chin Chow*.

Getting a bit brittle now.

More photographs. Stan and Lena and their children, one of me in my little car. Thirza with her girls – all very young. A lovely etching of the Crystal Palace. My letter from the ministry congratulating me on the standards of the canteen in the war. Bits of old shrapnel. I suppose Jack put those in there. I know I didn't.

The one photograph I have of Tilly and William. Mr Everton took it on their wedding day.

I start to put everything back because I can't cope with the sadness that is in here alongside the happiness. But something is caught at the back. I pull it out carefully. It's the last of Mother's handkerchiefs. I used all the others but I kept one so I should feel near to her. It's a funny yellow colour now and the lace – the lace from Mother's second-best petticoat – has rotted slightly.

But I hold it to my lips and, for a minute, I am twelve years old again.

Today is my birthday. I am going to go through the Channel Tunnel. There has been lots of oohing and aahing, and "do you think it's a good idea?" from my family. I said that though I wasn't especially bothered about going to France, for as long as I can remember everyone has been talking about this tunnel, and now it is finally there I want to go through it. And if they didn't take me, Thirza and I are quite capable of going on our own. Actually, Thirza doesn't want to come, she's always been a bit claustrophobic, but I didn't tell them that till it was all settled.

It's possible they may have been right. I am *very*

tired. The tunnel itself is a bit boring. We just sit in William's car and then get out at the other end. But then he drives us (on the wrong side of the road, which I do find a bit worrying) to this hotel for a birthday dinner. Everyone there is speaking French, of course, and as my only French word is *oui* it is just as well I am not on my own. But I sit back and let the others order for me. After all, if they don't know what I like by now they never will.

It is a truly wonderful meal. The French cook with such delicacy. It occurs to me that I have never used garlic on a regular basis, though I know that Harriet does, and used properly it enhances rather than distorts the flavour of so much. I shall buy some in Tesco. Fresh, not in little pots.

I am quite excited and thinking of recipes that it might be added to, when to my surprise I hear a violin playing "Happy Birthday" and in comes a very handsome young man. And he is followed by what seems to be the entire kitchen staff! A tall man in a chef's hat, who Jack tells me is the *maître d'hôtel*, is leading the singing in very broken English. Jack and William and Elsie and Harriet all get to their feet and join in. Then the *maître* (who looks a bit like Maurice Chevalier) produces a bottle of champagne and whoosh, there are bubbles everywhere.

I am really taken totally by surprise, as I was obviously meant to be. How clever of my family to have planned all this. And how lovely of these French people to be so happy for us. They fill our glasses with champagne and I stand, raise my glass, and utter my only French word several times: "*Oui, oui, oui, oui!*" Among the laughter and the kissing I know they understand perfectly what I mean.

Then we all come back through the tunnel again. But I am filled with the wonder of it. I seem to be living in the past a lot nowadays, and I remember the journey my brother Jack and I made from one side of Suffolk to the other when I went into service and it seemed to take forever. Eighty-three years ago. Another world. But I like this one best. And I am so glad that I went to France. Through the Channel Tunnel.

March, 1995

A strange gentleman has entered our lives. Well, he is a gentleman now. A bit of a ruffian on first acquaintance, I'm afraid. He appeared at the end of the garden in that cold spell at the beginning of February, dragging his tail behind him and limping on his front paw. An enormous bald patch on the top of his head. Howling piteously.

Rosalind diagnosed "traffic victim" over the phone and asked if we could get near him. No. We had tried but he was too scared. We were only able to put food down and watch him eating from a distance. Steve drove over with a cat-trap and said he would stay the night so he could release quickly anything else we mistakenly caught in it. But, bless him, our poor, injured, hungry and frightened lad walked straight in and as the door came down behind him just looked at us as if to say it's a fair cop, and got on with eating the food that had lured him into the trap.

A week with Rosalind and Steve and back he came to us, his tail foreshortened but his foot nearly better, and, as my granddaughter inelegantly expressed it, deballed. We put an advertisement in the paper, but no one claimed him. It's two years now since we lost Sophie, and longer for Darcy, so we were hoping no one would.

We couldn't think of a name for him, but Sebastian suggested Peter Abelard. Everyone seemed to think that was very funny and Elsie told me it was a tasteless joke, but somehow Pete stuck. So now Pete is a member of our household and sleeps alternately on our beds. And determinedly in front of the fire every evening. We are mutually delighted with each other's company, I think.

May, 1995

It is fifty years since VE Day. Victory in Europe. The whole nation is celebrating. Festivities and nostalgia all over the place. Vera Lynn everywhere. Rather more fun than it was at the time if the truth be known. We were too drained, and too poor, to feel anything but relief. And grateful to finally have time to mourn those we had lost.

There is a big fireworks display on the seafront tonight, and dancing. One or two couples are actually jitterbugging. That takes me right back. Bit too old for that nowadays. We are going to watch it all from Harriet and Jack's windows. Useful having a ringside seat.

It is a splendid evening. Glenn Miller's (among others) music played by an excellent live band, and loads of people in what are not bad imitations of wartime clothes. Red, white and blue lights and Union Jacks all over the place. Most of the children carry those funny bendy sticks that light up and they are also

289

wearing headdresses made of them, so the whole seafront seems to be made up of moving coloured lights.

There are a lot of veterans here, proudly in uniform. Thirza is wearing her WVS ambulance drivers' one, and it still fits her. I didn't think that putting my British Canteen pinny on would mean a lot to anyone, so I passed on that.

At about midnight everyone sings "There'll be bluebirds over the white cliffs of Dover". As the party finally breaks up and the crowd straggles away, a glorious tenor voice starts to sing, quite unaccompanied, "Lilli Marlene". As it soars through the night a silence falls over the crowd, even the children are quiet. When the song is finished an elderly man's voice calls out, "Thank you. Bless you for that."

It is a truly magical finish to a memorable day.

July, 1995

Phoebe very graciously allowed me to take her to see *Toy Story*. As she is ten now she intimated that it might be beneath her but I was able to tell her with absolute honesty that I was dying to see it and needed an escort in order not to feel too conspicuous.

In the event we both enjoyed it enormously. What a clever film. Vastly entertaining but I was also struck with the realism surrounding the fantasy, if you know what I mean. Like the children appearing to live only with their mother. A "one-parent family" as they call it nowadays. Too many of those in the war years, no choice for them then. Difficult for me to understand how anyone can make the decision that a child doesn't have a right to two parents where it's possible. I wonder how the kids will feel about it when they are grown up. Phoebe and I are in agreement that it is a splendid film and also that two parents are definitely better than one.

Afterwards, sitting in one of Andrew's Food for Living bars (they are everywhere nowadays) we agree that she will escort me to the planned sequel when it comes out. "I am so lucky," she says, "not only having Mum and Dad, but having a gran and a great gran."

I tell her that the good fortune is all ours in having her, but I think she knows that she has made my day complete. And I am tactful enough not to share with her my relief that her Uncle Andrew's enterprise has spared me from the dreaded MacDonald's so beloved of her generation.

September, 1995

I wake in the middle of the night with the spine-tingling awareness that something is badly wrong. I don't know what has woken me. Pete is with Thirza – no, that is what woke me up. Pete is scrabbling at my door.

I wish I could move faster – it seems to take an age to put my dressing gown on and reach the door but at last I'm there. Pete is in the hall and his eyes are like yellow lamps in the moonlight. I switch the light on and I say, "It's all right, Pete," and I know that I am saying it to reassure myself. Pete already knows that it is not all right.

Thirza's door is open and I can hear her harsh breathing and it is all wrong.

She is lying on her side and she looks up at me and

291

her face is screwed up in pain. "Hurts – heart," she croaks. I touch her face and know immediately that I have to get help. Thank God we let the children persuade us to have a phone upstairs. I dial Cynthia because I can't remember the doctor's number. I wish Sarah was nearer.

"Come quickly," I say to the sleepy response. "Cynthia darling, please come quickly."

I go back and hold Thirza in my arms and wait. I do the only thing I know how to do. I ask God not to take my sister. Not yet. Please God. Not yet.

He listened. Thank you, God. Thirza has angina. A sort of a heart attack, but a minor one. Makes me wonder what a major one is like. They say she has got to be careful, but she is not going to die. Not yet, anyway.

She's still at home and a charming young nurse is keeping an eye. Much better than having to be in hospital. If she starts to feel odd, and she says the pain is very easy to recognise, she puts one of these special tablets under her tongue. I am making sure she has them on her all the time.

The doctor is here to see her today and he asks if he could have a word with me. He says Thirza is recovering well but he is surprised that he has seen so little of us as we have been his patients for quite a few years. I point out that we have not been ill. He says he would have expected us, at very least, to have attended his "well woman" clinics. I have no idea what he is going on about. And I am too tired, with all the worry about Thirza, to care.

He suddenly bursts out laughing. This is so

unexpected and so contagious that I join in without really knowing what I am laughing at. He takes my hand and says, "Mrs Curtis, you are wonderful. And so is your sister. I think it possible you may both live forever. I feel privileged to have finally made your acquaintance."

Hmm. A rather odd way for a doctor to behave. But I quite liked him. And Thirza is nearly her old self again. So I don't suppose we will need to see much more of him.

October, 1995

A family gathering. Not like the usual ones. We have been expecting this ever since Thirza's heart thing. Sebastian and Cynthia, Margaret over from America, William and Elsie, Jack and Harriet. Right. We guessed it wasn't going to be merely a social occasion. But Cynthia has cooked a very nice lunch and although we may look as if we have been lulled into a false sense of security, the boot is quite on the other foot.

Cynthia starts the ball rolling. "Mum, we've all been thinking that you and Auntie Lillian might be happier if you came back to live in the granny annexe. We do worry about you both being on your own."

Thirza points out that we are not on our own, we have each other. William chips in with, "But look at what happened last month. You could have died."

I reply that we dealt with the situation quite adequately, and that in any case, we are going to die in the not too distant future. Wherever we live. This causes a certain lull in the conversation. Then, as we planned, we let them kick around a few more suggestions. After all, we do know that they care for us.

But – and now it is over to me – "Darlings!" (That shuts them all up. I used that voice when they were kids and am tickled to find I can still produce it.) "I am sorry if you worry about us. We, of course, have spent a lifetime worrying about you, so we understand very well. But, as every one of us knows, in the end you have to let people make their own choices. Right or wrong. Being old does not take away that right. Our choice is to go on living as we are. And enjoying our life together. We appreciate your concern, and also the fact that you are only a telephone call away. We love you all very much and believe that you love us enough to respect our wishes."

As we intended we've left them nowhere to go. Into the silence, naughty Harriet, always the actress, says "Lillian, that was scripted and rehearsed. You knew this was coming."

"Well," I say, "don't you think I was rather good?"

It breaks the tension. Everyone laughs and Cynthia has one more "Are you sure?" to which Thirza replies "Absolutely!" and Sebastian goes to put the kettle on.

Later, when we are home, Thirza says, "Well done, big sister. I think we pitched it about right, don't you?" I do. She takes my hand. "Do you think…?"

"Shhh," I say. "Not yet. Not yet."

She goes up to bed. Slower than me now for all she is younger. I sit on in the kitchen, with Pete purring on my lap.

Thinking.

January, 1997

Yet another birthday. Amazing. We keep celebrating each one as if it's the last and I sometimes feel quite embarrassed still to be around for the next one. Supper with Jack and Harriet tonight, and William and Elsie are taking me out at the weekend.

Thirza has just given me what must be one of the nicest presents I have ever had. From the whole family, she says. It's a video film, made by James especially for me, and every member of the family is in it. And they are not just saying happy birthday, but doing things that are part of their everyday life.

Rosalind and Steve working with a donkey in the sanctuary, Phoebe at her piano lessons with Wilfred lying behind the stool (he lifted his head to look at the camera, and I'll swear he grinned at me), Sarah talking to a receptionist in her surgery, and then another one of her helping Ben lay the altar in their church. And here's Andrew in one of his snack bars and he's holding up – oh my goodness, bless him, it's my Cornish pasty recipe. He told me it was one of his most successful lines ever. Nice to think I've had what Phoebe calls "input" into his venture.

Who...? Oh, it's Natalie and Mike and their partners and kids all on a cycle ride along a very sandy beach. Mike is yelling, "It's Camber Sands, Auntie Lillian, we knew you'd ask..." and now the children are pretending to fall off their bikes. Lots of laughter and legs waving in the air.

And Ivy...however long since we saw Ivy? Gosh, she is enormous, bigger even than Martha was. Still at her drawing board, for all she's nearly seventy. Good for her. That's Nerys and her family – do you know I think she has got even more beautiful in middle age, but oh dear, her dad has got very fat as well. Must have been in Martha's genes, it certainly wasn't in Father's.

There's Norma, doing a family barbecue on the beach. Thirza says James didn't actually go out to New Zealand, but got Norma to send him some film. Margaret, preparing for a radio broadcast, though she doesn't do so many nowadays.

Lettie, looking very frail, and oh, here is Edward, with his grandchildren. Hard to believe. No Timmy, of course, or Frank.

Nearly at the end of the film, and here are Cynthia and Sebastian with Thirza in between them. All waving madly and holding a big placard saying "Happy Birthday", then my boys with my lovely daughters-in-law waving madly from the deck of *Butterfly*. And just when I think it's finished, there's James himself, coming out from behind the camera, holding Pete.

"Keep watching, Gran," he says, and so I do, and the next person on the screen is...me! He filmed me without me knowing, sitting in Rosalind's garden last summer and talking to Thirza, with Wilfred at my side. I've got my best dress on and look rather nice. I'm relieved he didn't take me dozing with my mouth open. Even at ninety-seven, a girl has her pride.

What a wonderful, imaginative, clever present. I shall watch it all again immediately. And then I shall watch it again. And again.

February, 1997

Andrew popped in today, he comes to Brighton quite regularly as he has three Food for Living bars in the town. He's getting married to Poppy. I am very pleased but also surprised. I thought that having had one failure, he wouldn't want to risk it again. "You're about to have another great grandchild," he tells me, "and we want to do it properly."

What splendid news. He says they are going to have a very quiet register-office wedding, as they have both been married before. I must say I think that is sensible. The baby is due in July, and it is a boy. I can never quite get used to being able to tell that in advance. After he has gone I ring Elsie and tell her how pleased I am. She says she promised to let him tell me himself, though she's been bursting with the news for a couple of weeks.

I never expected Andrew to turn out so well. It's as if all the arrogance melted away when he had that run of disasters. Funny how this stuff makes or breaks people. It certainly has made Andrew. We were talking the other evening about the royal family. Disaster after disaster there, but it doesn't seem to improve them. Their Andrew, divorced from that lively redhead, and, of course, Charles and Diana. Sounds as if that was the marriage made in hell. I think that girl is well out of it. Her boys look OK. Let's hope she is strong enough to enable them to grow up like normal people. I wish her luck.

April, 1997

We can see the comet that they have all been talking about. Thirza and I wrapped up warm and came and sat out here in the garden with Pete and, all of a sudden, there it was. So bright and so beautiful. No wonder we

297

all think of God as "up there." How little we know really. How small we are in this great universe. But how awe-inspiring seeing such a wonderful sight. And, in a funny sort of way, a kind of symbol of hope. It seems like that to me, anyway.

I need a bit of reassurance. I sometimes think I'm losing the plot (isn't that a nice phrase? Phoebe uses it all the time, though with less justification, I think). I found a pound note in an old purse yesterday, and when I handed it to the girl in Smiths, she told me that they haven't been legal for years. Probably worth more as an antique, she said. Like me, I said. But I don't think she had much sense of humour. I did feel a bit silly, though.

Mind you, I'm sure everything does change at a faster rate than it used to, our Phoebe doesn't even do feet and inches, it's all metres and stuff. But at least she knows what a pound is, the weight kind, I mean. Though I have a suspicion she changes that to kilo-somethings in her head.

And today there is a whole programme on the radio about a common currency. So that money will be the same all over Europe. "The euro," I say to Thirza. "What a dreadful name. I hope we're gone before that happens here," and she agreed. Well, I ask you. All that hassle last time. Freddy and I nearly went round the bend trying to convert pence into what people insisted on calling "peas" and make sense of it all. In the end, it was just a big excuse to put all the prices up, I reckon.

Something like seeing that wonderful comet helps you to keep things in proportion though. Makes you concentrate on the important things in life. After all, I suppose if we do have to use these wretched euros, we will. And be glad we have enough of them!

May, 1997

Most of the family came round for election night, we decided to risk having a party. We all thought there might finally be something worth celebrating. Andrew supplied us with a wonderful buffet and we sat round the television, almost holding our breath as the first results came through. And at last - we have a Labour government again!

Margaret was reporting on it in America, but she rang us in the small hours. Knew we'd be still up and glued to the television, she said. We are agreed that Tony Blair looks like an honest chap. Oh, how I hope so. A landslide. He can hardly do worse than the departing lot – two MPs in prison, a couple more who probably ought to be, sleaze and lies everywhere, and Mr Major telling everyone how it's nothing to do with him and not his fault. Whose is it then? I don't see how he can stand in the middle of it all and not take any responsibility. Jack says that's what politicians do but I still believe that most people go into politics because they want to make things better.

Please, Mr Blair, don't let us down.

June, 1997

Jack popped in today to do a bit of gardening - the grass is growing almost as you watch. He was saying that Sarah is really excited about this cloned sheep, Dolly. She thinks it could lead to enormous advances in medicine. I hadn't realised that. To me it just sounds like something out of one of those horror films that they show late on the television and give you nightmares. Except you know that they are not real. And Dolly is. I wondered if he knew what Ben thought about it but he didn't. I must ask him. I suspect he has reservations, too.

Knowledge is supposed to be power, but power to do what? So often, all the wrong things. Well, I shall be on my way soon. Hopefully up with the comets.

September, 1997

Rosalind said she was taking Phoebe up to Buckingham Palace today so I asked if we could hitch a lift. We were going on the train but I thought that might make a long day for Thirza. Well, and for me. Rosalind came and got us, bless her, and we all took posies of flowers with us.

When we got out of the car the first thing to hit me was the amazing scent of the flowers. Hundreds and hundreds of flowers. And candles. And that enormous crowd, people of all ages and all walks of life, waiting quietly for the royal family to show some, if not grief, then respect, for this woman so many of us had come to care about.

Like most people here, we watched Diana struggling to grow into a good woman. We watched her cuddling AIDS victims and wondered if we would have dared. We watched her walking through fields that may or may not have been cleared of landmines and hoped that we would have had that much courage. Most of all we saw her being a good mother. And, we suspected, a good wife if she'd been given half a chance.

Difficult not to believe that her death would seem

very convenient to the family who appear to us to have used and abused her. As a last spiteful gesture, taking away her title. No HRH for the mother of a future king? But she was indeed the "people's princess." For all her failings, or perhaps because of them, she was probably this family's last chance at a continuing monarchy.

Loved. And beautiful and brave. And, of course, she will never grow old now. Always on the brink of being the person we hoped and expected her to become. Forever. Possibly, in death, more difficult to ignore and to overlook, than anyone could have dreamt.

So now we stand in this crowd. A small part of the waiting millions. Telling them honour her, or we will never honour you again. They've probably left it too late for most of us anyway. Cocooned in self-indulgence for too long. They've finally lowered the flag to half-mast. They are going to need to do a lot more than that. Those poor boys. What hope for them now?

October, 1997

This is such a delightful church. Norman, Ben tells me, and built by some French monks a thousand years ago. Still in quite good nick as far as I can see. Built "to the glory of God." I wonder how He feels about that. I expect He appreciates the odd monument or two. Among other things.

Ben has decidedly mixed feelings about some of those other things. He wanted a tough inner-city parish. Well, being Ben, he would, of course. But his bishop wanted him to have a bit more experience of being a vicar first, so when this quiet country living came up, he suggested Ben went for it. It seemed like a good idea. Sarah was offered the chance of being a junior partner in the village's only general practice and they expect to move on in about five or six years' time.

But. There is always a but, isn't there? This quiet country parish hosts an enormous power struggle. The sort that leaves politicians looking like amateurs at the game. And our poor, unprepared Ben is always getting caught in the middle. It all sounds pretty trivial to me. But Ben desperately wants to take the village church into the village, so to speak. He has a regular congregation of about 30 people in a village of about 1,400. He feels, with some justification I should have thought, that this number is hardly representative.

So Ben had the idea this year of asking Harriet if she would put on a passion play, using people, especially children, from all over the village. To process through the village on Good Friday, stopping at various points for prayers and hymns. Of course, Harriet said she would. I think she was quite excited by the proposal.

When he floated the suggestion initially his Parochial Church Council (everything has to have their approval, apparently) were quite enthusiastic. However, as soon as they realised he intended to ask people who never normally come to the church, support waned a fraction. It was the announcement that the local plumber was going to play Jesus that did it. The congregation was up in arms. An artisan playing Jesus! And one with a South London accent! Surely not. Hmm.

One of his churchwardens then intimated that perhaps the play should not include children from the

302

little council estate, unless they had been vetted, as "people might be offended by that sort of thing." A special meeting was called, theoretically to discuss the project. In the event it was a thinly veiled protest meeting.

The Good Friday procession was described as a publicity stunt. Ben has enough sense of humour to see the funny side of this, and agreed that yes, he was aiming to publicise the crucifixion. However, at this point the people on the estate got wind of all the aggro and said, "No thanks, we're not lowering ourselves to mix with that lot."

The last straw came when Sarah found she was being ostracised by some of her patients from the church. Frustrated and angry, Ben called it off. His congregation is now down to twenty-eight as two swept off in high dudgeon anyway. I expect the inner-city yobs will be a piece of cake after this lot.

However, today all is peaceful, an oasis of calm in this war zone, and this splendid building is full of family. Matthew William Spencer, son of Andrew and Poppy, grandson of William and Elsie, and great grandson of Lillian, is being baptised. And a great deal of fuss he is making about it. He's been yelling his head off for some time and seems to be gathering speed. Upholding a fine tradition, Ben assures us.

Sarah, James, Natalie and Mike are his godparents, and Ben is officiating. The occasion is made even more special as Sarah whispered to me just now that she is pregnant. I am so thrilled. This is wonderful news. I wondered why Jack and Harriet were wreathed in smiles. Harriet is an unlikely granny, and I tell her that she will set new standards for glamorous grannies. She laughs but I can see she is pleased with the compliment, which is nothing but the truth.

James is filming us all, of course. Very cock-a-hoop as he has just landed a contract to direct a new television serial about a sort of "punky" Robin Hood. "I think it is going to be big, Gran," he says, "and Morvina is playing Maid Marian." I don't like to confess that I have never heard of Morvina. Later Harriet tells me that she is a celebrity, though no one appears to know exactly why. Celebrity seems to mean people who are famous for being famous nowadays.

Andrew has dragooned his caterers into doing a magnificent spread. The cake is a simple white square with "Matthew William" written across it in royal blue. Too nice to cut, really. The church hall is built on a hill and the sun is setting over the valley, casting a rosy glow over everyone and everything. Thirza and I are standing at the window admiring this, when Jack comes up. "Mum, Aunt Thirza, look!" he says.

We turn and look down the hall. "What, darling?" I ask, puzzled.

"All of these people are here because of you two," he says. "This is your family. Almost" – he pauses for effect "dare I say – this is your lives! Aren't you proud?"

It must be all these years with Harriet that has made him so dramatic but, well, I hadn't thought of it quite like that. Nor had Thirza, obviously. We look at each other and grin. Yes, of course we are. Immensely proud of them all, and, I suppose, a bit proud of ourselves, too.

January, 1999

There is something faintly absurd about hanging around for ninety-nine years. Whatever can you say when your family ask what you would like for your birthday? I mean, if I haven't got it by now I am hardly likely to want it. I must stop being ungrateful. Sarah is here with little Lily and who could ask to leave more behind than a child named after them? She is gorgeous. Going to have red hair, I think. Her baby blonde has already got those amber tints. Thirza says she looks a bit like me but I can't see it, much as I would like to.

Thirza is a bit quiet. She had a call from Cynthia this morning, all the way from New Zealand, and then Norma came on the line for a quick chat. She said how much better Cynthia is looking already. Sebastian's death was such a shock to us all. I suppose because Thirza and I are so ancient we expect everyone to make it into their nineties or beyond. At eighty-three, Sebastian seemed a mere stripling. But we know that is daft. It is what people call "a good age."

Poor, darling Cynthia, waking up and finding him dead beside her. I can't begin to imagine how terrible that was. The only consolation being that it really was a terrific way for him to go. But very hard for those of us who loved him.

Cynthia asked me if I would write about him for the funeral, as I had known him longer than anyone. So I wrote about when I first met him, the sickly little boy, who became the soldier in Spain, then the RAF pilot, and finally, husband, father and part of our family. And a successful businessman. But most of all a brave, honourable man who worshipped his wife, and adored his children.

At the funeral Jack read what I had written. Then he talked about how during the war Sebastian had been his hero and how much he had looked forward to his visits. And how when Sebastian returned from being shot down over France he, Jack, drove Sebastian round the bend until he knew every detail of his escape back home. And how, years after, Sebastian had told him that, rather than disappoint him, he had been forced to make some of it up because of all the secrecy at the time. Funny, I had quite forgotten Jack following him around like a little dog that winter. Afterwards Cynthia came and put her arms round me and we both had a weep.

Cynthia has been looking more and more peaky. Chin in the air, and doing all the voluntary stuff she has done for years, not a quitter, but you could see she was empty inside. Putting on a brave face for her kids. Well, we all do that. There isn't really any alternative.

But Thirza heroically persuaded her to accept Norma's invitation to go and spend some time with her in the sun. I think I am the only one who fully understands how hard it is for her having her daughters on the other side of the world, and how much it cost her to send Cynthia off, too.

"After all, sweetheart," she said to Cynthia, "I've been around for over ninety years and if I do pop off while you're away, we both have the consolation of knowing that there hasn't been a single moment in your life that I haven't thanked God for you. I would much rather you go. I shall only feel guilty if you don't."

So we waved Cynthia off to New Zealand just after Christmas. A complete change of scenery will be good for her. Time does alter the way you see things. I don't know about this healing business. A wound always leaves scar tissue. But you start to remember the good times, and the things you loved best about a person, and smile at the memories of the laughs you had together. So in the end they are back with you in a way.

Family helps. I remember Lettie telling me that the worst thing after Timmy died was that she wanted to talk about him and everyone jumped away from the subject as if mentioning him had become taboo. They didn't want to upset her. Didn't want to have to cope with her having a good cry, more likely. At least family don't do that.

Jack and William are taking us both to a new restaurant in Tunbridge Wells for lunch. Harriet tells me James is coming along with his new girlfriend, Victoria. No one has met her yet, but Harriet has a feeling this is "the real thing." About time too. We are getting out the glad rags for the occasion. The purple hat again, I think.

March, 1999

James has come to say farewell, he's off to America. His *Robin Hood* series hit the jackpot out there. Even the ghastly Morvina went down OK. Perhaps they found it easier to accept Maid Marian as a six-foot-tall Swedish blonde. Anyway he's been offered a contract to direct a series about pirates. No one we've ever heard of is in it, but he says it's a big deal.

Victoria is going to spend a month out there with him but she is a serious career girl and has a fascinating job as an art historian working for Sotheby's. She says that she would probably consider living in America, but wants to make quite sure that she and James are right for each other. She is also checking that her career opportunities there would be at least as good as here.

I do admire these modern girls. No rushing into marriage for them. Heads all screwed on very tightly. At least until the old biological clock starts ticking and with any luck the careers are established before that particular panic sets in. She's a nice girl, not a bit the sort I would have expected James to fall for, but there you go. She's pretty, but you wouldn't notice her in a crowd. Though I suppose James did. Harriet says he mixes with the drop-dead-gorgeous ones all the time, and quiet but brainy Victoria is a new experience for him. Anyway, it seems to be working and she has Sarah's seal of approval. And Sarah knows him better than anyone, after all. The twin bond has always been very strong with those two.

Thirza's given him Margaret's new address in case he gets to New York. Margaret was going to retire this year, but she has been headhunted by a large financial organisation to investigate Third World debt for them. The job is for three years, and she thinks it is probably too good to pass up. "My last chance to make a real difference, and anyway, I'm very flattered," is how she described it, with typical modesty.

She has an office right at the top of the World Trade Centre, in what they call the Twin Towers, and when she came over for Sebastian's funeral she showed us some photos taken from the windows. Absolutely amazing views. I can't imagine working that high up. She and Richard are finally coming back in 2002 to make their home over here. "I'll have been away quite long enough," she laughed.

April, 1999

Thirza and I are off to see *Titanic*. We have discovered mini-cabs and it has broadened our horizons no end. We usually get a very nice young man called Nigel, who tells us he is only temporary, while he is considering his options. Thirza asked him the other day how long he had been working for the firm. He said six years. Hmmm.

Thirza has another attack in the middle of the film. The cinema is nearly empty, as it usually is in the afternoon, and I get her tablets out of her pocket and shove one under her tongue, then I massage her left arm. I always sit on her left side now, just in case. It doesn't last long, and we sit letting the film wash over us while she recovers.

"Wash over" is quite a good description, I suppose. All that sea. When she is better we agree that we are disappointed in the film anyway. Too much silliness detracting from the real-life tragedy, but we watch to the end. On the way home Nigel feels we should have liked it better. "It won all those Oscars, you know. And I bet you didn't know it was based on a true story." I can feel Nigel's options retreating.

June, 1999

Such a stupid thing to do. I am on my way down the garden to pull out some weeds and I don't see Pete lying under a bush and I trip over him. I am covered in bruises. He is most indignant but unharmed. I can't believe how long it is before I am able to get to my feet, though. My heart is racing and I feel quite ill. It makes me realise how lucky I have been all these years. It frightens poor Thirza. She wants to call Jack but I remind her of what we decided, all that time ago.

"I'm all right," I assure her, "and if Jack comes, the next thing we know we'll be sitting for hours in that wretched casualty department, and they'll all start on again about not living on our own." She goes quiet. Dear Thirza.

"It's nearly time, isn't it, Lillian?"

I nod. Still the big sister. "Elementary, my dear Watson, given our combined ages," I say. We've been listening to some Sherlock Holmes on the radio this week. We have a giggle and go and make some tea.

Shaken, but still here. For now.

August, 1999

We are on *Butterfly*, drifting along the river. Phoebe has given me a parasol and I feel as if I stepped back in time. I half expect to wake up and find that I am sixteen again.

Thirza is dozing opposite me. Snoring in a gentle, musical fashion. Wilfred is at my feet. I can hear the children (children! William was seventy-eight this year!) laughing quietly as they make sandwiches in the galley. The weather is perfect. The day is perfect. Thank you, God, if You are up there. And I'm quite sure You are somewhere. I can't look at all this peace and beauty and not believe in a benevolent deity somewhere. I hope I get the chance to ask You lots of questions.

And I hope You will forgive me.

November, 1999

I can see from my little bedside clock that it is only three in the morning. Pitch dark. What woke me? Funny how you know. Absolutely know.

I go into my darling Thirza's room across the passage. No noise. I take her hand. Warm. But quite, quite lifeless.

She still has the dressing-table set that Marcus gave her when they first married – two clothes brushes, two hair brushes, and a hand mirror in lilac enamel – and I pick up the mirror and hold it to her lips.

There is no mist on the glass.

Thirza. Darling sister. Lifelong companion. Gone.

Wait, dearest, I'm coming. Just as we planned. Just as we talked about. Just as we decided.

I keep the tablets in my bedside table. We thought that would make it easy for whichever of us was left. I am glad I didn't have to give them to Thirza. But I promised, as she did, that if either of us was in pain, or had a stroke or something terrible, we would be brave enough to do it.

And I know we would have done. Either of us.

All these years, I've had the morphine. After Freddy's death no one ever asked for it back. I learnt all about the doses during Freddy's illness. I shall break open the packets and put the evidence in the bin.

Who's going to check on two such old girls? No post-mortems for us. Good. I'd just rather the family didn't know. Of course they'll miss us but God knows we've had a good innings.

You can't mourn a couple of nonagenarians for

long. They are much too sensible for that.

I'm getting in beside Thirza. Oh goodness, Pete is coming in too. He'll be OK. Rosalind will take him.

I've had such a wonderful life. Ups and downs, good and bad. But I've been so loved. All my life.

It's time to go. Nothing to be gained by hanging around any longer. Pinning on a smile for the Queen's telegram. No thanks.

I've taken the pills.

There. Purr away, Pete. Purr me away.

Let me hold you, Thirza.

I'm coming, my darlings. Jimmy, Freddy, Martha, Collette, Tilly – Jack – brother Jack – oh my darlings – wait for me, I'm coming…I'm coming…

The End

Acknowledgements

I owe a great debt to my mother-in-law, whose stories of her early childhood in Suffolk were the original inspiration for *Lillian's Story*, and to Dora Bryan, who wrote the foreword for the original hardback, and to Tom Baker for his considerable encouragement.

I would like to thank the members of Shorelink Monday Group for their unflagging encouragement and enthusiasm, and especially Frank, whose request to 'write a short article for the magazine' sparked off *Lillian's Story*

I must also thank my lovely son, Alexander, for his unwavering faith in 'the product'.

And an enormous, quite incalculable, "thank you" is due to Ro, to whom I dedicate this book. His love, support and belief made all things possible during the six months that I was consumed by Lillian and her life. And they continue to do so.

—Sally Patricia Gardner, June 2005

Made in United States
Orlando, FL
24 August 2023

36408186R00188